MYSTERIA

MELANIE HIRAGURI

2020 White Bird Publications, LLC

Copyright © 2020 by Melanie C. Hiraguri
Cover by Trisha St. Clair

Published in the United States
by White Bird Publications, LLC, Texas
www.whitebirdpublications.com

ISBN 978-1-63363-461-9
eBook ISBN 978-1-63363-462-6
Library of Congress Control Number: 2020933565

PRINTED IN THE UNITED STATES OF AMERICA

For my Dad, Lawrence Hayward.
Thank you for passing on to me
your love for words.

Acknowledgment Page:

Writing a novel is like looking at yourself in a mirror. It takes you deep into yourself, to a place of vulnerability where everything about you is on display. But even without this, writing is difficult enough. There were days as I wrote MYSTERIA that I honestly felt like throwing my laptop across the room and giving up. Without fail, though, help would come. Sometimes, it was the quiet voice from deep within that provided the solution to my craft dilemma and kept me going. Other times, it was the timely voice of encouragement or craft wisdom from others that I needed. Many have helped me on this journey. I wish to acknowledge them here.

To my husband, Akira, and our children—Josie, Josiah and Julia—for letting me pursue my dream of writing and for believing in me.

To Trisha St.Clair for designing a truly magical book cover.

To Theresa Smith for the wonderful editing and advice.

To Mutsumi Kosaka for the author photos and for always listening and encouraging.

To Bruce McAllister, writing coach extraordinaire, for being my patient guide, champion and supporter.

To my friends Marcel Cabrera, Shane Evans, K'Lynn Bruchmiller, Sheli Livengood and Cami Carlson for the prayers and support.

To my fellow dreamers, Elly and Carrie Halim, for sharing your blue pearl.

To Evelyn Byrne-Kusch and the White Bird team, for believing in MYSTERIA.

And finally, to my Heavenly Father. Giver of all.

MYSTERIA

**White Bird
Publications**

Prologue

I remember clearly the night it came.

The hour was late, but sleep had yet eluded me and so I sat rocking in my chair, reading once again the well-worn copy of the Verses. My old shawl, a familiar comfort, lay across my knees, threading the memories of many years. I didn't know it then, but that same shawl was already working its way into another story, connecting my past to my granddaughter's future.

The night was hot and humid, and the breeze lacked the strength to stir the heavy air, though all the windows were opened wide. I quickly lost myself in the weaving of words— words that were not my own but of an older wisdom, from an even older time—until at last, my vision blurred and slid across the page. Then, with half a sigh and half a yawn, I closed the book and placed it carefully on the side table.

In the far corner of the room, my granddaughter lay sleeping in her little trundle bed. I turned toward her and froze, gripping the arms of my chair. My old heart began rattling in my chest so I could hardly breathe.

There, resting on the wall just above the sleeping child, I saw it, a wasp-like creature, at least eight or ten inches in length and so black it seemed to absorb all light and color. Wings, like delicate lace, folded tightly against the ebony body. They were oddly reminiscent of a shawl draped across grandmotherly shoulders. A white "V" curled along its back. It was a frightening creature, not only because of its size but because it exuded an uncanny awareness that no creature should ever possess.

My unease grew as I stared. I wondered what the creature was, where it had come from, and what it was doing here, in my cottage.

Slowly, a whisper began to rise from the edges of my childhood, a memory. It was a story that my grandmother had told me and that her grandmother had told her, reminding me of what I had once known—and nearly forgotten.

I looked at the creature again. Really looked. Memories stirred, and my mouth formed the word: "Mysteria."

I stiffened, frightened by the name.

Could this really be the creature of old tales? The creature I have heard about from the time I sat on my grandmother's knees? The creature I had dismissed as a fantasy?

I fumbled for the shawl in my lap and grasped it tightly. I cast around for more memories, but I knew so little about this creature. So little remained from the time that those stories were first told.

A gibbous moon arose, and. in the spreading glow, I realized that the creature had begun laying eggs along the wall. Small and sticky and clear as new-cut glass, the eggs caught and reflected the moon's light, glistening like tears.

The first egg was clear. The next, a milky-white. The eggs that followed were amber, then emerald and then azure—each one more jewel than egg. I stared in growing amazement.

This is no ordinary creature simply trying to keep its kind alive.

After laying each egg, she took what looked like a perfectly measured step, pausing only to lay another before continuing. The eggs were laid at a steady pace in what appeared to be a predetermined pattern. Everything looked rhythmic and unbroken, the creature neither stopping, slowing, nor doing anything in haste.

Within just a short time, there were more eggs on the wall than I could count—eggs of astounding colors—more varied than the shades of a rainbow. No two were alike. From each, a light emanated, faint at first, but growing steadily.

Circles of color had already begun to form along the bare wall. The lights expanded, growing brighter, their edges blurring. The circles began to overlap, and the colors blended further—blue and red circles mixed into purples. Red and yellow circles merged into orange. The picture being shaped by the circles was beautiful, intricate.

Planned.

I stared at it, certain there must be some meaning hidden within. But though the pattern continued to form, I could not understand it.

All the while, my granddaughter lay asleep beneath, illuminated by the eggs' glow. I could see her clearly from where I sat. She must be dreaming, for her face twitched. She cried out softly. Then, her thumb found her mouth, and she quieted.

The colors reached the corners of the wall where they bent, spreading onto the ceiling and the floor. Without pause, they continued outward into the room, filling in the places of remaining darkness. The light spread quickly, the leading edge reaching my feet within moments. I held my breath. Light and color wrapped around me.

My heart beat faster, stronger. I felt my blood course thickly, my bones harden, and my muscles strengthen. I glanced down to my lap and gave a start. My hands, curled by age and time, now appeared young, smooth, and strong.

Surely this cannot be.

And yet, as I stretched out my fingers and then drew them back into a fist, I knew that it was true.

What is this creature? I glanced at it again, fear knotting my stomach.

The glow continued to expand, the bright leading edge moving beyond me to fill in the rest of the room. The golden moment of youth went with it. I didn't have to look to see that my hands were again old. I knew.

Then, I noticed a scent spreading throughout the room. It was a sweet smell, delicate, almost like a fruit.

And strangely familiar.

Voices were moving about the cottage, too, voices other than my own. Their soft murmurings filled my ears. I heard whispers from the past, from the present, and whispers from what was yet to be. The voices were faint and fragile, like wisps of smoke. A simple breath and they might dissolve into nothingness.

The voices awakened memories of purple hanging blossoms on a mysterious vine that stretched tangled across my bedroom window when I was young, and my parents were still alive. It was that same sweet, grape-like scent that was now drifting about the cottage. I took a deep breath.

Scent merged with memory, the two becoming one. Story began following story from my childhood. I saw my parents' faces vividly before me, heard their voices, their laughter. Then, I felt a warmth growing in my heart—powerful and real. It was their love, spreading through me, filling me.

The sweetness of the scent filled my lungs. Whispers again disturbed the air around me—other voices. I saw more images from my past—blossoms hanging in large clusters, blossoms I wove into my hair, blossoms loosening, drifting with the wind. Their sweet perfume saturated my memories.

And—I realized, turning in wonder toward the

Mysteria—*they're all coming from her. And her eggs.*

The eggs, glowing warm and alive on the wall, now surrounded her. More were still coming. The whispers were loudest there.

I looked at my granddaughter curled up beneath, breathing it all in as she slept, hearing the voices, dreaming. They were part of her, now—the voices and the scent—part of her memory, her story. Just like they were part of mine.

Liliya would carry that perfume with her, all of her life, in her own stories, and in the stories the Mysteria was giving her, sealed away within each egg. At last, I understood. That's what the eggs really were—stories. Stories the Mysteria was giving to my granddaughter. In time, Liliya would tell those stories, and even if her listeners had never heard of the Mysteria, they would feel her touch in the fragrance released through them and through her words. The sweet fragrance would remind her listeners of what they could no longer remember, who they had once been—or could still be. Their own stories.

Like it has for me.

My old hand rested comfortably against my heart, against the warmth I could still feel there. Warmth that was a part of me, a part of *my* story.

Leaning back in my chair, I glanced toward the open window. The night had nearly passed. A pink blush brightened the horizon. Already, the first thin fingers of dawn were slipping through the eastern window. Shadows retreated before them. I watched as the light spread across the room—touching last the eggs on the far wall.

Suddenly, I sat up and stared, rubbing my eyes. The eggs were gone. I blinked, peering at the place where they had been—but no trace remained.

The Mysteria, her work now complete, simply unfolded her wings. With a slight push, she lifted her great body into the air. She flew out the open window in silence—just as she had come—taking with her all color and brilliance, wrapping it around her dark body like a silk scarf. As I watched her go—

a tiny black speck disappearing against the brightening sky—I felt a heat beginning in my hand. And something else. I looked down, and in the middle of my palm lay a blue pearl egg—smooth and wet and sticky—smaller than a single grain of rice. It glowed faintly. I stared at it, wondering what it could mean.

Bright, clear, and perfectly formed, it was more beautiful than any other the Mysteria had laid that night. I held it up in amazement, trying to examine it more closely. But as the light touched it, it, too, disappeared—just like the others. I turned and stared out the open window behind me where the Mysteria had disappeared.

My now empty hand lay clenched in my lap, but I could still feel the warmth in it, growing, spreading. Images and voices had begun wrapping around me, around my tongue—giving me words. I shivered. Then, I heard Liliya beginning to stir in her little bed, awakening, and my shivering increased. I could see it all unfolding before me. My granddaughter would soon leave me and be raised by another. I pulled my shawl tightly around my shoulders and huddled within it.

It was her story the Mysteria had given me, Liliya's story.

Chapter One

A gentle breeze blew in from the sea, and Liliya looked up. *Still too tired.* Her thoughts dragged along, disjointed. *Too tired to move.* She stared dully at the waving grasses, green broken only by occasional swatches of red, white, and yellow flowers that faded as they spread into the distance.

"Liliya, tell me another," he said again.

She turned her head slowly and blinked. Only Eli remained. The rest had gone. *They always leave.* She sighed heavily. *Always, that is*—she made a great effort and fixed her eyes on the young, ruddy-faced boy—*except for him. He never leaves, no matter what. Ever since*—

"Please, Liliya," he begged. "Tell me another."

"No." She winced, staring at the ground. "I can't."

"Please."

"No!" she snapped. But as the boy's face fell, she felt her

own shame rise. "I'm sorry, Eli."

He couldn't help being the way he was any more than she could.

The boy dug his bare toes into the brown earth.

"Eli?"

He didn't answer, and she frowned. She wasn't sure now whether he was sulking or thinking, but knowing him as well as she did, it was probably the latter. She often had to stop her words midstream, just to give him time to catch up.

"Eli, I can't tell anymore," she explained, trying to be patient. "Don't you understand what just happened?" She wrestled with her fear, biting her lip so hard she tasted the coppery taste of her own blood.

It had been a story. Just a simple story. But it got away from her. And, now— Now—

"I couldn't control it," she whispered.

Again.

She was angry, not at him, but at herself. She turned away, chasing her troubled thoughts off into the distance, where the blue sea and the grey sky blurred. She couldn't meet Eli's eyes. Not now. Not yet.

Slowly, the sun dipped into the west, setting the clouds aflame. The sky burst into brilliant color—orange, pink, and purple fire. Then, the colors began to bleed and fade, like her anger, and the shadows came.

Liliya drew a hand across her eyes, and her gaze returned.

In the fishing village below, the first evening shadows were beginning to stretch long from the squat buildings. Lamps were being lit along the streets. Families, friends, and loved ones had begun gathering on the docks. An evening ritual. They were there to welcome the fishing boats returning from sea—sons and fathers and grandfathers coming home.

Liliya did not move to join them. Nor, for that matter, did Eli. It had been years since either had. A lifetime ago, it seemed. Eli remained because he had no one left to welcome. She remained because she'd never had anyone.

"Liliya?"

She turned toward him and sighed.

He was staring at her and smiling. He didn't give up. Eli never gave up. He still pleaded, leaning forward now with growing eagerness.

"Liliya, just one more," he begged. "Please."

She pressed her lips together. Eli didn't understand, could never understand. Like the stories. He just kept asking. He always wanted more.

"No, Eli."

"They're not all like that," he muttered disappointedly, plucking a blade of grass.

Her breath caught sharply in her throat. "What did you just say?"

"I like your stories, Liliya." He looked at her, his eyes bright, untroubled. And empty.

She stared at him, hoping there would be more because sometimes there was. But there wasn't.

A heaviness filled her heart.

"No, Eli. No more," she said finally. "I'm finished for today. Now, help me up."

Simply accepting her words, Eli took her hand firmly and pulled, his nine-year-old body lifting her easily.

Liliya never tried to explain her weariness to him. She didn't understand it herself. What was, just was. Eli stood beside her patiently as her legs steadied beneath her.

"I'm ready now," she said quietly. With effort, she turned her face away from the sea, the breeze, the fading sunlight. "Let's go."

Leaning her own slight body against his sturdy frame, Liliya made her way down the worn path of the hill, all the way to the front door of the old Healer's cottage, one among many dotting the hillside. She rested her hand against the rough, wooden door.

"Thank you, again, Eli." She smiled faintly.

He nodded, smiling back. "Tomorrow, Liliya?" he asked, as always.

"Yes, tomorrow."

"More stories?"

"Yes, Eli," she sighed wearily. "More stories." *There are always more stories.*

His eyes brightened. "Ok."

"See you tomorrow, Eli."

"Bye, Liliya." He broke into a run and darted away.

Her eyes followed him. And then, because she couldn't help herself, she called after him, repeating the same thing she always said. "Make sure you go home before it gets too late. And try not to upset your uncle."

But he was already too far away to hear her.

Suppressing another sigh, she turned and reached for the handle to the door.

Chapter Two

"Grandmother, I'm home," Liliya called.

The door opened wide, letting in air and what remained of the light.

"Liliya. There you are. I was beginning to wonder."

The old Healer turned from the stove, wiping her hands on her apron. Looking at her granddaughter, she shook her head slightly and smiled. Liliya stood framed in the door, squinting. The vivid colors of the days' sun, the wildflowers, and the grasses still lingered on her granddaughter's face and in her hair.

"You're like the ocean breeze yourself, coming in like that." The old woman chuckled softly.

"The hill's like that," her granddaughter said quietly. Her eyes drifted to the open window, to the sloping edge of the green hill, just visible in the deepening shadows.

She nodded. "So it is, child. So it is."

Liliya closed the door and gave her a half-smile. "By the way, I'm sorry I'm late," she said.

"I suppose a few minutes more or less won't change the fate of the world or the outcome of our supper." She returned her granddaughter's smile before resuming her preparations. "So, how was the storytelling today?"

"Ok," Liliya said.

Stripping the fragrant leaves from the stems of the herbs, her grandmother nodded again. She had learned a long time ago not to insist. Liliya would tell a story if it was meant to be told.

From the corner of her eye, she studied the girl's face, examining it more closely. Then, seeing the tracks of recent tears, she bit back a sigh. *So, it was that kind of story. No wonder. The poor child.* She knew just what to do.

Hands on her hips, she turned and faced her. "Well, don't just stand there, girl. Wash your hands and help me cut up these vegetables for supper!"

"Yes, Grandmother," Liliya responded quickly.

They worked side by side in companionable silence, peeling and then chopping the potatoes and onions, the herbs. In almost no time at all, her grandmother was already stirring the ingredients into her savory fish broth.

The soup bubbled and steamed on the stove, filling the small cottage with its comforting fragrance. Sitting at the table, Liliya had her chin propped up in her hands, watching quietly as the soup cooked. She sniffed the air appreciatively.

"Mmmm, smells good."

"Hungry?"

"Yes," Liliya answered. "Very."

"You're always hungry, child." She shook the wooden spoon at her granddaughter and laughed. "Do something useful. Set the table, would you? It's ready."

"Yes, ma'am." Liliya rose from her seat, a grin on her face.

She listened to her granddaughter opening and closing

cupboards behind her. Liliya gathered all she needed and carried it to the table. Liliya divided up the cups, bowls, and spoons and laid them in their places. Then, uncovering yesterday's baking, she sliced off two thick pieces of the brown bread and set them on empty plates. Then the old Healer herself carried over two steaming bowls and they took their seats. Pressing their palms together, they gave thanks and then began.

Liliya spooned her soup hungrily.

The old woman watched the girl as they ate. Even though Liliya's appetite was good, it was obvious to her that something was bothering the girl. She was unusually quiet. Chewing her bread thoughtfully, she began pondering how best to draw it from her.

"So, how's Eli?" she asked finally.

Liliya paused in her eating and frowned. "As demanding as ever." She drew in a breath and then blew it out slowly. "He's so stubborn and selfish. All he ever wants is more stories." She pursed her lips together.

The old woman looked at her in surprise. Liliya usually spoke much more kindly about Eli.

"And is that such a bad thing?" She set down her spoon.

Liliya looked up defensively. "No. Yes. I don't know." She shook her head and then frowned again.

"Did Eli do something, then?" she prodded gently. She watched her granddaughter carefully.

"No, no. It's not that. Never Eli," Liliya sighed. "I mean—I really don't mind telling him stories. I want to. It's just..." The girl's face had gone slightly pale. She twisted her hands in her lap.

"It's just what, child?"

Her granddaughter licked her lips nervously. "Grandmother, I—" Liliya lowered her eyes.

"Liliya, tell me," she urged.

"I—" The girl covered her face. She spoke muffled into her hands. "I told another one."

The old Healer's eyes widened, and her hands began to

shake. "Another? Like Eli's?"

"Yes. Nearly so."

"Oh, child!" she cried, rising quickly and circling the table. She pulled the girl into a tight embrace.

"Grandma, I didn't want to. Really. I tried, but I couldn't stop it." She could feel hot tears where Liliya's face pressed into her dress. "And now Amanda—"

"What about Amanda?" she interrupted, pulling back from the girl to look at her.

Liliya's face went pale. "Her father won't be recovering from his sickness," she said softly.

"Oh, Liliya. Are you certain?"

Liliya nodded miserably.

"That poor, poor girl."

"It's all my fault—" Liliya moaned.

The old woman heaved a heavy sigh.

"They wouldn't listen to me," she continued, choking back a sob. "I got angry. And the story—it just came out. They're afraid of me now, Grandma. Afraid of my stories." She looked up suddenly, her cheeks flushed and damp. "All of them."

The old woman brushed the girl's long hair out of her eyes.

"I'm not. And neither is Eli," she said gently.

Liliya shook her head. "Eli should be," she said bitterly. Her gray eyes darkened, filling suddenly with guilt and self-hatred. Then she hunched over, wrapping her arms around herself. "They're right, you know." Her voice was flat. Emotionless. "Right to be afraid of me."

A stab of pain went through the old woman's heart as she stared at the girl. But there was nothing she could do. She knew no herbs that would ease the girl's burden, no herbs that could relieve the hurt. Never before had her knowledge as a Healer so completely failed her. Even her words faltered. Her eyes rested heavily on the child. There was only one thing left she could give. Herself.

"I love you, child," she whispered, and her heart nearly

broke.

Liliya's sob caught in her throat. Her eyes filled with fresh tears, but this time of a different kind.

"I love you, too, Grandma." She wrapped her arms around the old woman's neck and clung to her like a small child, burying her head in her shoulder.

The old Healer held her, stroking her hair, waiting. She didn't have to say anything more.

Gradually, the storm of tears stopped. Liliya pulled from her arms. "I'll do the dishes tonight," she mumbled, embarrassed.

"I was going to remind you it was your turn, anyway." The old woman forced a smile. She gave the girl a playful swat.

Liliya gave a faint smile in response and rose. In silence, she began stacking the empty bowls and cups. Then she carried them to the washtub by the stove.

The old woman watched as the girl poured the water from the kettle over the dishes. Steam rose in white clouds above them. Liliya added cold water and then plunged her hands inside. The sounds of small splashes and dishes clinking and scraping together filled the cottage. The stack of drying dishes grew beside her. Suddenly, Liliya's busy hands paused in the soapy water. She stiffened. The room fell silent and still.

The old Healer, rocking in her chair before the fire, also paused. "What is it, child?" she asked.

"A story," Liliya whispered.

The old woman sobered. "Let it come."

"But—"

"Just let it come, child."

"But Grandma, what if—"

"I trust you."

Nodding, Liliya swallowed. Her mouth opened. In a soft, tremulous voice, she began to speak. Her words floated throughout the cottage, their touch gentle and light. Liliya visibly relaxed as she stared into the distance, speaking out the words. A soft coloring tinted her cheeks.

Nodding to herself, the old woman resumed her rocking, her eyes half-closed. The girl's calming voice filled her ears, her thoughts. All around, the colors inside the cottage were brightening, their edges smudged by a sweetly scented breeze blowing in through the open windows. It was the wisteria blossom, the fragrance that always accompanied one of Liliya's *tellings*. The old woman breathed in deeply. She felt green words, purple words, and blue words wrap around her. A song began to form in her mouth. She recognized it as a lullaby from her childhood, long ago. Memories came with it: she remembered a warm, comforting lap, soft kisses planted on the top of her head, brown eyes crinkled with laughter. Finally, a face began to form.

The old woman stared at the vision, her throat tightening. A single word formed in her mouth and then broke from her lips.

"Mama."

She stopped her rocking. The word hung before her, heavy with old longing.

Mama?

She shook her head. It had been years since her mother had been alive. Years since she had last thought of her. Her mother had died young of a terrible, wasting disease while she—just a young child—had stood by helplessly, filled with remorse. It was for that reason she had dedicated her life to learning the secrets of the plants and herbs. Why she had become a Healer. But the knowledge she gained had done nothing to lessen the guilt she carried inside, nor alleviate her pain. Her learning had come too late to help her mother. It wasn't until Liliya came into her life—a helpless orphan in need—that the old woman felt the lessening of her guilt. At least, that's what she'd always told herself.

But inside, still hurting, that younger, remorse-filled self had always remained with her. And now, it was that younger self that Liliya's story was forcing her to face.

Liliya's words continued, the story reaching deeply into

her, unlocking her heart. More memories surfaced. Emotions and past hurts, feelings she'd kept hidden away and buried deeply within herself appeared, one after another. Then at last, from the deepest and most vulnerable part of herself, the heart's cry of that younger girl-self broke free and rose.

Mama, I should have helped you—

The old woman began trembling. Her lips parted, completing the old words. "I'm so sorry." The echoing hurt she heard in her voice startled even herself.

She stared at the younger face in her memory, the girl she had once been—and like a mirrored image, the girl stared back.

It was still her, she knew, but *she* was more now—and old. She raised her wrinkled hands before her, before the reflection. For a moment, the old and the young merged, both becoming pieces of who she was today, in this moment of time.

They were one and the same.

"Help me," the girl whispered.

And at last the old woman understood. She had never forgiven herself.

She stared hard at her reflection, at the girl-self she had been,

"It's not your fault," she spoke firmly. "It's never been your fault. You did all you could."

The girl in the mirror squeezed her eyes shut—and when she opened them again, she smiled and nodded.

All around the cottage, colors suddenly brightened and shimmered. The sweet scent of the Wisteria drifted about the cottage. Deep within the old woman, a peace welled up and filled her. She heard Liliya's voice behind her, growing softer. The mirror vision faded. The memory faded.

"You did all you could," the old woman whispered again—this time to herself. Then she, too, smiled.

She turned and looked at Liliya, bent over the washtub. The faraway gaze was still bright in the girl's eyes. The old woman's smile faded, bittersweet. For the first time, she felt afraid.

Her stories are growing stronger.

Already, Liliya's voice was rising and falling again. The stories were continuing. The old woman couldn't say when the words and the story had shifted, but she felt herself caught up with the movement of them. She was swept into another place. A new series of images came into focus before her, one after another—a clear brook winding through a green forest, a doe stepping out with her little spotted fawn, a green meadow sprinkled with yellow flowers, the sun setting red over a snow-topped mountain. These stories she did not know, but she welcomed them. They were gentle and full of beauty and life.

She leaned back, no longer afraid, receiving the words and images, letting them wash over her, renew her—heal her. Her heart strengthened.

Chapter Three

Clang! Clang! Clang!

The village bell rang loudly, sounding the alarm.

The old Healer looked up from the bundles of herbs she was tying to the open windows, her eyes widening. *It's coming.*

Already the wind about her was picking up.

Liliya! Outside! Her thoughts turned wild.

"Grandmother!" Liliya ran into the cottage, breathless. Her arms were full of the warm, fragrant clothes she had just gathered. "What is it? What's happening?"

From the cottages nearby wooden shutters slammed shut. Doors were locking. Villagers huddled in the dark shadows of their homes and waited.

The old woman grabbed the girl by the shoulder.

"Liliya, you must leave. Hurry. It's coming. It's coming

back. We can't let it find you. We can't let it have your stories. Here." She pressed the half-filled water bag into Liliya's hands. "Take this."

She pulled out an old sack and began rushing about the room, throwing whatever she could find inside: dried fruits, hard cheese, and bread. She yanked open the cupboards, the contents spilling onto the floor as she grabbed small sacks of wheat and barley and dried meat and tossed them in, as well. Then, she grabbed Liliya's winter cloak from its hook, and rolling it tight, stuffed it on top. Lastly, grunting and breathing hard, she dragged the heavy chest from under her bed and flung the lid open wide. Liliya appeared by her side, too late to help, as the old woman fell to her knees and rummaged frantically through the contents, pulling out a black shawl. As she held it up, the golden threads caught the dim light and shimmered.

"Grandma, you don't mean?" Liliya gasped, staring wide-eyed at the shawl.

"It's time, child," she said gravely.

Liliya's face paled.

"Didn't you hear me?" She took the girl by the shoulders once more and shook her. "It's like I've always told you. It's coming. You're in danger. Your stories are in danger. You have to go. Now!"

"Grandma, please. I don't—"

"Liliya, take the stories. Go North."

"North?" Liliya whispered. She cast a glance toward the northern window. Fear and longing crossed her face.

Taking her by the chin, the old woman turned the girl's head so that they were staring at one another once more. She looked into the girl's gray eyes, wide with fear, and swallowed the lump growing in her own throat.

She was remembering the pale, unconscious child that had been brought to her nearly fifteen years ago, cold and stiff with seawater. She remembered her own hands hovering over the tiny girl, feeling the child's spirit trembling there, just beneath the surface, awaiting release. She remembered her fierce struggle to save the child. The feeling of relief and joy when the child had at last opened her eyes. Those same gray eyes.

And now she must release her.

"Yes, child. North," she whispered. Her hand hovered over the girl's heart once more. "Go find your story. It's the only way."

How she wished theirs had been different, that Liliya's could have been a simple, normal life. But it was not to be, had never been meant to be. She had known that from the moment the girl opened those gray eyes.

"Grandma." Liliya's voice broke. "What about you?"

The old woman wrapped her arms around the girl, embracing her in a hard hug. "I love you child, always have. Like you were my very own." Slipping the sack's strap over the girl's head, she turned her around and pushed her toward the door. "Now, go."

"But, Grandma," Liliya pleaded. She dug in her heels, looking back over her shoulder.

The old woman forced a brave smile. "I'll hold tight to our stories. I won't let it take them. I won't forget. I promise. Now run," she told her, "and don't stop. Not until you are far, far away."

Another cold gust blew through the open window and she could see the wave of goosebumps rising on Liliya's arms. The Wind was getting closer.

"Go, child." Her voice broke as she spoke the words of journey, words of prayer and hope. "May the winds always blow soft."

Tears were wetting Liliya's cheeks. "And may the waves bring you home," Liliya finished in a whisper.

"Now go!" she shouted.

Taking one last terrified look back, Liliya tucked the sack against her side and ran. She ran as fast as she could—on and on—away from the rising Wind, into the future.

"Liliya, stop!"

She stumbled in confusion. Turning and seeing Eli, she

gasped in dismay.

"Eli, go back." She pressed a hand to her chest, feeling her heart racing underneath.

"Liliya, where are you going?" His feet pounded the dirt, running until he caught up with her. "Can I come, too?"

A gust hit them, swirling their words.

"Eli, I'm not going back."

He just stared at her in confusion.

The wind blew stronger. In it, Liliya heard a faint wailing. Her heart froze in her chest. She knew that sound. She had often heard it in her nightmares.

Another gust, and her long skirt was wrapped around her legs, nearly bringing her to her knees.

"Let me come, Liliya. Please?"

"Eli, I—" she began in protest.

Then she felt it, the rising Wind, growing stronger as it roared onto the shore behind them.

Cold tendrils stretched out hungrily, reaching for her stories, insatiable, searching. The hair on her arms stood on end.

It's too late, already too late. It's here.

"No!" she cried.

Her ragged breath caught in her throat. *It will not have them. It will not have me.* Liliya took Eli's hand in hers, tears now streaming down her face.

"Run, Eli. Run!"

Worse and worse.

Behind them, growing louder even than the crashing of the waves against the shore, she heard something else and trembled.

It was the Wind. And it was laughing.

Chapter Four

On and on, Liliya and Eli ran, away from the Wind.

Clutching her side with one hand and Eli with the other, Liliya pulled the younger boy along with her until his steps dragged wearily beside her. Up they climbed, then down, and then up again, adrenaline, fear, and raw desperation driving her forward each step. They ran what seemed like forever, a blur of measureless time. But they did not stop. Once more, the road began to descend, pulling them with it. Liliya's pace quickened. Eli's shorter legs could no longer keep up. He stumbled and fell.

"Eli!" Liliya cried.

She just managed to avoid a tangle of legs before he pulled her to the ground with him. Together they tumbled down the hill, landing in a heap at the bottom.

Liliya lay dazed, gasping for breath.

What just happened? She glanced around in confusion. *Where am I?*

The sun was again shining warm and bright overhead. She squinted, blinking rapidly. It was quieter, too, she realized, and the Wind was no longer blowing so strongly.

Carefully, she sat up. Suppressing a groan, she began untangling herself from her skirt, from the broken branches and twigs. She hurt all over. She had a raw scrape along her calf, another on her elbow. She wracked her brain trying to recall what her grandmother had taught her. Maybe she could find some yarrow or goldenrod. She automatically began ticking off the plants she knew with healing properties. Then, she caught sight of the smaller figure beside her. He still hadn't moved.

"Eli?" Her voice was hoarse. She touched his arm lightly. "Eli? Wake up. Oh, please be ok," she begged.

He moaned softly, his head falling heavily from side to side. Blinking, he opened his eyes. He stared up at her, focusing on her face. The brown of his eyes appeared almost black against his very pale skin.

"Eli, are you all right?" Liliya whispered anxiously. She was near tears.

"Ok. Liliya," he stammered. He licked his dusty lips. Then raising a hand, he fingered a lump forming on the side of his head. "Ouch." He grimaced. "No."

"Don't move yet. Ok?"

He gave a slight nod and then squeezed his eyes shut.

Somehow, she still had possession of the water bag, and what was even more amazing, it was undamaged. She yanked the strap over her head and removed the cap. Carefully, she put it to his lips. He drank thirstily. Water dribbled down his chin. Color began to return to his cheeks.

"Better?" she whispered.

He nodded again.

"Can you sit now?"

"I think so," he said.

"Here."

With Liliya helping, he rose to a sitting position. "What happened, Liliya?"

"We escaped," she said shakily, hardly daring to believe. "For the moment."

She cast her eyes around them once more. She still recognized nothing.

They were in a sort of small valley or gully. To the left, she could see where the road divided the land, an endless line, stretching out before and behind them. Nearer, she glimpsed her old rucksack, the one that her grandmother had so hastily packed, caught sideways in a bush. Many of the contents were scattered.

"Wait here," she told Eli. "I'll be right back."

Limping, she made her way over. She quickly retrieved the sack and its contents and then turned back toward Eli, still gazing warily about. She kept an ear tilted as she walked, listening. She was almost certain she had heard faint voices again, stirring in the wind. A shiver slowly traveled up her spine.

"It's still behind us," she said softly as she returned.

Her eyes were fixed on Eli. He was now struggling to stand.

"I know, Liliya," he grunted. His voice was strained. "I heard it, too."

Liliya took his hand and helped him. Feeling that it was cold and clammy, she studied his face worriedly.

Arnica. That's what I need for Eli. I'll have to find some.

She glanced around, almost as if expecting to see the bright yellow flower. But of course, there wasn't any. Arnica blossomed in late summer.

She turned back to Eli.

"It's going to be ok." She gave him a reassuring smile, squeezing his hand gently. "But we can't stay here. It's too dangerous. Can you keep going? Just for a little while longer?"

He nodded.

"Good." She smiled again. "I'll help you."

Already her eyes were sweeping across the land, mapping out the path they must go.

"Come on."

She wrapped an arm around him. Carefully, she navigated through the smoothest sections, leading Eli back toward the road.

Suddenly, Liliya's hair whipped up and around her wildly. She staggered. A powerful gust had blown up and over the hill, blowing so hard she could hardly see. Angry wails and screeches filled the air. She and Eli pressed their hands to their ears and huddled together. Then, just as suddenly, the wind stopped. The valley became silent and still once more.

Liliya lowered her hands and then began peeling the strands of hair from her eyes and lips with shaking fingers. She brushed them back over her shoulder, angrily. *It will not have us.*

"You still ok, Eli?" she asked. Her voice shook despite herself.

He was rubbing sand and grit from his eyes. "Yes," came the faint reply.

She took a deep breath, squaring her shoulders. "Come on, then. Let's go." She gritted her teeth. *I can do this. For Eli.*

"Ok, Liliya."

Neither asked where the wind had come from. Both already knew.

The day was growing late. The sun rested heavily on their left shoulders. Liliya set off determinedly, bringing Eli along with her.

Go and keep going, her grandmother had said. *And don't stop until you are far, far away.*

The grasses stretched green all around, the blades bending only slightly as the breeze became milder. They heard no more from the Wind, and gradually the tension in the air became less charged. Liliya felt some of the tension in herself lessen, as well.

Then she heard it from within…voices were beginning

to stir. They were awakening. Liliya groaned softly. "Why, of all times, now?" she asked.

A story was taking form, rising out from the edges of her thoughts. She felt it and nearly cried. Already she was so tired. And there was Eli.

Her thoughts became more scattered.

She struggled against it, trying to resist, but it was no use. The story, like a powerful ocean wave, pulled back and then surged again, washing over her, separating her thoughts.

Too late. Too strong.

Colors swirled around her. She grabbed Eli's shoulder and held on when the familiar heat rushed through her.

He grabbed her, his eyebrows tight with worry. "Liliya? What is it? What's wrong?"

"A story." She winced, closing her eyes briefly. Her head pounded. The remainder of her thoughts were immediately swept to the edges of her mind, where they unraveled, drifted, and were for the moment forgotten. She was no longer aware of the road, no longer aware of Eli. New thoughts, other thoughts, began to emerge—pictures and images and voices.

A wisp.

A thread of the past—a ghost of a memory.

A story.

Liliya tried to grasp it, but it eluded her, teased her, remaining just out of reach. She waited. The story formed around her, drawing her within. Then, the words came— words joining more words. She opened her mouth.

Liliya found herself in another place, another time. A young sun shone bright and warm overhead. It was a land alive with green and growing things. Animals of all kinds walked around unafraid. She breathed deeply, and her lungs filled with fragrant, pure air. It was a beautiful place, a rich place, a place teeming with abundant life.

Liliya looked around slowly. The words of the story continued.

In the distance, she saw the silhouette of a family. They were walking together, close, completely at ease with one another. She heard the soft sounds of their voices floating over the low hills, their light and easy laughter.

Then the vibrant colors began to fade. Liliya felt a coldness descend. A heavy dread settled over her heart.

Into that land, a storm came, driven by a dividing Wind. It blotted out the bright sun, bringing shadows and darkness. The hearts of men were split. Separation and forgetfulness came into the world. Destruction followed. The Wind pounded the earth, snapping trees in half, pulling others up by their roots and tossing them broken to the wayside. Rocks tumbled. Crystalline streams ran red with mud.

Liliya felt the Wind rise around her, too. It was tugging at her long skirt, pushing her, blowing her hair in all directions so that she had to stretch out her hands before her, blindly. Fear filled her. She stuttered as she spoke.

The scene changed again.

Liliya blinked and looked around. She pressed a hand to her chest. Her heart was beating rapidly.

She stood once more in sunlight, in the same place she had seen the family. Only now, it was a broken land. The children were gone. The father walked in silence, alone.

His head was bowed, his hand held protectively against his heart. He turned his face slowly, toward the setting sun. The light blazed around him. Then, with care and firmness of purpose, he began making his way through the destruction, through the brokenness. He followed a path Liliya could not see, a path she somehow knew would lead him back to his family. She watched, as he grew smaller in the distance and then disappeared. Then, drifting out from the edge of the growing darkness, Liliya heard a faint echo of laughter.

She wrapped her arms around herself and shuddered.

"Liliya?"

She blinked and returned. Her eyes quickly took in the changes—the now rolling landscape, the long, winding road—and finally came to rest on the small boy beside her.

"Eli," she breathed.

She had forgotten about Eli.

As she looked at him, she began searching his face. Something was different.

"Eli?" She said his name again, almost fearfully.

He gazed at her with eyes that were large and clear and fully there. Suddenly, he placed his hands on his hips and stamped a foot.

"It *was* the same wind, wasn't it?" he insisted.

The Wind. Again.

"Wasn't it?"

"Eli." She kneaded a hand into her forehead. Her thoughts tumbled in confusion. Pictures from the story replayed before her. Pictures of her grandmother. The cottage. "I don't know. Probably," she sighed.

Why, Eli? Why did you come now—of all times?

"It was," he repeated stoutly.

She eyed him wearily but didn't say anything. She knew he was right. When he spoke like this, he was always right. And it scared her.

"I know it was," he grumbled.

So do I, she thought miserably. *But I just don't want to admit it.*

Her limbs felt leaden, and weariness dragged on her but she tried to ignore it. There was always weariness after telling a story, and sometimes it was deeper than at other times.

"Let's just go," she said heavily. "We have to keep going."

Pressing her lips together, she took a step, leading the way. She didn't say anything more; she was too tired.

Eli followed.

The weariness increased as they walked. Liliya's steps grew heavier. Her thoughts dulled. Without realizing it, her feet began to slow. Then, she felt Eli wrap his strong arm around her waist. She looked down, meeting brown eyes full of concern, and smiled.

"Thanks, Eli," she whispered. She shook her head in an attempt to clear it. "I guess I probably should have taken a short rest."

"Do you want to sit down now?" he asked.

She smiled and shrugged. "No. I'll be ok. It'll pass if I actually give it a minute."

He frowned. "If you say so."

She paused and turned her face upward, breathing deeply. A cool breeze touched her cheeks. Gulls were riding the same breeze high above them, skimming the edges of white clouds scattered across a blue sky. Their faint cries reached her ears. They were beginning to circle back toward the sea, flying away in groups of twos and threes. Liliya listened sadly as their cries faded into the distance.

Suddenly home seemed very far away.

Then, at last, only one voice remained. Liliya heard it echoing lonesomely among the clouds. She stared up at the small speck, shielding her eyes with her hand.

"Go back," she whispered.

Another breeze blew, carrying with it the smell of the sea, the smell of home. Her throat tightened.

"Go back." Her whisper grew hoarse. "Go back while you still can." With effort, she pulled her eyes away.

Around them, grass-covered hills stretched unchanged on either side of the bare road, broken only occasionally by dark green mounds of bushes. She fixed her eyes on the road ahead, where her own journey lay. Suddenly, she felt the urge to put as much distance between them and the Wind as was possible before night fell.

"You may be right about the Wind, Eli," she said slowly, her voice sounding strangely calm, even to her. "But even if it was the same, it doesn't have us now." She clenched a fist. "And it won't. Not if I can help it. Come on." She lifted her chin. Her strength was back. "I'm ready now. Let's go."

"All right, Liliya," he grinned, nodding. "I'm ready, too."

They began walking quickly, side by side, determined to outrace the Wind.

Chapter Five

"Liliya, I'm hungry."

Liliya turned to look at Eli in confusion. Something about his voice sounded different, changed.

"I'm hungry," he repeated, pouting slightly.

She stared at his face—hard and frowned. He *was* changed. He had gone back to wherever he hid, retreating into himself. His large brown eyes were, once again, dull and empty.

She sighed. She had hoped this time that he might stay. She gave him a sad smile. "So am I," she admitted.

With all that had been happening, food had been the last thing on her mind. Eli's mentioning it had just reminded her of how hungry she really was, how hungry they both must be. She glanced at the road behind them, the road they had just traveled. It remained empty and quiet, and evening was at last gathering on the edges. Liliya paused and listened, making a decision. She had heard no voices for quite some time.

Safe for now.

"Come on," she said. She noticed how long her shadow stretched out before her, how late it had grown. "I've got just the thing." She smiled.

Eli followed eagerly.

Liliya led them just off the road, beside a stream. Weary, she sank down on the rocky bank and dipped her sore, dusty feet in the cool water.

"Sit down, Eli." She patted the ground beside her.

Eli dropped down obediently.

Opening her rucksack, she began rummaging through the contents. She pulled out a small loaf of the brown bread her grandmother had put in it. Tearing the loaf into two pieces, she handed the larger one to Eli, keeping the smaller for herself.

Neither spoke as both ate hungrily. When they had finished, Eli stretched out flat on his stomach. He drank long and thirstily from the stream. Then, he crawled back up the bank next to Liliya, his lips and chin still wet. He smiled contentedly. Yawning and rubbing his eyes, he positioned himself comfortably between the tree roots and let out a deep sigh.

"That was good, Liliya."

"You're welcome, Eli." The corner of her mouth twitched.

He rubbed his chin, wiping away the last of the water, and yawned again.

A breeze began to stir, and Liliya stiffened, listening anxiously. She heard voices in the wind, moving above and around her. But they were different from the fearful voice of the Wind. These voices were gentle and quiet. These voices were safe. They reminded her of the voices she had heard from the hill above the cottage. She leaned back and relaxed, her eyes half-closed. Around them, the shadows continued to darken and deepen.

When she finally looked back toward Eli, she couldn't help but smile. The boy had curled up on the ground beside her and fallen asleep. As she gazed at his peaceful, untroubled face, marred only by the darkening bruise from their tumble down the hillside, she sighed.

"Eli." She shook her head. "Why did you come with me?"

Eli's thin arms and legs stuck out from the ragged ends of his trousers and shirt. As she watched him shiver in his sleep, she felt a softness fill her heart. Tucking a few loose strands behind her ear, she leaned over and opened her sack once more, rummaging inside. It wasn't long before she had found what she was looking for and pulled out her own winter cloak, the one her grandmother had made for her just last year. After shaking it out, she wrapped it around him, tucking him in warmly. Then, she sat back on her heels and studied his face.

He was smiling in his sleep.

"Are you ever going to come back to me for keeps, Eli?" she whispered softly. She brushed her fingertips lightly across his bruised cheek.

With the sun gone, the temperature dropped rapidly. She began to shiver, rubbing her arms as she stared up at the awakening night sky. Never before had she been outside so late. It was a lonesome feeling.

One by one, stars were coming out, small bright points of light appearing against an inky black backdrop. She watched in growing amazement. The stars were brighter and more numerous than she had ever seen before, filling the night sky until it was simply dazzling. They winked and blinked at one another animatedly. She could almost hear the words they were saying, the stories they were sharing.

As she stared, the night around her grew darker and colder. She grew colder with it.

Finally, she gave in. Reaching into the sack one more time she pulled out the black shawl. The golden threads caught the starlight and shimmered faintly. She wrapped it around herself slowly, mindful of its mystery. She didn't know its story, only that she and it were connected to some unknown past. She ran her fingers lightly down the smooth fabric, tracing the golden threads. It was the first time she had worn it since she had been found wrapped in it over fourteen years ago. As she huddled in it now for warmth, she found it surprisingly familiar, surprisingly comforting, and surprisingly warm.

She leaned back and continued to stare into the darkness. Her own weariness began to come at last, in waves, and she found herself slowly sinking beneath them. Soon, her eyelids began to droop, and her breathing became softer and more regular. Her chin came to rest on her chest. Then, an even deeper stillness gathered around her.

Chapter Six

Morning came, and Liliya awoke with the first faint rays of dawn. For a moment, she didn't know where she was. Then she looked around, and everything came rushing back.

Wind.

Running.

Eli.

She glanced at the still lump beside her.

"Eli, wake up." She shook him.

"Awake," he mumbled and then rolled over.

"No, Eli." She smiled faintly. She shook him again. "It's morning. Time to get up."

"Just one more minute."

"Come on, Eli," she coaxed, rolling him onto his back. "Get up."

But he only snuggled more tightly under the cloak.

She pursed her lips together, thinking. Then, breaking into a grin, she grabbed the cloak and gave it a strong yank. "Come on, lazybones. No more sleeping," she laughed. "The sun's up!"

Eli gave a noncommittal grunt and then reached a hand behind him, searching blindly. "Liliya," he complained, shivering. "C-c-cold."

"You won't be once you get up and start moving," she said without sympathy. She rolled up the cloak and packed it away with the shawl.

Eli slowly opened his eyes and lay squinting in the brightening light. One by one, he began stretching his limbs, and then finally, he stretched out his whole body.

Seeing him stir, Liliya rose stiffly and began to shake out her skirt, attempting to brush off the leaves and dirt. As she became more fully awake, she took in their surroundings again.

"Eli, hurry up," she insisted.

But Eli had never been one to wake quickly. Still complaining, he sat up and rubbed his eyes. After a nearly head-splitting yawn, he crawled slowly to the bank and leaned over, taking a long drink from the stream.

Liliya eyed him impatiently as she combed her fingers roughly through her tangled hair. Once Eli had finished his drink and risen to his feet, she slung the sack over her shoulder and began to thread her way back to the road.

"Come on, Eli, we're going," she called over her shoulder.

Eli, still shaking the sleep from his thoughts, followed behind, yawning.

Fearful of the Wind behind them, Liliya kept them walking all day, stopping only to eat a bit more of the brown bread before continuing. The breezes grew softer, and Liliya no longer heard in them the occasional harsh whisper, nor felt the cold fingertips brushing her cheeks. But even so, her fear did not lessen, nor did her dread. The same urgency—coupled with desire—was in her steps, driving her forward.

The North is still far away.

"Liliya, where are we going?" Eli asked.

They had been walking for at least an hour.

"Away, Eli." Her voice was quiet. "Far away. North."

"Is that where you come from?"

She looked at him in surprise and then said faintly, "I think so."

Her grandmother had told her many times that she bore the mark of the people of the North—the light coloring of her hair. Maybe it was true, but she didn't know for certain because all the people Liliya ever met had brown eyes and dark brown hair—brown like the rich, fertile earth beneath their feet. But Liliya's hair was a lighter brown, many shades lighter than those around her, and her eyes—well, they weren't brown.

"Is it far?"

"Yes, Eli, very far. A many, many days' journey."

Eli stared ahead mutely. Finally, he spoke again. "I miss the village."

She glanced behind her at all she, too, left behind. "I know," she said softly. "So do I."

She slowly turned her gaze forward toward the North. She knew with certainty that was the direction she must go. That *her* future lay there.

But Eli? Her thoughts stalled. *He doesn't have to go, does he?*

She turned to him sharply, grabbing him by the shoulder. "Eli, do you really want to go with me? Really and truly? You could go back, you know. To the village. It's not too late." Her voice was uncertain.

His eyes brightened. "Are you going back, Liliya?"

"No," she said quietly. Her hands dropped heavily to her sides. "I can't go back. I have to go on."

Eli frowned, the light faded from his eyes. "Oh."

They began walking again in silence.

Liliya plucked a leaf from a bush lining the road. She began to tear it, letting the pieces fall from her fingers as she went. She plucked another and then another.

"Why not?"

Liliya tried to bite back her irritation. "Why not what?"

"Why can't you go back?" Eli asked.

"The Wind, Eli," she said in exasperation. "Can't you remember?"

"The wind?" he asked blankly. Then, understanding flashed in his eyes. "Oh, yeah. I remember. The Wind."

"It's back there, and it's coming. After me—and my stories. I have to go North, Eli. I have no choice." She looked at him, new doubts rising above her frustration, chased by her fear. "Maybe you should go back after all." Her eyes darted back toward the way they had come. "You could help Grandmother."

"I'm not leaving you, Liliya," he protested.

"But what about your uncle? Won't he be worried?" She stared at him.

"He won't miss me." Eli kicked at the dirt, his bright face darkening for just a moment.

"It's dangerous, Eli," she said bitterly, her voice fading. "Just to be with me." The full weight of what was behind her, pursuing her, had her trembling.

Eli's eyes flashed with determination. He stuck his chest out and said stoutly, "I'm not afraid."

She stopped and looked at him hard. "No," she whispered. "But I am."

He smiled and slipped his hand into hers, comfortably. "I'm staying with you, Liliya."

She stared at his smaller hand in her own and sighed. She had nothing to offer him—nothing except her friendship— and her stories. Yet, that was all Eli wanted, she knew. All he had ever wanted.

"Yes?" Eli looked up, the question in his bright eyes.

"Yes," she heard herself whisper.

Her eyes, once again, followed her path straight into the far unknown. Stories untold stretched out before her, pulling her. Eli's eyes followed her gaze, taking the same path. The

North was ahead.

Slinging her rucksack over her shoulder, Liliya set her jaw firmly. They would continue together, all the way.

"Come on, Eli." Taking a deep breath and then exhaling, she took a step forward, planting her feet solidly in the bare dirt road.

Eli, in imitation, did the same. Then, looking up at her, he grinned. "Together, Liliya."

Despite herself, her doubts, and her worries, she had to smile back. She quickly placed one foot in front of the other and began leading the way. The past and all they knew—the village, the sea—would soon be left behind. Ahead were places they had never gone before. Ahead was their future.

Eli kept pace beside her, step by step. They went together.

In each footprint, they left the dust of their past, mingled with the new dust of the road. With each step, their past and their future met.

Chapter Seven

When night fell again, and it became too dark to see, Liliya finally allowed them to stop. There was a sharpness to the air, a chilliness. They shared another loaf of the brown bread, wrapped themselves in the cloak and shawl, and then lay down. They were too tired to talk. Huddled together, they fell asleep almost immediately.

The moon rose silently above them, shining its pale, cold light. Wispy clouds stretched over it, clouds that quickly built and thickened. The moon faded behind them. Then the breeze picked up, blowing even cooler. A few scattered drops of rain fell.

"Hmmm?" Liliya murmured, her voice thick with sleep. She opened her eyes to darkness. She shook her head to clear it and sat up.

More drops fell, raising the dust.

"Rain?" She stared at the dark sky in surprise.

"Liliya?" Eli mumbled sleepily, "What's the matter? What's happening?"

"It's starting to rain."

She leaned forward to peer into the gloom. The shawl began to slip from her shoulder, and she clutched it absently, pulling it up and wrapping it tightly around her.

"It's pretty dark out there, but do you think we could try to find some shelter? These trees won't stop the rain." She chewed her lip pensively. "Eli?"

When he didn't respond, she turned toward him, thinking he hadn't heard. But he had only gone back to sleep.

"I guess that means we stay," she sighed.

The sky in the distance lit up and then darkened again. Several seconds later, she heard the soft rumblings of thunder. She stared harder into the darkness, her anxiety growing. She had never liked thunderstorms.

Suddenly, the wind picked up, and with it, rain began to fall.

Liliya wrapped the shawl around herself even more tightly.

The night sky lit up once more, followed closely by a soft clap of thunder. The storm was heading their way.

"Eli, wake up." She shook him. "There's a storm coming."

She rose to stand closer to the tree.

Drops of rain had begun to slide from leaf to leaf, merging with others, growing in size until they finally landed about her feet with great wet splashes.

"Eli, get up. Hurry. Over here," she called urgently.

The rain began to fall harder.

Eli rose and, half-stumbling, half-staggering, managed to make his way over to her, dragging the cloak in the dirt behind him. "Liliya." He yawned, still half asleep. "What—"

"Eli!" she cried, grabbing the cloak from him. "What are you thinking?" She shook it out and then wrapped it around him again, tightly. "I don't need you getting sick on me," she muttered. "Now, stand over here. Next to me. Next to this tree," she ordered.

Eli scooted in close to her. "Sorry, Liliya."

They stared into the blackness.

After a while, Eli began rubbing his eyes and yawning again. He leaned back against the tree, his eyes growing heavy. Suddenly, lightning flashed in the distance. He jumped and stared wide-eyed.

"A thunderstorm is coming," Liliya said quietly.

A gust blew, and the tops of the trees waved in the darkness above them, sending more drops of rain scattering below.

"Is it the Wind, Liliya?" His voice sounded shrill.

"No…" She paused, feeling the darkness with all her senses. There were no voices, no grasping fingers. She rubbed her smooth arms. No goosebumps. "Just a regular storm," she finally said.

And yet, I have to wonder.

The rain pounded harder. They remained under the tree, growing colder, wetter, and more miserable by the moment.

Lightning flashed through the sky once more, followed almost immediately by a loud rumbling of thunder. A few seconds later, the sky was brightened once more, this time almost directly above them.

"Liliya?" Eli huddled in the cloak, shivering. He stared at her anxiously.

"It's going to be ok, Eli." She forced a smile. "I promise."

Crack!

The sky lit brilliantly above them. In that brief moment of light, their eyes met, wide with fear. Then, the sky darkened once more.

"Liliya," Eli wailed. "I don't like the thunder."

Neither do I. She was shaking inside.

"Nothing to worry about, Eli." She spoke with greater confidence than she felt.

The rain poured, the wind gusting.

"When's it gonna stop?"

"I don't know. Soon." *I hope.*

She was so cold. She had to clench her jaw to keep her teeth from chattering. Water splashed around her feet. Her skirt clung to her, sodden.

Crack!

Eli jumped again, making a whimpering sound. "Please, Liliya, make it stop," he begged. He was trying to cover his ears and hold onto the cloak at the same time.

White lines tore jaggedly through the clouds.

"Hold on, Eli!" Liliya shouted. She was looking straight up. "It's right over us."

The rain pounded the earth, soaking through their outer garments. They bowed their heads, blinking cold water from their eyes.

Crack! Boom!

A tree on the other side of the road suddenly exploded into flames. They both jumped and screamed.

"Here, Eli. Take my hand," Liliya shouted.

Even in the semi-green-gray darkness, she could see him trembling. So did she. They pressed in against each other.

Crack!

Forked lightning ripped across the sky overhead.

They stood huddled together under the falling rain, not daring to move, not daring to speak, and wishing they were anywhere but where they were.

Crack! Boom! Crack!

The storm passed overhead. Lightning and thunder soon began to fade into the distance.

The winds quieted. The rain slowed and then stopped. At last, all that remained was the sound of water dripping—dripping from the leaves and the branches, dripping from their clothes and their hair. A stillness followed.

Their eyes swept uneasily over the damage left behind—broken tree limbs, flooded dips and valleys here and there, and wisps of smoke and steam rising from the now blackened tree trunk.

"Is it over?" Eli asked.

"Yes, I think so."

"Good," he whispered hoarsely. Then, his face crumpling, he buried his head in her chest and burst into tears.

"Oh, Eli," Liliya soothed. Her own tears joined his. She wrapped her arms around him tightly. "Shhh. It's ok now."

Then distantly, as if an echo of the retreating storm itself, Liliya heard the faint rumbling sound of laughter—a sound even colder than the rain. She shivered and clutched her wet shawl. She had no more doubts about who had sent the storm. *It's still behind us, still following.*

Trembling, she lifted her eyes and found courage. "Eli, look," she whispered. Tears threatened her once more.

In the east, the sky was just beginning to pink, breaking between the clouds. The night had ended.

Chapter Eight

The sun rose higher and warmer. Liliya tried fixing her gaze on the road ahead, but she felt so tired. She yawned again and then clamped her mouth shut. Her thoughts drifted before her loosely—with the breeze and with the grasses. Every once in a while, she tilted an ear behind them, listening for the voice of the Wind. Each time, she heard nothing. All she really wanted to do was lie down and sleep, to forget everything, even if just for a little while. But at least she had one thing to be thankful for…their wet clothes had dried on them as they walked.

"Liliya, what's that?" Eli shook himself awake and pointed.

"What? I don't see anything." She squinted.

"Over there. Those black things."

Following the direction he was pointing, Liliya shaded

her eyes, trying to see farther ahead.

"Are they houses?" he asked.

"I don't know, Eli." She thought she could almost make out several black blurs along the landscape. But then again, it could have just been more road. "Maybe."

"They look like houses," he persisted.

She squinted again, straining, but her eyes only blurred worse. She gave up with a sigh. "I'm sorry, Eli. I can't make them out," she admitted. "I guess your eyes are just better than mine." Eli stared a little longer. "They're houses," he concluded, satisfying himself, at last. "I'm sure of it." Then, his mouth opened wide in another ear-splitting yawn.

About midday, they began to come upon farmhouses, spread far apart from one another. Liliya and Eli stared at them curiously. The houses were small, though larger than the cottage of Liliya's grandmother. Each was surrounded by yellowing fields of grain with white clumps of sheep and goats dotting the green hillsides. Many of the houses were squat and low and made plainly of earth and rock with green grass and flowers growing on some of their roofs. White billowy clouds raced one another across the blue sky above them, occasionally blotting out the sun.

Liliya and Eli relaxed. Their eyes wandered the countryside from farm to farm. It was a peaceful country, a pleasant country, a place where they could breathe easily.

"I like this place," Eli said simply.

A sweet floral scent drifted in the air, faint but familiar.

Liliya smiled as she recognized it. "Me, too."

The road stretched out before them in soft curves as it wound through the countryside. They passed more farms and more houses, catching glimpses of daily life. Men, bent under the sun, worked the fields. Children weeded gardens. Shepherds stood guard on the low hills. Sometimes Liliya and Eli smelled baking bread. Other times it was the rich meaty smells of stew. The homey smells mixed with those of the animals, the grasses, and the dark soil beneath them.

As they continued, they came to another farmhouse, built

closer to the road than any they'd seen so far. Squawks of angry chickens filled the air. Dogs barked. They heard someone shout.

Liliya's feet slowed. She and Eli approached warily.

Suddenly, the flock they had been hearing appeared in a flurry of feathers and noise, crossing the road directly in front of them. The hens' necks and wings were stretched out as far as they could go. Behind the chickens ran a red-faced girl, carrying a broom and shouting. Two scruffy-looking dogs rounded a corner behind her, running and barking at the girl's heels.

Liliya and Eli froze and stared, their mouths open.

The girl took a swipe with her broom, and the flock turned, crossing the road again. She chased after them, yelling even louder.

Liliya had to bite back her smile. Eli giggled openly.

In the midst of the chaos, a familiar feeling began tugging at the edges of Liliya's thoughts. Whispers were rising, the voices faint. Stories were forming.

Liliya looked about them more fully, taking in the ordinary farmhouse and the usual yellowing fields beyond. It was an average farm, smaller than some of the others she had seen, but not the smallest. She swept her gaze over the clean and well-ordered yard. She noticed a row of covered cages in a small enclosed area. Between the wooden slats, she glimpsed gray, brown, and black bits of fur, sometimes a tip of a long ear, sometimes a fluffy tail.

She smiled as she recognized them.

"Get over here. No. Not that way. Here!"

Liliya turned. She was just in time to see a streak of white scurry into the henhouse. The girl slammed the door shut and latched it.

"Gotcha!" she shouted triumphantly.

A roar of indignant squawks came from inside.

"That'll teach ya to obey, ya foul feathered beasts!" She gave the wooden frame a good kick.

More squawks and protests erupted loudly. A cloud of

feathers rose and then slowly drifted back down. She blew out a great, angry puff of breath. It sent the feathers scattering again.

"Serves ya right, ya tiresome old biddies," she grumbled.

Rubbing a red mark on her hand, she grimaced. Then, turning and seeing Liliya and Eli for the first time, she stopped, almost mid-stride. The two dogs halted beside her, their tongues hanging long out the sides of their mouths. Her brown eyes narrowed as she shifted her gaze back and forth between them, first in impudence and then in outright challenge.

"What are *you* looking at?" the girl panted. Her eyes were dark against her flushed face. A streak of dirt smeared one cheek, a few feathers clung wildly to her hair. She looked again from Liliya to Eli. "Who are ya, anyways?" she demanded. "I've never seen either one of ya around here before."

Liliya returned her gaze. She trembled slightly as the colors around them suddenly brightened, and a sweet fragrance began drifting through the air. Then, words came. Story words. Liliya felt them forming on her tongue. She was about to open her mouth when a sharp tug on her sleeve pulled her back—sending the words unraveling.

Eli was staring at her through narrowed eyes. He had hold of her and wasn't about to let go. He shook his head slightly.

"Thanks," she whispered. *This is not the time to lose myself in a story.*

"So, are you gonna tell me yer names or not?" The girl's voice rose like hackles.

"Yes. Sorry," Liliya said hurriedly. "This is Eli, and I'm Liliya." The words seemed to echo in her head.

The girl straightened to her full height, considering them slowly. The smaller of the two dogs licked her hand and whined softly. She fondled an ear without breaking her gaze. The larger dog sat and began scratching at a flea.

"I'm Alanna," she said, at last. "So, do ya live around

here?"

"No." Liliya hesitated. "We—we're just travelers."

"Where *do* ya live, then?" the girl pressed. She placed her hands on her hips and tilted her head to the side.

"We—" Liliya stared at the place where the road disappeared into the distance, troubled. Words took shape in her mind: *Nowhere, everywhere, and all the places in between.*

"I don't know," she answered finally. It was the truth.

The young girl gaped, incredulous.

"Don't cha have anyone? Any family?" she asked. Her accent grew stronger. "You canna be that much older than me by the looks of ya." She addressed Liliya but stared at them with curiosity.

"No. Not anymore." Liliya put on a brave face, straightening her spine. "I take care of myself now."

She felt another tug and looked down into the brown eyes of Eli. She gave him a warm smile.

"I mean, I take care of *us*," she said quietly.

Eli stiffened slightly, throwing back his shoulders. "*We* take care of us," he corrected.

Another smile tugged at Liliya's lips. "You're right, Eli. We take care of each other."

The girl stared quietly, letting her gaze sweep over them once more. Then, her eyes came to rest on Liliya.

"How old are ya?" she asked.

"Fifteen."

"And him?" The girl pointed a finger.

"Nine," Eli answered proudly.

The girl looked at them both in disbelief.

"It's really just the two of ya? All alone?"

Liliya nodded. "Yes."

"What's it like?"

"What?" Liliya sputtered in surprise.

"Out there." She gestured impatiently toward the road. "What's it like *out there?*"

"I, uh, don't really know. I mean, we just—"

"Come on."

"What? Where?"

"To my house, of course. Come on." The girl laughed. "Ya can tell me there."

"Wait a minute," Liliya began to protest. "I don't think—"

"Ya hafta come to my house." The girl made an impatient stamp with her foot. Then, she grinned. "Come and meet my mamma." She spoke faster, her words chasing one another in her eagerness. "Ya can tell her, too."

"But—"

"I bet she'll even let ya stay."

"Wait, I—"

Ignoring her, Alanna grabbed Liliya's arm and pulled. The dogs began barking once more, excitedly, racing out ahead and then circling back, snapping and growling playfully with each other.

"You, too." She gestured toward Eli, grinning excitedly. "Come on."

As the girl tugged with a greater strength than her smaller frame suggested, Liliya found herself being half-pulled, half-pushed toward the girl's home.

Just as she reached the door, Alanna turned toward the dogs, almost as an afterthought. "Stay!" she commanded.

The dogs dropped to their haunches, disappointment on their fuzzy faces.

"Mamma!" Alanna yanked open the door with a bang, causing the loose hinges to rattle. She stepped inside quickly. Liliya and Eli followed less enthusiastically. They stood just behind her, next to the door.

"Mamma!" she yelled again, louder.

"Alanna," an exasperated voice called. "What's wrong? What are you going on about?"

Alanna's mother emerged from a side room, her face flushed, her hands covered in flour. She was a woman of small stature with soft, brown hair pulled tidily from her face. She had a set of deep-thinking, dark eyes—with a hint of a deeper spark. She looked very much like Alanna, only an older, more mature version.

"What's this, Alanna?"

Her floury hands went to her hips as she tilted her head. Liliya recognized it as the same gesture Alanna had made earlier. The woman looked the children up and down with a critical eye.

"This is Liliya, Mamma. And Eli," Alanna burst out breathlessly. "They don't belong to any place. All right if they stay? Just for supper and the night? Please," she begged. "They've got stories!"

Liliya felt her cheeks flush crimson and took a step backward.

"Thank you, but we can't," She blurted. "We really need to be going. Now, in fact. It was very nice meeting you. Alanna. Ma'am." She smiled her politest smile and then turned quickly to Eli.

"Let's go, Eli," she hissed. She wrapped an arm around his shoulders and began steering him toward the door.

"No. Wait."

Liliya and Eli both stopped and turned slowly.

Alanna's mother was looking out at a darkening sky, at the rapid building of gray clouds in the distance. She sighed loudly.

"I can't just let the two of you go like that. Leastways, not with another storm coming." She pressed her lips together.

She turned her gaze back to them. She studied Liliya a moment, considering. Then she shifted her gaze toward Eli.

"You two have honest faces. You will stay with us until the storm blows over," she said decidedly.

"What did I tell you?" Alanna whispered loudly.

Liliya turned to her, embarrassed. Once again, she could feel her cheeks heating.

"Alanna! Where're your manners, child?" her mother exclaimed. She gave Liliya an apologetic smile.

Alanna placed a hand over her mouth and giggled.

A smiled tugged at the woman's lips, too. Then, she

sobered, and her gaze became more thoughtful. "That's a lovely shawl, dear. I don't think I've ever seen the like."

"Thank you, ma'am." Liliya looked away. Her voice became uncertain. "It was my…" She searched for an answer. "My grandmother's."

"Oh. I'm so sorry." The woman's eyes filled with compassion. "I had no idea. Please, please feel welcome. We're the McClellans." Her smile was warm.

"Thank you."

"Alanna, show them where they can put their things."

Suddenly she looked down at her apron, her floured hands, and gave a start.

"Oh my, I nearly forgot. The loaves. And John and the boys'll be back soon." Her face flushed. "Excuse me, please."

She hurried back toward the kitchen. Just before disappearing, though, she called over her shoulder, "Make sure you wash up for supper this time, Alanna. And use the soap!"

"Yes, Mamma!" she shouted. "I will."

Alanna turned toward her guests, grinning like a pleased cat. "Follow me," she ordered. "You can put your things in my room. Though it's not really a room, more like a loft. Well, half a loft, anyway. Papa built it. The boys have the other half." She spoke rapidly, hardly drawing breath. "Mamma and Papa have that room over there." She pointed toward a closed door.

Liliya listened to her, nodding every so often. Eli followed silently, his eyes wide like saucers.

"Up here." Alanna pointed and scurried up a ladder.

Liliya followed right behind, less nimbly, and Eli more so.

"You can put your sack over there." Alanna gestured toward the far corner. "That's where you and I will sleep. The boys are on the other side. He'll be with them." She pointed a finger at Eli.

Liliya looked around slowly.

Waves of weariness began coming over her. Eli, beside

her, yawned loudly. The sleepless night was catching up with both of them. Clamping her lips to stifle her own threatening yawn, she hoped they could make it until bedtime.

"I'll show you where we can wash up now. We'd better hurry, though. Mamma gets awful mad if we're late. And Papa? Well…" Her voice trailed off.

Liliya just nodded again before following the girl back down the ladder. Her head felt as if it were stuffed with wool, her tongue wooden. Lucky for her, for the moment, Alanna didn't seem to mind her silence.

She didn't think she could have spoken even if she tried.

Chapter Nine

Alanna's father, Mr. McClellan, and the twins, Matthew and Thomas, returned home from the fields just as Mrs. McClellan was getting supper on the table.

"What's this?" Mr. McClellan asked, even before sitting down. He gestured toward Eli and Liliya and frowned with displeasure. "More of Alanna's mongrels?"

"Travelers," his wife said soothingly. She pulled him toward his seat. "Just a couple of children passing through. I offered them a place to stay for the night."

"Look like a couple of beggars if you ask me," he said irritably. He took his time looking them over. Liliya felt herself stiffening under his hard stare, her cheeks heating. But she did not break eye contact. He finally blinked and shook his head. "Strange pair," he muttered, taking a sip of his water.

Liliya heard Alanna exhale softly beside her, and she

nearly did the same. Instead, she reached under the table and gave Eli's hand a squeeze. He hadn't spoken more than two words since they'd entered the house.

Mr. McClellan pressed his hands together, and everyone quickly joined him.

"For what we are about to eat, we give thanks," he said solemnly.

"Let's eat!" Matthew burst out, reaching across the table for a slice of bread.

Thomas laughed. Having been quicker, he was already biting into his slice.

Dishes around the table were quickly emptied. Mrs. McClellan refilled their bowls over and over again with the good mutton stew she had prepared, thick with potatoes, carrots, onions, and fresh parsley. She'd also baked fresh brown loaves of bread, passing around thick slices spread generously with her creamy white goat butter.

Liliya and Eli ate quietly, listening as the conversation ebbed and flowed around them. They were too tired and uncomfortable to try and follow it, much less take part.

It turned out Mr. McClellan talked nearly as much as he ate.

"The spring barley is ripening rapidly," he said proudly, lifting his chin. "And it should be ready for harvesting within another couple of weeks." He dipped his bread in his soup before biting off a large corner. Mouth bulging, he chewed and swallowed. "All our hard work is finally paying off."

"That's good," Mrs. McClellan murmured.

"We'll be harvesting the summer corn next," Matthew spoke up.

"And then the wheat and oats," Thomas added, not wanting to be outdone.

"We'll certainly be busy." Mr. McClellan winked at his two boys. "But nothing we men can't handle, eh?"

"No, sir." They both straightened in their seats and grinned proudly.

Mr. McClellan turned his sharp gaze on Alanna, and his

smile slid from his face.

"So, girl. What kind of trouble did you get into today? Besides the obvious." He cast a dark glance toward Liliya and Eli.

Alanna met his stare uneasily, trying not to squirm. "Nothing, Papa." She coughed nervously.

"She helped me with the baking and the house-cleaning," Mrs. McClellan said, laying a hand on the girl's shoulder.

"And did ya take care of all of those creatures outside like I asked ya?"

Alanna made a short bob of her head. "Yes, sir, I did," she said evenly. "Even the chickens."

"Well, I suppose that's worth something."

He turned back to the boys, who still shoveled food into their mouths, and the smile flickered back onto his face.

Alanna's face fell.

"It looks like it's going to be a good year for us," Mrs. McClellan addressed her husband, deftly turning the conversation.

"It certainly does," he agreed amiably.

"Maybe we can even make those repairs to the barn like you've been wanting," she added.

"We just might be able to do that." Mr. McClellan leaned back in his chair and sighed contentedly. "We just might."

His eyes rested upon the two strangers sitting at the end of the table. He stared at them in silence, regarding them with a growing displeasure.

"And just where did you say you two were from, girl?" Mr. McClellan finally addressed her.

Liliya, carefully setting down her spoon, raised her eyes.

"Little Haven," she answered.

"Ahh, from the sea, then, aren't you?" He again glanced from one face to the other.

"Yes, sir," she nodded.

"Lived there your whole life?" He raised a heavy eyebrow.

"As long as I can remember, sir," she said truthfully.

"You don't look like the sea folk." He stared at her face intently. "He does." The man pointed to Eli's brown eyes, his ruddy complexion. "But you—" He looked again at Liliya and frowned. "Yer hair color's more like the people of the North, but yer eyes—" He paused. "I ain't never seen eyes like yers before."

She felt color blossoming on her cheeks.

"Yer not relations, neither, are you?" His dark eyes bore down on her.

"No." Liliya twisted her hands in her lap and looked down.

Mr. McClellan stared at her, waiting for more, but Liliya just pressed her lips together in stubbornness. That was a story she couldn't tell, wouldn't tell. Especially not to a stranger like him. Her hands clenched and unclenched in her lap. An uncomfortable silence settled around the table.

This time, it was Eli who reached out, unseen, and took her hand in his, smoothing it open. She latched onto it desperately, threading her fingers through his.

Mrs. McClellan cast her husband a disapproving frown.

"Eat some more, children," she said kindly, ladling another spoonful of stew each into Liliya's and Eli's dishes. Then, leaning across the table, she refilled Matthew's and Thomas's empty dishes as well.

The twins shared identical grins and then jostled elbows for the remaining pieces of bread.

That night, Liliya shared a bed with Alanna. It felt strange not having Eli beside her. She lay on her back listening to the steady drumming of rain outside, the soft, regular breathing of Alanna beside her, and the rustles and murmurings of the boys on the far side of the room. Her thoughts came to her in an endless stream, driven by worry and fear and the unknown future. She rolled from one side to the other—back and forth—all the while trying not to wake Alanna. But despite her aches, weariness, and lack of sleep from the night before, she couldn't settle. Her eyes remained open. She rolled onto her back. Staring at the ceiling, she sighed, frustrated.

Then, from the other side of the room, she heard it: Eli's answering whisper. He too had been awake. He, too, was listening.

"Goodnight, Liliya." His simple words rose quietly through the darkness, washing over her like a soothing balm.

"Goodnight, Eli." She smiled, relaxing at last. Closing her eyes, she sank, almost at once, into deep and colorful dreams.

The rain fell heavily all night, slowing to a light drizzle just before sunrise. Everything outside was left cold, wet, and dripping—the clouds, still heavy with rain, threatened more.

Following Alanna to the kitchen, Liliya was relieved to see only Mrs. McClellan at the table.

"Good morning." Mrs. McClellan set down her cup of tea and rose. "Did you sleep well?"

"Yes, ma'am. Thank you," Liliya answered politely.

Eli nodded shyly.

Mr. McClellan and the big boys had already eaten, she told them as she ladled hot porridge into three bowls. They had slipped into their oilskins and boots and gone to check on the grain fields a while ago.

Alanna dropped into her seat and grinned. "Boy, am I hungry this morning!"

"When are you not?" her mother laughed.

Liliya and Eli sat down beside her.

Mrs. McClellan placed the steaming bowls in front of each of them. "I'm afraid you two won't be getting an early start this morning," she said, glancing toward the window where the sky grew darker. "It looks likely to storm again at any moment. Anyway, I'd rather not have you take the chance and then be caught out in it later."

Liliya met her eyes briefly.

Nodding to herself, Mrs. McClellan continued, "Stay 'til lunch. Most likely it'll clear up by then."

"All right. If you say so, ma'am," Liliya said quietly. Then she added, "Thank you."

Eli began kicking his short legs under the table. Liliya wasn't sure whether that meant he was happy, or, like her, impatient for them to be on their way.

"You're welcome." Mrs. McClellan turned toward them and smiled. "Now, eat up while it's still hot."

Liliya gave her a polite smile in return before digging a spoon into her oats.

After breakfast, they helped Mrs. McClellan and Alanna with the morning's household chores. They cleared and wiped the table, washed and dried and stacked the dishes, and then swept the floors clean of dust and dirt.

Alanna's mother boiled a pot of water for tea. When they had finished their chores, they all sat around the table sipping the steaming hot liquid and nibbling warm, freshly baked cookies sprinkled with sugar and cinnamon. Liliya took the opportunity to offer her small bag of wheat for their hospitality.

Alanna's mother stared at the sack in surprise. "I can't take that. Keep it, dear."

"No, please," Liliya insisted. "I can't really use it, anyway. I have no way to grind it or even an oven to bake it in if I did. Please take it." She knew it was only a small token in comparison to all they had been given, but it was all she had to offer.

"'Tis true," Mrs. McClellan admitted. She accepted the small gift with a graceful bow of her head. "Thank you, my dears."

Afterward, Liliya and Eli followed Alanna outside. Eli scattered cracked corn for the chickens and then refilled the water troughs while Liliya helped Alanna with the rabbits. They began by cleaning each of the cages and then adding handfuls of fresh green grass and clean water. Soon the rabbits were all munching the long blades, happy and content.

They came to one of the last cages, and Alanna motioned for Liliya to stand back and remain quiet. Speaking in a soothing voice, she opened the cage and reached a hand inside. Carefully, without any sudden movements, she examined the animal within. Then, with a brightening smile, she stepped to the side and opened the cage door wide.

"It's ok," she coaxed. Her voice was soft. "You can come out, now."

Her gentleness surprised Liliya. It was a gentleness she had not expected coming from the bold and impetuous girl.

Something inside the cage rustled.

"That's it. Come on," Alanna encouraged.

The animal emerged cautiously, blinking in the brightening sun. He rose up on his hind feet and stared at them with bright black eyes. A soft chattering sound emitted from his throat.

"A raccoon?" Liliya said in surprise. She stared at the animal's black mask.

"I found him," Alanna explained.

The little bandit sniffed the air and then dropped back down onto his four paws. He began digging and scratching in the dirt.

Alanna shooed him. "You're free. Go on."

He took a step and paused, staring at her with confused black eyes.

"Get along with you." She stamped a foot. "Go home."

He took a few more paces and then stopped again to look back.

"I said, git!" she bellowed.

Frightened, the young raccoon turned and ran, dividing the tall grasses as he passed. He disappeared into the green.

Liliya watched him go and then turned toward Alanna, questioning.

"He's all better." Alanna sniffed, rubbing her nose. She stared at the faint trail where he disappeared. "He's going back to his home. Where he belongs."

"You helped him?"

"Yes. His foot had been torn on a stick," she said softly.

Liliya stared at the girl as if seeing her for the first time.

"What?" Alanna shrugged. "I like animals—" she paused, mischief brightening her dark eyes, "—that is, all animals except for chickens." An impish grin stretched across her face. "In my opinion, chickens are good for only one thing. Soup pots."

Liliya laughed.

They came to the last cages.

"I found those two fighting." Alanna shook her head disapprovingly and clucked her tongue. "Bad-tempered little things."

When she opened the doors, Liliya saw that each held a young gray squirrel. Alanna checked their wounds before giving them nuts and seeds and fresh water.

"Don't they ever bite you?" Liliya asked incredulously.

"No. Never. Why would they?" She looked back at Liliya, just as incredulous.

She closed the doors and carefully latched them. Then, she turned over two empty crates and sat down. Sunlight was just peeking through the clouds in long yellow streaks. It reflected off the drops of water left behind by the storm. The air warmed.

"Here." She patted the crate beside her.

Liliya sat down.

Alanna leaned over and opened a cage. She reached in and pulled out a baby rabbit.

"Oh," Liliya gushed as she saw it.

Smiling, Alanna handed the warm bundle of fur to Liliya. Then she took out a second rabbit for herself. They sat quietly, not speaking, breathing in the fresh, damp air as they stroked their rabbits' soft backs.

Eli was playing on the edge of the yard, chasing some small creature she couldn't see. Liliya smiled as she watched him.

Suddenly, a loud sigh burst from Alanna. Cuddling her rabbit to her chest, she rose to her feet and began pacing back and forth. Once more, the colors around them began deepening.

Liliya watched and waited.

Finally, Alanna paused, turning her dark eyes on Liliya.

"I've never been one to sit still for long," she said fiercely. "Or stay indoors. Papa says I'm far too wild and independent for a girl. I do try sometimes to be quiet and sedate—but I can never really be the way he wants." She frowned.

Liliya nodded, stroking the soft rabbit in her lap. "It's not who you are, is it?" She spoke quietly.

"No." Alanna raised her chin defiantly. "It's not. And ya know what else?" Her eyes suddenly blazed with passion. "I wanna do more than just live my whole life on some little farm. I wanna go places, see things, meet people—"

Liliya listened without interrupting, giving an occasional nod. She continued stroking her rabbit.

"—But I'll most likely be stuck as a farmer's wife my whole life. At least, that's what my papa would have for me. And that's practically worse than death." Alanna groaned loudly. The rabbit in her arms began to squirm. "Oh, I wish I was free. Like you." Her gaze fell on Liliya, full of envy. "Maybe I should just run away," she burst out. "Far away. Where I can do whatever I want without anyone telling me different."

"But why?" Liliya asked in surprise. "You have everything here. A family. A place where you belong. A home—"

"Whaddya talking about?" Alanna took a step forward, clutching the now nearly frantic rabbit to her chest. "You don't know. You don't know anything about it. Yer on your own. Yer free."

"I may be on my own, but it's not by choice," Liliya replied bitterly.

"Hmph." Alanna tossed her head. "I just wanna be myself. Who I am. That's all. What's wrong with that?" she challenged.

"Nothing." Liliya sighed and looked away. "Nothing. Except when it hurts others."

The fire in Alanna's eyes suddenly went out, and her shoulders slumped. She sat back down.

Both were thinking of Alanna's mother.

The fragrance of grapes began to wrap around them, faint but growing stronger. Liliya raised her eyes and breathed deeply. Her skin tingled. She knew that smell.

Whispers filled her ears, words were forming. Liliya turned toward Alanna, but it was no longer Alanna she saw. She saw the Alanna she would become—the Alanna of the future. The words swelled and grew, filling her thoughts— becoming story. Taking another deep breath, Liliya opened her mouth:

The sun rose early over the mountain—streaks of yellow, orange and pink painting the sky with color—

All around them, the McClellan farm grew brighter and more vibrant. The grasses of the fields stood tall, waving their slender arms in the breeze. Flowers opened wide, stretching out their petals to catch the falling sunlight.

An old man, a Healer, packed his bags—herbs and bandages and medicines—for another crossing. This time, he would travel East to West. He would heal where he could and then move on.

"What fun!" Alanna exclaimed. "Traveling all over. Helping people." Her face grew wistful. "If only such a life was mine."

Liliya paused. Suspended between the story and the present, she stared at Alanna. Words and story formed and reformed. New words came. Words from another place.

"It will be," she said.

Alanna sucked in a breath and stared at her.

Liliya met her stare boldly. Then, opening her mouth again, the story continued with new characters.

A young married couple shouldered their heavy packs for the first time. They were ready. Like others before, they, too, had chosen the lives of Healers—traveling from village to village to care for the sick and injured. They set out hand in hand, their hearts joyful. The sun rose brilliant overhead. They looked forward to the day. Their first village, they knew, was waiting for them—just beyond the turning of the road.

Liliya's voice fell silent again, almost as quickly as it had begun. The story was finished. It had told of a beginning, a story yet to be lived. It was a promise.

Bowing her head, she stared at the ground, suddenly too tired to move. The usual weariness had come over her. One hand rested, unmoving, on her small rabbit.

Alanna, too, sat silent and thoughtful, her hand unconsciously stroking her rabbit's velvety fur. Suddenly, she turned toward Liliya and frowned.

"You don't really believe all that, do you?" she demanded. "All that about me traveling and being a Healer?"

Raising her eyes, Liliya met Alanna's intensity with her own.

"It will happen," she said slowly. "I know."

Alanna returned to her deep thoughts, her lips parted with words that didn't form. The rabbit on her lap wriggled and hopped off.

"Oh!" she gave a startled cry. She scooped it up and cuddled it safely against her chest. She looked at Liliya, again, her eyes still full of doubt.

Liliya's clear gray eyes met hers with confidence.

Slowly, Alanna's face brightened. "I'm not sure why, but I believe you." She gave a sudden laugh. Then, she smirked. "I guess that means I don't have to run away. Too bad, too. It might have been fun."

Just then, Eli came running. "Liliya! Look! I caught it."

He held a small striped lizard in his hands.

"That's good, Eli," she said weakly.

He froze, looking at her strangely. "Hey! You told a story," he said slowly. The happiness faded from his face.

She nodded.

"But you didn't call me," he added, disappointed. "Why not?"

When she didn't answer, he glanced at Alanna's shining face and frowned. "It was for her, wasn't it?" he said accusingly. He had forgotten the lizard still in his hands.

"I'm sorry, Eli," Liliya whispered. It seemed she had

been apologizing to Eli a lot, lately.

He looked at her again, and his brown eyes filled with concern. "Are you ok?"

"Yes. Ok."

"Do you need anything?"

"No. I'll be fine. Just give me a minute—or two." She smiled faintly.

"What is it? What's wrong?" Alanna asked. She looked from one to the other in confusion.

"Nothing." Liliya managed a dismissive shrug. "The stories just tire me. Sometimes."

"More like always," Eli grumbled before sitting down by her feet. He released the little lizard and watched with little interest as it scurried away.

Liliya gave him a sideways glance and then pursed her lips. She sat unmoving, her head still bowed. She closed her eyes. *What if*—she thought of Eli. *But no,* she stopped herself. She couldn't ask that question. She didn't dare.

She took a deep breath, filling her lungs over and over until she felt her strength beginning to return. Then, she opened her eyes and raised her head.

"Sorry." She gave reassuring smiles to both Eli and Alanna. "I didn't mean to frighten you," she said slowly. "I'm ok now." She rose to her feet, still a little unsteady, but she was good at hiding it.

The sun was now shining bright and warm overhead. Liliya looked up and squinted, shading her eyes with her hand. She took another deep breath and released it. More strength returned. Her thoughts cleared further. She handed the small rabbit back to Alanna.

"Eli, I think it's time we were going," she said quietly and firmly.

"Good." He jumped to his feet eagerly.

Good. Her thoughts echoed him.

She glanced once more at the blue sky. Not a cloud was in sight. She tilted her head and listened. No Wind, either. She smiled.

"Let's go." She turned and began walking toward the house.

Alanna returned the rabbits to their cage and followed behind, thoughtfully.

At the house, Liliya retrieved her sack from the loft and then met everyone near the door. Mrs. McClellan joined them from the kitchen.

"For you both." She smiled, pressing a clean cloth full of something warm into Liliya's hands.

Eli sidled up beside Liliya and leaned over her shoulder to look. Carefully, Liliya unwrapped the cloth. What she saw nearly brought her to tears. Her wheat had been ground and baked into five small loaves.

Eli wrapped his arms around Mrs. McClellan. "Thank you," he murmured, going up on tiptoes to kiss her cheek.

"You're welcome, child. Just baked this morning." She blushed prettily, her eyes suddenly too bright. "They should keep for several days. Just make sure you two eat them before they go bad."

"Thank you, ma'am. We will."

Liliya packed the loaves carefully in her sack and then pulled the cinch tight.

"No. Thank you." Mrs. McClellan wrapped an arm around Alanna and drew her close. The air around them was fragrant with the smell of summer grapes and new dreams. "Alanna just told me you were a Storyteller," she said softly. "Thank you, dear, for your stories. And for giving my Alanna hope."

Storyteller?

Liliya looked from Alanna to her mother and then back to Alanna questioningly.

Alanna gave a small bob of her head. Her mother did the same.

It was the first time she had ever been called that.

Liliya swallowed and smiled, felt her cheeks warming. "Let's go, Eli." She put her arm around him and led him away.

"May the winds always blow soft," Mrs. McClellan

called after them warmly. "Goodbye, children."

"Goodbye!" Eli cried over his shoulder.

"Goodbye!" Alanna echoed, jumping up and down and waving. "Goodbye!"

"And may the waves bring you home," Liliya whispered, fixing her eyes on the road ahead.

Chapter Ten

The man raised his head and sniffed the air rushing past. Mingled smells of beasts and earth and man told him that another village was not far ahead. Crouching back over his horse, he whispered in his ear, urging him faster. And like the wind itself, the horse ran, his black mane and tail streaming like ribbons behind. Sunlight flashed from his hooves. Clouds of dust rose up thick wherever they passed.

The empty lands they traveled soon gave way to a scattered community of farms. They slowed to a fast trot as the man began sweeping his gaze from side to side, searching.

They had found nothing so far—in any of the villages they had passed. But that didn't discourage him.

If anything, it only strengthened his determination. He continued the search.

Suddenly, a spot of brightness in the distance caught his attention. He pulled back on the reins, tightening his knees as the horse reared. They came to a clattering stop.

The horse stood quivering, his long legs trembling beneath him—but his stance was proud. He held his head high, and his ears alert. Light foam flecked his neck and chest, darker patches appearing where his coat was wet.

The man, too, bore signs of hard riding. His breaths came in hard, quick pants. Grit and travel clung to him. But he took no more notice of it than his horse did. Tall and straight in the saddle, he tightened the dark cloak around his shoulders and peered through the settling dust. Villagers retreated before them, but he paid little, if any, attention. He saw them only from the edges of his awareness, faint spots of light in a fog of darkness. He already knew that what he wanted was not among them.

He searched, instead, the scattered farmlands beyond, seeing all the way to the farthest borders. Here and there, he noticed areas that were brighter and more colorful than others—and they all seemed to be concentrated around one farm.

He focused his gaze there.

The farm was small, he decided, and just as unremarkable as all the others. His eyes swept quickly over the rolling green hills surrounding it, the brown patches of naked earth, the rows upon rows of yellow and green stalks of growing grain. His gaze remained in some places longer than others before they finally narrowed on a fixed point. He stared intently at a row of roughly made cages. An excited chill worked its way down his spine. The colors were brightest there.

Just like the Wind said they would be.

His lips pulled into a tight smile. Throwing his dark cloak over his shoulders, the man raised his head and spoke, casting his words into the breeze.

"Speak." The answering response came almost immediately.

Icy fingertips scraped along the man's cheek. His skin tingled with the sudden charge of energy in the air.

"I have found a trail," he said. His blood pounded in his ears.

"Excellent. Follow it."

The voice thrilled him, drove him. It was all he lived for. He bowed his head in obedience. "Like a hound."

The icy wind caressed his cheeks once more, causing shivers to run through him.

"I will send my delay ahead of you," the Wind promised. "I know you will not fail me."

Then the voice was gone, leaving the man cold, empty, and alone. He raised his eyes slowly, warily. He sniffed.

Something else still lingered. A sweetness. It was faint—but vile. The light fragrance brushed the edges where his memories lay dark and silent. He clenched his teeth. A sudden hunger seized him. Greedily he reached for the memories, but his hands passed through. Sniffing again, he realized that the smell was already fading. Gone. And with it went the ghost-like memories.

Disappointed, he turned to scan the line of empty road. Whatever had made it, it was still out there, he knew. Just ahead. He would find it. Carefully, he fixed the scent in his memory. It would be there when he needed it. He would not forget. He had only to follow the trail. He would be the hound he was.

Wasting no more time, he tightened his grip on the reins. "Yah!" he cried, giving a sharp kick.

Pulling at the bit, the horse roared, leaping forward into a run. The sharp clatter of hooves drummed in the man's ears, matching the rhythm of his own heart, beat for beat.

Chapter Eleven

Liliya and Eli left the McClellan farm and turned their faces north. The open road stretched ahead, empty. The sun was shining bright, warm, and bold overhead, but Liliya hardly noticed. They were once again alone, and she was afraid. Her thoughts had already returned to the Wind. She wondered where it was now and how much distance remained between them. She worried they had stayed too long.

Liliya set a steady pace, hoping to make up for lost time. They walked all that day and the next. The landscape before them changed slowly from flat, green tilled farms to the occasional small tree and then more trees and then finally, larger trees.

Eli kept his eyes fixed on what was ahead. Mouth opening and closing, he pointed every now and then, uttering excited little bursts. Liliya strained her eyes to see what he was seeing. At first, she could see nothing. But after a while, even she began to make out the dark shapes of huge, old trees—the largest she had ever seen—lining the far horizon.

"Liliya," Eli squeaked again.

"I know," she whispered in awe. "I can see them now, too."

Gradually, the trees increased in number, growing all the way up to the edges of the road. Liliya and Eli soon found themselves in the midst of them, speechless with amazement.

Unlike the spindly, wind-bent trees of the coast they had known, these trees were enormous and proud. Their trunks were so massive that Liliya and Eli together couldn't have wrapped their arms around them. Looking up into their tall, leafy bowers, Liliya felt very small in comparison. It was like nothing she had ever experienced before. The silence, too, was uncanny. It was so quiet and still. The thick trees seemed to absorb every sound that fell beneath them.

And—she smiled—*it's nice and cool.*

Liliya walked with soft, light footfalls, her mind filled with wonder and awe as she stared and listened. Eli walked beside her, just as silent, in his own thoughts.

The trees continued to thicken and broaden around them, the light becoming dimmer. Even the air itself beneath the trees became heavier and denser. Here and there, where the sun managed to slip a finger between the leaves, the air sparkled gold with dust particles. The bands of light appeared in odd places—some near, some far—but never quite close enough to touch.

There were stories here, too.

Liliya walked along, filling her lungs with the rich, earthy scent of old forest—fragrant like aged wine. Stories saturated the spaces around her, stirring her own stories within. Words and voices clamored excitedly, pouring into her thoughts, filling them. The words grew heavy on her tongue. The familiar heat rushed through her and, at last, she opened her mouth. One word fell from her lips.

"Beautiful."

The single word rose, fell, and spread throughout the forest. A sweet, heady fragrance was released with it, blending and mixing perfectly with the scents of the forest already there—the earth and flora and fauna. Liliya felt her own stories begin to settle and still within. The voices grew quiet—and then she understood. This forest didn't need any more stories. It was complete. Her single word had been all it needed.

"Liliya?"

"Yes, Eli."

"I think I could almost tell the stories here," he whispered. His face was shining.

"I know what you mean, Eli," she said quietly. She took a deep breath of the sweetness. They were walking in story, breathing story, being filled by story.

"This place is story, Eli."

Eli nodded.

"Beautiful," she said once more—softly this time—for herself.

Never before had she been in a place that needed no stories, a place so completely *itself.* For the first time, she was at rest.

"Beautiful." Eli tested the word, feeling it on his tongue. Then he looked up at Liliya and grinned. "I like it."

The day passed, dreamlike and unnoticed. They walked until evening fell and then settled themselves comfortably between the knobby roots of the trees. The soft rustling of leaves filled the darkness above them.

Eli slept curled up on the winter cloak. Liliya slept beside him, wrapped in her shawl. They slept deeply, undisturbed—except for the one time the Wind appeared in Liliya's dreams. She awoke to darkness, her heart pounding in her chest. But the leaves' soft voices comforted her and soothed her back to sleep.

The night passed, and day came again. Liliya opened her eyes to a dim but steadily growing brightness. Sunlight was filtering through the leaves above her, creating a green and golden ceiling like an ethereal vision of heaven. She gazed up in wonder.

"Beautiful."

The word formed without her thinking, and she smiled.

With the freshness of the morning came new smells—wood and earth and flowers—and a faint tang of the sea. The familiar smell brought Liliya a sense of comfort and security, even far from home.

Eli was beginning to stir beside her, and she turned.

"Good morning, Eli." She rose quickly to her feet, spreading her arms wide. "And what a morning it is, too." She laughed lightly.

Eli sat up, rubbing his eyes.

"Morning, Liliya." He yawned and then gave her a sleepy smile.

Liliya broke one of the small brown loaves Mrs. McClellan had given them and passed half to Eli. As she chewed and swallowed, she thought of Alanna, wondering what the girl was doing at that moment. She almost laughed as she imagined the younger girl collecting the morning's eggs, chasing the clucking and complaining hens out of her way. Thinking of Alanna, Liliya's heart lightened. She knew the girl's life would be a happy one. Those stories had already been told.

The sun rose higher, though deep under the trees, the only change was a slight brightening of the dimness. Liliya washed down her last mouthful of bread with a swallow of water and began packing.

"Eli, hurry up," she called.

She rolled up the cloak and put it in the sack on top of her shawl.

"Almost ready, Liliya." He stuffed the remaining breakfast in his mouth. His cheeks bulged. "Mmphfe—"

She laughed. "Come on, then." She offered a hand. "Let's get going."

With a grin, Eli grabbed hold and scrambled to his feet.

The air was cool as they set out. Liliya and Eli followed

the road North as it wound through the trees. They traveled all day through seemingly endless forest. Then, once again, the light began to fade, and they had to stop for the night. They slept under broad-leafed trees, now interspersed with needled pines. As before, the night was peaceful and calm. And this time, not even the Wind marred Liliya's dreams.

Chapter Twelve

The next day, they rose early and continued. The trees around them had begun to thin. They caught glimpses of road winding further ahead and treeless lands beyond.

"We're almost there," Eli said excitedly. He gave a little skip.

"That's good," Liliya said.

Her thoughts were elsewhere. Glancing behind, she suddenly stopped and wrapped her arms around herself.

"Liliya?" Eli stared at her with a puzzled expression.

Liliya shivered slightly, and the hair on her arms began to rise. She heard it again: a faint voice carried on the breeze.

"Eli, we have to walk faster," she said urgently. "We mustn't linger."

The forest was warning them.

"Ok," he said slowly. His frown turned even more

confused.

"It's ok." Liliya took his hand. "Don't worry." She began to chew her bottom lip.

They hurried along—not quite at a run—but fast enough to feel their own hearts beating. The trees thinned as they went, growing smaller and farther apart. They came to the edge of the forest. Beyond lay rolling hills and flatlands covered by waving grasses. And the road. They could see it clearly, now—stretching out in a line ahead of them. It was so straight it might have been drawn with a ruler. Without pause, Liliya and Eli followed it, stepping out from under the shade.

Instantly, they felt the bright sun on their heads—a sun they had forgotten. It was hot. The dirt under their feet was also hot, as well as dry and dusty. They walked all morning, making only brief halts to share the water bag before continuing again. Liliya was afraid to stop any longer.

"I'm tired, Liliya," Eli complained. "And hot, too."

"I know. But we can't stop yet."

"When, then?"

"I don't know. Later," she said shortly. "I'll let you know when."

Liliya grabbed his hand and pulled him along. Eli followed unhappily. By afternoon, a village began to take shape in the distance.

A sense of foreboding came over Liliya as they approached the village. Her steps slowed, and for just a moment, she hesitated, looking for an escape. If there had been any other route, any other way, she would have taken it. But there was only one road, and only one way led to the North. Fixing her eyes straight ahead, she led them into the village.

It was gray, colorless, and large—much larger than her own small village by the sea. It was also noisier, busier, and dirtier. Tall buildings and stores cast dark shadows across the road. Liliya shivered every time she and Eli had to walk through one. She was always glad when they returned to the sun.

They followed the mixed crowds—well-dressed villagers walking or riding on horseback and slow-moving carts being pulled by lumbering beasts.

Liliya, in her bare feet and simple homespun dress, felt awkward and out of place among the fashionable, shoe-clad people of the village. She watched uncomfortably as they hurried by, making wide circles around her. Some went so far as to straighten their collars or brush imaginary dust from their garments. Not one person offered a smile or a kind word.

Liliya began to long for the simplicity and peacefulness of the trees and grasses, the quiet solitude of the open road. It was one thing to be alone among trees and birds and grasses; it was another to be alone among strangers.

"Come on, Eli," she whispered under her breath. She led him hurriedly, weaving through the crowd.

The afternoon air warmed, growing sultry, and no breeze seemed to pass between the buildings to offer relief. The putrid smells of the village—like rotting fruit and decay—clung to their clothes.

Liliya wrinkled her nose in disgust. She was liking the village less and less.

From almost every direction came sounds, movement, and more smells. Turning in the direction of shouts, they saw thick, barrel-chested men tossing heavy sacks from one to another in a long line. The flat sound of metal striking wet meat pulled their eyes in another direction. Recognizing a butcher shop and a butcher hard at work, Liliya instantly pressed a hand over her mouth and turned away.

"Come, Eli." She gagged.

"What is it, Liliya? What's wrong?" He twisted his head, trying to see behind them. "What was that?"

"Never you mind, Eli. Just keep walking." With a firm hand she steered him straight ahead.

All around more village smells rose—the acrid and pungent smells of smoke and dust, the sweat of beasts and men and industry.

They continued working their way through the dense

crowd. One by one, the rickety carts turned off onto narrow side roads. The road became less crowded, and they began to weave their way more easily through the remaining villagers.

They passed a school filled with children—some even younger than Eli—poring silently over books.

"Look, Liliya." Eli pointed in amazement. "They're reading!"

"Keep your voice down, Eli," she hissed. "I see them."

They passed a blacksmith, every precise stroke of his hammer sending bright sparks into the air. A tanner, rubbing a hide until the sweat ran down his face and chest. A red-faced baker, placing steaming pies in the window to cool.

Catching the warm scent of apples and spices, Liliya's and Eli's mouths watered, and their stomachs growled. They walked faster.

There was so much to see. Everywhere they turned, there were shops with things for sale. Liliya and Eli had never seen so many things. Their own village by the sea had boasted a few shops, and those had only basic supplies. It had never prepared them for a place like this. Here, there were dressmakers' shops, mercantile stores, and dry goods stores—more than they could have imagined.

And yet, contrary to all they saw, Liliya sensed emptiness. Distortion and confusion penetrated everything. The feeling was so unlike the beautiful forest they had just passed through. Rich in its own stories, the forest had a voice. The forest knew who it was. The people in this village were like noise without words.

Liliya guessed there must be very few stories in this place. And very few words. She looked around slowly, searching the hard, gray faces. Her heart sank as she found nothing to read there. Despite all they had, the people of this village were poor, destitute. She doubted there were stories at all.

But Liliya had stories. Lots of stories. If she could give them.

As if awakened by her thoughts, the stories inside began

to stir. They were slow and thick-tongued. Liliya had to strain to hear their voices. Words connected to words—still unhurried—words that were not her own, words building into story. Finally, the familiar heat she had been waiting for rushed through her. She clutched Eli's shoulder as her thoughts became blended with others.

"Liliya, what's the matter?" Eli asked.

She felt his hand steadying her. "Story," she smiled.

He stared at her and then spoke quietly. "They won't listen."

She turned to him, squinting through her pain. She felt her thoughts slipping, but she held onto them. "Probably not," she agreed. "But if ever there was a place in need of stories, this is it," she said, then gritted her teeth. Her thoughts became more confused. *Was that the Eli from inside? The Eli I remember from before?* She struggled. "I have to try, at least." Her tongue felt thick. "If I don't, the Wind—" She glanced behind them anxiously.

"I know. It will come," he finished.

She nodded and closed her eyes. The rest of her thoughts were swept away as the story unfolded.

New words, story words, filled her mouth. She began speaking them out as they walked the colorless, dusty streets. Word after word came, sentence after sentence. Colors swirled around her, blending and mixing. A sweet scent arose, fresh—and fragile. Liliya opened her mouth:

In the early days, when the grass was still green and purple Wisteria grew wild, an old woman lived in a tiny house on the edge of the village. People's lives were open, then, and their hearts were generous.

Liliya cast her words everywhere, scattering them like multi-colored seeds. Children and adults paused as she passed by, but they did not really listen. The words fell to the ground where they were crushed and trampled underfoot, and the colors—fading—bled out of them.

She continued, refusing to give up.

A change came over the village. People decided their

own needs were enough. They had become too busy pursuing their own prosperity to be bothered by anything else. One by one, they began to shut their doors.

"Enough!" A voice sliced into Liliya's words. "We don't want to hear any more."

But the old woman's door remained open. Always. Anyone with a need came to her: the poor, the sick, the hungry, the lonely. She helped them in her simple ways.

A crowd of people gathered. More voices began to shout. Liliya could feel the rising anger. Her words came faster.

Yet, the old woman knew a time was coming when the last door—her own—would also be shut. She tried to warn them, but no one listened.

"How dare you!" the villagers cried. They reached down, picking up sticks and stones, whatever lay about their feet.

"That's nothing but an old nursemaid's tale."

"Just a bunch of lies."

"We have become prosperous." Eyes shone.

"We are wealthy." Ugly smiles spread across their faces.

"We are important."

"We are everything."

Lightning flashed. Black clouds built rapidly in the distance, bumping and scraping together. The delicate scent Liliya had smelled turned rotten—sickly-sweet. Wrinkling her nose and grimacing, she pushed down her rising panic, hurrying to complete the story.

When the old woman died, the villagers lost more than they could ever know, never understanding that—

"Ouch!" Liliya cried.

A large stone clattered to rest by her feet.

"There's more where that come from, girl!" a livid voice shouted.

Liliya swept her gaze around slowly. Tears filled her eyes as she cradled her throbbing hand. More arms were readied to throw.

"Liliya!" Eli cried. "No!" He stepped in front of her protectively, his hands held up. "Don't hurt her!" he yelled at the crowd.

The remaining words of the story withered on Liliya's lips, dying, and her voice dried up. "I'm ok, Eli," she whispered. She began rubbing her injured hand, blinking away her tears angrily.

The story was gone. The words were gone. All now lay lifeless and broken at her feet.

More lightning lit the sky overhead. Thunder crackled.

Liliya and Eli cringed.

The villagers glanced around uncertainly. Even then, they were not ready to be afraid. They could not see their danger. Liliya's words had failed.

They took another threatening step.

"It's time to go, Eli. Now," Liliya said urgently. She took his hand, and they began backing away from the hostile crowd. Then, turning, they both ran.

"That's right. Go! And don't ever come back!" the villagers shouted, throwing their sticks and stones at their retreating heels.

"We don't want you."

"We don't want your stories."

Liliya and Eli sped along; they did not slow. Eli, pumping his thin arms, did his best to keep up with Liliya's longer stride. The houses lining the sides of the road began to stretch farther and farther apart. The edge of the village was just before them. As they neared it, a strong gust whipped around from behind. Liliya caught a whiff of the rain it was bringing and glanced nervously over her shoulder. The sky had grown even darker, blotting the last of the sun. The threatening storm was nearly upon them.

Lightning again lit the distance. Another powerful gust pushed past them.

Liliya heard a faint voice in it and began trembling. She grew cold all over.

"We have to get away from here. Hurry, Eli," she cried. Biting her lip, she clutched Eli's hand and pulled him along, running as fast as she could. She was no longer just running from the village or even the storm, she was running from the Wind.

"It's coming, isn't it?" Eli gasped, breathless. His feet pounded the earth beside her.

Liliya didn't answer, but the look on her face must have said enough. Eli didn't ask a second time.

They passed through the outer borders and were met again by the wide empty road. But even then, Liliya did not stop. The Wind was still behind.

They continued most of the night—running, walking, and then running again. Their feet stumbled and tripped over tree roots and stones, as they were shadowed by darkness. Only when it became too dark to see the road ahead did they finally give in and stop. Then, throwing themselves on the ground, they slept, exhausted.

Dreams came instantly to Liliya, dreams that were nightmarish and full of wild and shrill voices. She slept fitfully. Then just before dawn, she awoke with a start and sat up, shaking. She listened. A gust passed over them, shrieking and wailing. An uncanny stillness followed. In the emptiness, Liliya heard it for the third time—cold laughter. And she knew. The Wind had arrived at the village.

Her head sank heavily to her knees. Warm tears slid down her cheeks.

"I tried," she whispered. She touched her injured hand, staring at the dark bruise visible even in the moonlight. "I really tried."

The stories inside wept with her.

Liliya did not go back to sleep. She sat the rest of the night in silence, waiting for the sun. When the horizon finally turned pink, she woke Eli. She didn't tell him about the village. Handing him a corner of bread, she just hurried him back to the road. They ate as they walked. They did not look back.

Chapter Thirteen

The days grew hotter.

Liliya and Eli walked now through a land empty of stories, color, and scent. There was little life at all. It was a land dying. The earth beneath their feet was hard, like granite, and the ground infertile. Only a few pale and scraggly bushes managed to take root here and there in the cracks and grow. Liliya thought them pitifully courageous things for trying to grow in such a harsh environment.

Dry lands gave way to more dry lands. They walked and slept. Each morning when the sun rose—flat and dull and brassy—they rose with it and continued. The land around them remained empty and silent and still. Even the stories inside Liliya had become voiceless.

Gradual changes measured the distance they traveled.

The hard, flat road slowly became a road that wound over

and through dry, rolling foothills. As they followed it, small loosened stones rolled beneath their feet, puffs of dry dust rising with each step. They dug in their toes as they scrambled up the sides of the hills. Then, slipping and sliding, they made their way down the other side. Always, it seemed, another hill stood before them. It never changed. They plodded along, their backs bent beneath the glare of a sun too bright against the bleached, dry earth.

One late morning, Liliya lifted her weary, burning eyes and glimpsed lines of faded color in the distance—blues and greens. They were just beyond what looked to be the last line of hills.

"Eli." She paused and licked her cracked lips. Wiping the sweat from her eyes, she pointed hesitantly. "Do you think—"

Eli looked up and then broke into a wide grin.

"Yay!" he shouted hoarsely. "The end of the hills."

Liliya grinned, too. It was as if a weight were suddenly being lifted from her shoulders. She glanced again at Eli, taking note of his very flushed face. Her grin faded.

"Here, Eli," she said softly. She passed him the water bag. "Drink."

After he had, she took a small swallow herself. Then, straightening, she gazed ahead again, brushing the damp hair out of her eyes, at what she hoped would be one of the last large hills before them.

"Ready to see what's beyond these awful hills?" she asked, giving him a crooked smile.

"Of course," he laughed.

She chuckled. Slipping the strap back over her head, she turned.

"What are we waiting for, then. Let's go."

They began climbing the steep path, using their hands as well as their feet. They reached the top and slid down the other side. One more hill perhaps. They scrambled up eagerly. When they arrived at the top, they both clutched their sides, panting, and froze.

It was better than they could have imagined.

"Liliya."

Liliya nodded silently, her eyes hungrily taking in everything. There was so much *color.*

Pale, dry earth gave way to glorious greens that stretched out almost as far as they could see. The green was crisscrossed with occasional lines of blue and gold. In the far distance, they could make out blue and purple smudges of tall mountains against a soft gray sky.

"Is that the North?" Eli pointed to the mountains.

"Yes. I think so." She shaded her eyes. "Grandmother said it was on the other side of a long chain of mountains. I suppose that's it." Her voice fell quiet as she stared.

"What do you suppose we'll see down there, in all that green?" Eli asked, suddenly.

"I guess we'll just have to wait and see."

"Do you think there'll be villages?" He frowned.

"Most likely."

He scratched his nose thoughtfully. "Forests?"

"I wouldn't be surprised."

"Rivers and streams?"

"Of course."

"Birds?" he asked, getting more excited. "And wild animals, too?" He was practically bouncing on his tiptoes.

Liliya laughed. "Yes, Eli. Yes. Of the wildest kind, likely enough. But enough questions. Like me, you're just going to have to wait and see. Ok?"

"Ok." He grinned happily.

As Liliya gazed at the sea of green stretching out before them, the sunlight dancing gold off the ribbons of water, she knew with certainty that whatever they found, there would be more stories. She could already feel them.

"Well, what are we waiting for?" Eli cried. "Let's get going."

He began the descent eagerly.

"Wait, Eli!" Liliya said. "It's still a long way away."

"That's ok. We've already come a long way." He

laughed and then called over his shoulder. "I bet I can beat you down!"

The Wind was far behind, or so Liliya hoped. They'd neither heard nor felt it for many days. And hills stood between them—hills that even the Wind would have trouble crossing.

Her breaths came easier.

"You're on!" she called after him.

They raced one another down the hill, each trying to be the first to reach the inviting edge of green at the bottom. They whooped and laughed. Dust rose in clouds behind them. Then the land leveled and smoothed.

"I win!" Eli shouted.

Liliya slid to a stop beside him. They had made it.

They stood for a moment in wonder, catching their breaths. Verdant greens stretched out before them in all directions. Liliya's eyes hardly knew where to look first. Eli was beside himself with excitement. Then, their eyes met— gray to brown. Their grins mirrored one another. Laughing suddenly, they began to run once more. They stretched their arms out as they went, trailing their fingers along the green tops lining the road.

Eli giggled. "It tickles."

Liliya grinned. "I know."

"And it smells good, too."

She laughed. "I know, Eli." For the first time in days, her heart was wonderfully light.

After the dry, barren and colorless lands they had traveled, the green was like an oasis. Their eyes drank in thirstily all they saw until they could hold no more. Then, they left the road and waded right into the midst of it. Once they were completely surrounded, they sank down and rested.

Liliya lay on her back, staring at the waving grasses above her. Spotting a red ladybug among the green stems, she sat up. She coaxed the small creature onto her finger, watching as it crawled from one hand to the other, back and forth. Then, finding it could go no higher, it opened its black wings and rose into the sky.

Liliya pulled her knees up to her chest and smiled. She watched as the ladybug disappeared into the blue sky. Eli was on his stomach, just a few paces away, poking at an ants' nest he had discovered. Liliya smiled again. *It feels so good to be among living things again.* She took a deep breath of fragrant air. *Good to be among so many stories.* But when the voices in her began to stir, too, her feelings of joy changed to fear. She glanced at her hand where the bruise had once been. She hated to admit it, but she wasn't ready to tell more stories. Not yet. She was relieved when the voices fell silent again.

They spent the night on the soft grasses, breathing in the sweet, rich smells around them. Liliya crossed her hands behind her head and stared up at the clear black sky, dotted with white stars. She was so tired she could hardly keep her eyes open. She rolled to her side. Eli was already asleep, curled up on the cloak. She smiled sleepily.

"Good night, Eli," she murmured.

Wrapping her shawl lightly around her, she closed her eyes. She was still smiling when she fell asleep.

They continued the next day.

Liliya and Eli delighted in everything they saw. All about them, the lands remained green and fresh, the sun warm on their heads. Insects buzzed lazily.

As the sun rose higher, dark smudges appeared on the horizon. Eli stared at them without saying a word. Soon, the dark smudges took on a shape that even Liliya could recognize. Another village lay ahead.

Liliya carefully hid her unease. "Well, Eli," she said, forcing herself to smile, "I suppose that answers at least one of your questions."

Eli nodded and then frowned. Their steps became less eager. It was late afternoon when they arrived.

The village—they were relieved to see—was modest, with only a few of the most necessary stores, as well as a mill and a blacksmith. The houses and cottages that made up the rest of the village sat fairly close together, simple and unadorned. Liliya and Eli followed the smooth and well-worn road. A few of the villagers eyed them curiously, nodding politely as they passed. One even offered a small smile.

As they walked, colors and scents gathered around them, and Liliya, again, felt the familiar stirrings of the stories within.

What? Here? Now? She froze.

Her hand unconsciously fingered the place where she had been bruised. Suddenly she was afraid. "I—I don't know if I can," she moaned, bowing her head. She was shaking.

The stories continued to stir, their voices growing louder.

No, she pleaded silently. She fixed her eyes straight ahead, deliberately avoiding eye contact with anyone. *Maybe if I hurry.* Chewing her lip harder, she picked up her pace. A little further and she caught sight of the outer edge of the village. Open road and green grass lay beyond.

"Eli, I think we made it." Liliya pointed. Hope was beginning to rise within her.

But as they approached the open road beyond the village, a dry floral scent swirled around them, tugging on her gently. Liliya felt her gaze drawn from the empty road and beyond to an old cottage squeezed between two larger houses, just within the village's border.

"No," she whispered.

Liliya clung to the thought of the empty road. Already, she could feel the words of stories forming and filling other parts of her thoughts. She couldn't peel her eyes away. Her feet slowed.

Oh, please. No.

She stared at the cottage. Worn with weather and time and sorrow, it stood nearly lost in shadows. Her feet stopped.

Eli stopped too. He stood beside her as though confused.

Sighing heavily, she laid a hand on his shoulder. "Give me a minute," she said in defeat. "There's something I need to do."

He looked at her a moment and then slowly nodded his head. "All right, Liliya."

She gave his shoulder a small squeeze. "Thanks."

She looked around again. Her gaze came to rest on an old woman sitting in the dirt before the small cottage. How she had missed her before, Liliya did not know. She studied the old woman in silence.

The woman was staring ahead, her eyes pale and sightless. A few small children were gathered in the dust around her—not quite school-aged but not quite so small, either, that they had to be within constant view of their mothers. The children were listening, their eyes wide, as the old woman told stories from her youth. She spoke of a time when grass grew everywhere, and the air was fresh and the spaces wide. Wild creatures roamed freely, making their homes in the tall grasses. Then, men came. They broke the land and built their lives among them.

The gentle colors weaving through the woman's story contrasted with her voice—bitter and hard and sharp. As Liliya listened more, she felt the words of the woman's story rising and falling within herself, almost like an echo, resonating with her own stories.

Then, mid-sentence, the woman abruptly stopped. She raised her sightless eyes toward Liliya and stared. Her face darkened into a scowl.

"Whoever you are, don't just stand there. Come. Sit," she said gruffly, slapping the ground next to her. "Or go away."

The stories' voices grew louder in her. Liliya gave one last look toward the road and then turned away with a sigh. She motioned for Eli to follow her. Accepting the old woman's invitation, she squeezed between two of the children. Eli sat across from her on the other side.

The stories had won.

As the old woman resumed her speaking, another story rose up in Liliya, simultaneously. She saw pictures of a young woman—happy and carefree—pictures of the old woman's life. Liliya watched them unfolding in amazement. Then, the pictures darkened and turned black and she could see nothing more. The old woman had come to the end of her story.

"And now I see nothing but the visions in my memory, and they, too, grow dim with time." The old woman turned her head again toward Liliya. She bristled. "But you—you also are a Storyteller. I heard it, by the way your pulse quickened as I told my own story. Yes?"

"Yes," Liliya answered truthfully. "I suppose I am."

The old woman's gruff exterior softened slightly. "Then let's see what you can do," she said. She folded her arms over her chest. "Tell me a story, girl."

Liliya swallowed nervously.

"Go ahead, Liliya," Eli whispered. "You can do it."

She nodded and licked her lips. The stories were ready. They had been waiting. She could do it.

Liliya took a deep breath. Blood rushed into her head. Colors brightened around her. Her senses sharpened, and she instantly smelled the rich beasty animal smells of the village, the sweetness of dry grasses, the dusty earth below her—and age. The smell of old age on the woman. Words formed on her tongue. Strong and powerful, they filled her mouth and she began speaking them out. The story that had come was the old woman's story—not a story of her future—but a story of her past, her forgotten past.

The old woman closed her eyes as Liliya's words washed over her and around her. A flush of color came to her withered cheeks, and her thin lips hinted at a smile. She sat with her hands clasped in her lap. Liliya noticed that they were trembling.

The story told of forgotten memories and buried emotions—the husband of the woman's youth. It told how rich and full the old woman's life had been during those few years when it was just the two of them together, living their lives in the wild, unbroken land.

"I can see him! I can see him!" the old woman exclaimed excitedly. "Yes. There he is." Her sightless eyes shone bright with an inner vision. "I had forgotten how handsome. He was so handsome. And his eyes—blue. Blue like the sky." Tears began making slow tracks down her wrinkled face. "How could I have forgotten the color of his eyes?"

It had been the happiest time of her long and lonely life.

Liliya's voice grew softer. She told how the old woman was now widowed and alone and had been for decades. She told how the village, over the years, had spread and built up around the old woman, pressing in on her until there was hardly any room left to breathe. She told how the old woman had been squeezed into a dark corner and left there until she herself had almost forgotten.

Until now.

Tears fell down Liliya's cheeks when she came to the end of the story, mirroring that of the old woman's. But it was not *the end*. Liliya had more stories, stories so eager to be told that their words nearly entangled one another.

Liliya quickly dried her cheeks. Before the old woman could say anything, she took another breath. Opening her mouth wide, she began again.

Stories filled her, and Liliya spoke them out, one after another. She told stories for the old woman, stories for the children. She told stories that spoke directly to the secret dreams and sorrows hidden away in their hearts, stories of their pasts and their futures. She spoke the stories out to a people and a land parched and dry, thirsting for stories. She told stories until her voice grew hoarse with the telling. She told stories until she could speak no more. Then, at last, her voice fell silent and the voices within fell silent with her.

Liliya raised her head and looked around wearily.

Wonder filled the eyes of those before her—and peace and hope and courage.

She stared in surprise. *My stories are growing stronger.* Then Liliya became aware of the richness of the colors around them, the brightness of the earth, and the sky. A sweet fragrance drifted in with the breeze, blowing away the dust. She swallowed nervously. *So is my storytelling.*

"Your voice, it has a different accent. You're not from around here, no?" the old woman asked.

"No," Liliya rasped. Her thoughts unraveled.

"And you are staying somewhere tonight. Yes?" Her sightless eyes fixed on Liliya.

"No. I'm just traveling through." She pressed a hand against her throat and grimaced. She offered no other explanation. She was so tired that even her hands seemed heavy.

"Not tonight." The woman gave a papery laugh. A claw-like hand, dry and thin—but warm—grasped Liliya's arm possessively. "You, girl, will stay with me tonight." She turned to the children and waved a bony hand toward them. "Go, children. Scat."

Liliya stiffened. Her heart began pounding in her chest. She wanted to pull away, but the woman had managed to get a tight grip around her wrist.

The children rose to their feet. Giggling, they scattered in different directions. Liliya watched them go, her fear growing.

"I'll see you all back here tomorrow," the old woman barked after them. "Don't forget, now."

Their titters of laughter faded into the distance.

The old woman turned her sightless eyes back on Liliya. "You will come," she said. It was not an invitation, but an order.

"But—I have someone with me. A friend."

"What? Where?" The old woman tilted her head as if listening.

Eli stepped forward and laid a hand over the old woman's.

"Right here," he whispered.

She wrapped her hand around his much smaller one. "Then you'll just have to come, too," she said matter-of-factly.

Eli's face paled, but he didn't pull away.

Liliya looked around, wanting to escape—to run, to refuse—but she already knew she would not. She had one last story for this hard, old woman, a story she had been reluctant to tell.

She swallowed and turned toward the sightless face, her heart sinking. Her blood ran cold.

"We will stay with you tonight," she whispered. Then, she shuddered.

Eli's mouth dropped open.

Glancing at him, she mouthed, *I'm sorry,* and looked away.

The old woman cackled triumphantly and released her vice-like grip. Then, shuffling to her door, she motioned curtly. "Come."

Liliya, rubbing her arm, followed her inside. Eli trailed just behind.

They entered the cottage, and the old woman shut the door behind them. The room grew dark.

Chapter Fourteen

Liliya stood blinking, casting her gaze around the tiny, unlit single room. She kept glancing nervously toward the closed door. Eli stood behind her, so close she could hear his breathing.

As her eyes adjusted, she saw that the cottage was sparse, with only one chair set before a low stone fireplace, now cold and bare. A narrow, sagging bed with a ragged quilt pulled over the top filled one corner. A table with a single chair set before it filled another. A small stove stood in the last, the pipe rising crookedly up and out through the low ceiling overhead. To this, the old blind woman went. With practiced skill, she built up a small fire, her hands seeing what her eyes could not. When it was going well, she filled a blackened kettle and set it on top to boil.

"Sit," she barked at Liliya, pointing toward the chair by

the fireplace.

Liliya walked slowly to the chair and sat. It leaned precariously to one side, and she had to balance herself so she wouldn't fall.

"Eli," she whispered, pointing to the floor next to her. "Over here."

Eli dropped heavily beside her, resting his chin in his hand.

"Liliya," he whispered loudly. "What are we doing here? Why can't we just go?"

"Hush, Eli," she said softly.

He pouted.

Liliya glanced anxiously in the direction of the old woman, but if she had heard Eli, she didn't show it. Liliya let out a breath in relief.

The old woman shuffled across the room to the table, mumbling to herself. Liliya watched as she dropped a few curled leaves into a teapot.

"I ain't got but one cup." She turned her sightless eyes upon Liliya. It was more a statement of fact than an apology.

"Oh," Liliya stammered. "That's all right. I've got one of my own." She opened her rucksack and began rummaging. At the very bottom, she found her small tin cup. It was the first time she had used it since it had been packed. "Eli and I don't mind sharing."

The old woman gave a nod and then began mumbling to herself again.

Liliya's eyes shifted from the old woman to her sack and then back again. She bit her lip. After a moment's hesitation, she tucked her hair back behind her ear and then reached in again. She pulled out the last of the cracker bread her grandmother had given her. It was broken into many pieces but still good.

"I've a bit of cracker bread we could share, too, if you'd like," she offered quietly.

The woman turned sharply, her face suddenly greedy. She shuffled over and snatched the small package from

Liliya's hands.

"Yes. That will do," she murmured happily to herself, her fingers exploring the package. "That'll do just nicely." Hugging it possessively against her chest, she carried it over to the table. She set it next to the teapot, her fingers lingering on it for just a moment. Then, muttering again, she went to the stove and opened the door.

The room took on a soft red glow.

The old woman leaned close—so close the deep crevices of her wrinkles were illuminated. She took a long stick and tapped the fire gently, feeling the shape of the burning mound. Then, placing a split wedge on top, she closed the heavy door. The room fell dark once more.

She rose, and her sightless gaze fell on Liliya. The shadowy lines of her face deepened. The old woman began arguing with herself, muttering under her breath. Liliya could only make out an occasional word. Then, abruptly, the old woman frowned and turned away.

Liliya was filled with unease.

She turned to check on Eli. He was still sitting on the floor beside her, entertaining himself with some made-up finger game. She smiled faintly. Nothing ever seemed to bother him for long.

Across the room, the tea kettle began to whistle, bubbling, and hissing on the stove. Grunting, the old woman hobbled over as quickly as she could. She poured the hot water into the teapot, splashing a little on the table in her haste. Then she returned the kettle, placing it off to the side.

"Tea's near ready. Bring yer cup," she said simply.

"Yes, ma'am."

Liliya rose carefully from the chair and walked over to the table.

"S'pose I have ta," the old woman was muttering. "No other way ta be knowing fer sure."

Liliya glanced at her warily. As she neared the table with her cup, the old woman grabbed her, turning her so that they faced one another. It happened so quickly Liliya had no time even to cry out in surprise. She froze.

The old woman stepped closer, leaning in.

Liliya could smell her foul breath. Her eyes began to water. She tried not to gag.

The old woman's sightless eyes grew wide. "Mysteria," she panted. Her breath washed over Liliya in warm puffs. "Do you know?"

Liliya's muscles suddenly became like water under the old woman's tight grip.

"Mysteria," she demanded again. Her fingers tightened. "Do you know her, girl?"

Liliya didn't recognize the word. She didn't even remember hearing it before. But it touched her deeply—more deeply than any word had ever touched her. She felt she *should* know it.

"No. No, I don't," she whispered. She felt her cheeks burning.

The old woman's face darkened into a scowl. "'Tis as I thought." She dropped her hands heavily to her sides. "Doesn't know," she muttered. Then, turning back to Liliya she spoke sharply. "Sit, girl. Listen. I ain't gonna say this but once."

Liliya slowly sank to the floor, right where she was, her eyes locked on the old woman's sightless face.

The woman fumbled behind her, feeling around for the chair. Grabbing hold, she dragged it across the uneven floor and then sat stiffly. For a moment, she stared at Liliya. Then, she leaned forward.

"It's what give ya them stories," she hissed.

Liliya suddenly felt cold all over.

"Them stories that burn fire in yer veins." She paused, tilting her head slightly as if listening. "Them stories that are—alive in ya."

Shaking uncontrollably, Liliya wrapped her arms around herself and lowered her head.

"Ya know what I'm saying, don't ya?" She laughed a bitter laugh. "Don't ya, girl?"

"Yes," came the faint whisper.

"I *was* right," she muttered to herself. Her face hardened. "Then keep listening, girl. There's more." Her voice grated. "There's *her*."

The wood inside the stove suddenly caught and flared, glowing red through the cracks in the old stove. The dim light cast strange shadows about the cottage, obscuring even the old woman's face.

Liliya listened as the old woman spoke, the tightness in her throat increasing. It was as if words were finally being put to what she had always known, words that confirmed what she had already suspected about her stories for a long time, words that were uncomfortably familiar.

"The Mysteria," the old woman's voice deepened. "A creature from the beginning of time itself, when the first words were spoken. It's she that give ya them stories, girl—in them eggs of hers." The old woman fixed her gaze on Liliya, her sightless eyes dark and full of secrets. "She that made ya her—Storyteller."

Liliya swallowed hard. She was suddenly remembering what Alanna's mother had said, just before she and Eli had departed. Her throat tightened.

"And—them ain't just stories she give ya, girl." The old woman lowered her voice cryptically. "They *do* things."

The small cottage fell silent but for the hiss and sizzle of burning wood.

Liliya turned to stare at the red cracks in the stove. She chewed her bottom lip nervously. Her hands were cold.

"You've seen it, yes?"

"Yes," Liliya answered faintly. "Yes, I have."

A harsh cackle rose from the old woman's throat.

"But I don't understand," Liliya whispered.

The old woman straightened. Her sightless eyes fixed on

Liliya like a hawk. "They's stories," she said. "*Her* stories."

"But—"

"Her stories. From her," she repeated impatiently. "She give 'em to ya." Her eyes grew clouded. "And now they be yers."

"From her." Liliya shuddered. "The…" She fumbled for the word. "Mysteria."

Instantly, voices began whispering around them, filling the air with words and untold stories. Liliya started in surprise. Ghosts, fragments of old memories, and older stories hovered in the shadows. Colors deepened, their edges beginning to blend and blur. Then she smelled it, wafting through the small cottage—the sweet fragrance of the wisteria blossom.

"They're strong in ya, girl." The old woman's face grew dark. "Very strong."

"Mysteria," Liliya whispered again. Then, touching her fingers to her lips, she trembled. *I did know. I have always known.*

Eli slipped beside her and put a hand on her arm.

"Mysteria," he said softly. His brown eyes studied hers with concern.

She stared back, but no words came to comfort either of them.

The old woman rose and went to the table. Her face became closed. "Come. Time's a wasting," she said gruffly. The conversation had ended.

They shared the woman's weak tea and the last of Liliya's cracker bread for their supper. The woman was too old to ask any more questions about Liliya, too tired to care. They ate in silence. When they had finished, the old woman rose stiffly and rinsed their teacups in the same bucket of water she had used to fill the kettle. Still wet, she placed them back on the table, dripping.

"You sleep there." She pointed a knobby finger toward the space on the floor in front of the cold fireplace.

"Yes, ma'am."

Her eyes followed the woman as she felt her way to her bed and lay down heavily without another word. Sighing softly to herself, Liliya carried her pack to the empty space and set it down. Digging into her rucksack, she pulled out the winter cloak. She spread it on the rough wooden floor and motioned for Eli. He lay down upon it. Then, wrapping the shawl around her shoulders, she lay down on her back beside him.

The room fell silent.

Eli raised himself on an elbow. Staring down at Liliya, he smiled. "I like your stories, Liliya," he said softly. "I'm glad you're going to keep telling them."

Liliya tensed, gripping her shawl.

"Go to sleep, Eli," she grumbled. She rolled to her side, turning her back to him.

"Good night, Liliya," he said happily.

Sleep was long in coming. Liliya lay quiet and still, watching the shadows stretch and deepen around her. In the semi-darkness, she listened to the heavy rasping sounds of the old woman's breathing on the far side of the room, the softer breaths of Eli beside her. Outside the four thin walls, she heard the fainter sounds of the village, still awake.

Her thoughts drifted and meandered loosely. She thought about her stories, about the Mysteria. She thought about the Wind, the sea, the waving grasses of her hill. She thought about her grandmother. She wondered what her grandmother was doing right now, far away in the old cottage. She hoped she was all right. The familiar ache began to swell in her chest and she quickly squeezed her eyes shut. She would not cry. Not anymore. It was too late to cry.

What time sleep overtook her, Liliya did not know. But it did not happen until long after the dark had become so thick around her that open or closed, her eyes saw the same.

Liliya awoke with the first streaks of dawn. She stared at

the dark ceiling before hearing the old woman's shuffling steps in the room behind her. Then, memories from the day before came rushing back.

"The water's near boiling," the old woman said gruffly. "Get up. Tea is ready in a minute. I know yer awake."

Liliya sat up obediently and smoothed down her messy hair. Her eyes felt gritty, her mouth dry, and her throat hurt.

"Yes, ma'am. Thank you," she croaked. She stared at the woman in surprise. "How did you know?"

"I heard the change in yer breathing."

Liliya nodded slowly.

Turning to Eli, she shook him. "Wake up, Eli. It's morning."

His eyes snapped open, and seeing Liliya, he instantly broke into a smile. "Good morning, Liliya."

"Good morning." Liliya couldn't help smiling back. "Get yourself up. Quickly now." She gave his arm a squeeze.

He rose and handed her the cloak. She stuffed it hastily into the pack. A few minutes later, she joined the old woman, already seated at the table.

"Good morning," Liliya said brightly.

There was no place to sit, so she stood. Eli sidled up beside her.

"After ya break yer fast you'll tell me a story. Yes," the woman stated matter-of-factly. It was not a question.

Liliya groaned inwardly. *So there isn't even to be a good morning in response?*

"You have one, still, I know." The old woman turned her sightless eyes upon her.

Liliya bit back a sigh. "Yes," she admitted reluctantly. "I still do."

"Here." The woman pushed a plate of overripe fruit towards them, motioning that it was for both of them. "Eat."

It was a simple breakfast of figs and more weak tea.

Liliya flicked several small flying insects away and then handed a fig to Eli before taking the other for herself. She ate hers slowly.

No one spoke.

In the growing light, she could see more clearly than she had the night before. She studied the old woman curiously.

The woman's hair was unkempt, a mass of gray tangles. Her hard face was lined with wrinkles that seemed to stand out even more than they had the night before. Liliya studied the face, the wrinkles—each one, she was sure, with its own tale to tell. The woman was angry and bitter and full of contempt. Lily knew from the stories that, but for a few golden years, the woman had lived a painful, lonely and unhappy life.

And now she was being asked to add to that pain.

Liliya put the last bite in her mouth, but the sweetness had gone.

"Ya finished?" the old woman asked impatiently.

She swallowed. "Yes."

"Be telling yer story, then."

Liliya hesitated. It wasn't a story she wanted to tell, even if she did know how to begin.

"Come, girl. Speak it out," the old woman insisted. Her sightless eyes flashed with irritation.

"But..." Liliya sighed heavily. "My story for you is not a happy story. I can feel it."

The woman growled, "Life isn't all happiness, girl. Out with it."

"But this story tells about the end of your life," Liliya protested. She stared at the old woman's face earnestly.

"Ah, so that's it, is it?" A bleak understanding came over the old woman, and she leaned back in her chair. "I should have expected as much." She grew silent.

"I'm sorry," Liliya whispered.

"For what, girl? Telling me something I already knew?" she snapped. Then her voice grew softer. "You've got a tale, might as well tell it."

"But aren't you afraid?" Liliya couldn't help asking.

The old woman let out a cackling laugh. "Afraid? Of course not. What is old age and the withering body if not an outward reminder of the strengthening spirit within? What is the dimming of eyes but the opening of a window into the soul?"

Liliya's breath caught in her throat.

"You think I don't know? That words *fail* me?" The old woman turned to Liliya, her face dark. Then, her voice hardened, growing cold. "No! For I, too, was a Storyteller. I, too, have heard the voice of wisdom—"

The dusty scent of dry flowers filled the room. Liliya shuddered.

"And I have made my own choices," the old woman finished bitterly. The scent slowly faded.

Liliya stared at the old woman in sorrow.

"Then, you're really sure you want to hear it?" she said softly.

"Very sure, girl." Her voice faded. "Truth is, I'm tired. Tired of being tired. Tired of fighting, of waiting. I know my time is near—and I am ready to welcome it, I am. You will tell me the story now. Yes?" Her voice was less demanding. And this time, she was asking.

"Yes," Liliya said softly. "I will tell it."

Taking a deep breath, Liliya began. She told the final story for the old woman, the story of her end of life.

Lines of hard life vanished from the old woman's face as she listened. Peace and gentleness washed over her. Liliya saw a softness there, a glimpse of who the woman once was— once upon a time, at a beginning long ago. Then, the story ended, and Liliya fell silent.

"There's nothing more I could ask. I thank you, 'tis true." The old woman stared at something in the distance, something only she could see.

Liliya waited.

Finally, the old woman spoke again, her voice quiet. "Be sure ya hold tight to them stories you've been given, girl. Keep telling them."

Liliya nodded. "Yes." She reached out and lightly touched the old woman's arm. "I will."

The old woman scowled and pulled away.

The final story had been told, and it was now time to go. Her heart heavy, Liliya retrieved her belongings. As she stood by the door, her eyes fell upon the old woman crouched on the floor, stoking her fire, lost in her own dark world. She stared at her sadly.

"Be gone with you, girl," the old woman barked.

"Yes ma'am," she said hurriedly. "Thank you, ma'am. Goodbye, ma'am."

Liliya stepped outside the cottage, Eli right beside her. A warm wind whipped about them, winding her skirt around her legs. Liliya held her breath and listened anxiously, but it was just a wind, not the Wind. She exhaled. *Not yet.*

They turned their faces away from the dusty cramped village, away from the lonely cottage, away from the blind old woman, and headed for the road. The wind continued to blow in moist gusts, and the smell of rain was in the air.

Liliya was suddenly glad, a fierce sort of glad. The coming storm suited the wild confusion of thoughts and emotions within her.

"Well, that's the end of that." Eli smiled happily, skipping along.

"Yes, that's the end," she said slowly. She touched her fingers to her lips, speaking soundlessly one more word.

Side by side, they passed through the borders of the village.

Chapter Fifteen

The tall stranger, barely visible in his dark, travel-stained cloak, sat down to eat inside the dimly lit inn. He was just reaching for his wine when he caught scent of a sweet fragrance. His hand froze, suspended over the cup. He raised his nose quickly to sniff, but already the scent was fading.

Again.

"That scent!" He slammed his fist onto the table. Wine sloshed over the rim of the cup and onto his hand. He barely noticed.

Those nearest glanced at him warily, then slowly returned to their meals as if nothing had happened.

Suddenly, he wasn't as hungry as he had thought. Or at least the hunger for food had been replaced by a different kind of hunger—a deeper hunger. He rose quickly, scraping the chair across the wooden floor as he pushed back from the table. He left his food and drink untouched.

The Wind whispered a warning, and for a moment, he stiffened. Then, he clenched his hands.

"The Wind be stilled," he hissed under his breath. Throwing his cloak over his shoulder, he wound his way around tables as he headed toward the door.

"Sir, where are you—" the innkeeper called.

The man never heard the rest. The door swung shut behind him with a hollow thud.

"You want to know where I am going?" he muttered to himself darkly. "Only where you cannot."

Grimacing, he stepped into the sun, wrapping darkness around him so tightly that he made no shadow. In the middle of the road, he stopped. His eyes darted in all directions.

Villagers were walking back and forth along the busy narrow street. His ears filled with the deep murmurings of their conversations, the sounds of the villagers' feet against the hard-packed earth, the soft swishing of ladies' skirts. The people approached where he stood and then made wide circles around him in passing. Then, further along, they bunched up again, forgetting him.

Like always.

Standing motionless, he continued to search the busy crowd. He sniffed, but all he smelled was sweat and dust and traces of wariness. The crowds thickened, the circle around him grew smaller. A farmer, bent under a heavy sack, stumbled into him as he was jostled by the crowd.

"S'cuse me, sir." The man bowed and grunted under his load. "So sorry, sir."

The man hissed angrily and took a step backward. "Have a care, fool. Watch where you're going."

"Yessir. I will, sir. Sorry again, sir." His shuffling steps hurried past.

Potato farmer, the man sneered, passing him over quickly to scan the crowd once more. He wasn't sure what he was looking for, but something. He would know it when he found it—scent or no scent.

As he continued to sweep his eyes over the crowded, dusty streets, the emptiness in him began to pick up stories in the people around him. There were many stories here, he realized, more than he had at first suspected. His eyes rested a moment on several individuals, and he pressed a hand to his stomach. S*ome, it seemed, had even more than others.*

He continued his search. Raising his nose, he sniffed the air again but found no lingering trace of the scent. It was gone.

His stomach rumbled loudly.

He thought briefly of his untouched meal—by this time grown cold. But he knew this hunger would never be satisfied by mere food. He pressed his knuckles into his forehead and growled. There was only one thing that could satisfy this hunger.

He raised his eyes decisively.

No. There would be no rest for him here tonight. He would leave immediately. He could always find another place further down the road. And if he did not, sleeping under the stars was no new experience for him. It was always the lights that troubled him, now, not the night. He could hide in the night.

Besides—he smiled coldly—*scents are often stronger in the night.*

He spun sharply on his heel and returned to the inn. He would leave. Now. He wouldn't waste another moment. He yanked the door open. "Innkeeper!" he roared.

Standing just inside the entrance, he swept his gaze over the sparsely crowded, darkened room. His eyes adjusted to the darkness almost instantly.

"Yes, good sir?" The red-faced innkeeper, wearing a stained apron, hurried over. He huffed and blew breathlessly. "Did you want a room, sir?"

"No." The man spoke through gritted teeth. "I was just here. I left a meal untouched just moments ago." He raised his chin. "There's been a change of plans. I won't be staying here after all."

The innkeeper stared.

The man rose to his full and commanding height. "Ready my horse. I wish to be leaving immediately."

The innkeeper scratched the day-old growth on his chin. "Well, now—"

"My horse," the man demanded. At the innkeeper's puzzled response, he growled and added, "The black one. In the last stall."

Being easily forgotten has its disadvantages at times.

"Yes, sir, but—" the innkeeper began to protest once more, "I don't—"

His words were left unfinished as the dark man pressed several heavy coins into his fat hand. "That should more than compensate for any inconvenience I may have caused you."

The innkeeper's eyes widened briefly at the sight of the bright coins. He clamped his fist over them greedily.

Money always helps them remember—the man smirked—*and if not remember, at least it makes them move.*

"Yes, sir. Of course, sir." The innkeeper began scraping and bowing. His previous hesitation was forgotten. "Anything I can do to be of service, sir. Anything at all."

"Just get my horse!" the man roared. "And be quick about it." He had no time or patience for dull-minded innkeepers fawning at his feet.

"Yes, sir." The innkeeper shuffled off, eager to please. He hurried as fast as his short, fat legs would carry him. "Right away, sir," he called over his shoulder, grinning widely.

The tall man sighed. *These fools don't deserve the few memories they still have.*

His spirit was restless, and he began pacing the crowded room. The hunt goaded him, urged him. When he finally heard the footfalls of his horse rounding the corner of the inn, he hurried out to meet them.

His horse whinnied loudly, tossing his head up and down.

"Easy, boy." He placed a hand on his warm neck. "It seems we are off again," he said quietly. "No rest yet for either of us."

The horse nickered softly, his ears twitching.

The man tied down his belongings. When he had finished, he wrapped his black cloak tightly around himself. The embroidery work caught the filtered sunlight overhead and shimmered faintly. Taking hold of the reins, he leapt lightly into the saddle.

The fat innkeeper was already waddling back to his inn. The man smiled slowly.

Why not?

He lifted his lips and laughing, called upon the Wind.

Instantly, lightning flashed in the distance, and he heard the rumbling response. The Wind would blow through the inn, taking the village—and the innkeeper and all the others like him would be theirs. More victims, more weak-minded souls, more stories. Just like all the others before.

His thoughts turned to the sweet scent taunting him.

More stories? Oh, yes. He stared into the distance, following the road as far as he could see. He chuckled darkly to himself. *The best prize of them all was still ahead.*

He would hunt it down, and he would find it. Then, he would summon the Wind, and all those stories would be theirs—his and the Wind's. And when that happened, he would no longer be hungry. He would, at last, be filled.

Holding the reins in one hand, he reached down and patted the horse's thick neck with the other. He whispered something in the quivering ear and then, straightening, smiled. With a loud cry, they set off at a fast gallop, the horse's hooves kicking up clouds of dust along the dry road.

The Wind had promised, after all.

Chapter Sixteen

Liliya and Eli walked all morning. Silence and emptiness filled the spaces around them. Liliya was glad to be alone with just Eli again—away from the noise and crowds and dust of the village, away from the hard, embittered old woman, away from the old woman's stories. Her rampant thoughts had left her bewildered, confused, and—she admitted to herself—a little afraid. She had far more questions than answers. She understood far less than she had before.

"Mysteria," she said slowly, feeling the word wrap around her tongue. *Such a strange word. An even stranger name.*

The breeze ruffled her hair, and she shivered.

"Liliya?"

"What, Eli?"

He glanced at her sideways. "You ok?"

"Yes, Eli," she said quietly. "I'm just fine." Staring straight ahead, she kept walking.

Eli trotted alongside, glancing at her face from time to time. Finally, he slipped his hand into hers.

"I like your stories." He smiled.

The sun was beginning to emerge from behind scattered clouds, shining warm and bright. Liliya wrapped her cold fingers around his.

"Eli, I—"

His eyes brightened.

She looked at him and sighed heavily. The stories were as much a part of her as her own memories. They always had been. But it wasn't a story she had for Eli, this time.

"Mysteria," she said quietly.

He waited, expectant.

Voices began stirring inside. Their familiar soft whisperings filled her ears. The stories were a part of her. Liliya shifted her gaze, following the empty line of road ahead. And she now knew the Mysteria was a part of her, too.

"Are you gonna tell me a story, Liliya?"

"Another time, Eli."

There is always another time.

The remainder of the day passed quietly, and evening gathered around them. Eli yawned loudly, and his feet slowed. Liliya's slowed with him.

"Let's make camp here, Eli."

Eli yawned again and nodded. "All right by me."

They ate their small meal hungrily. Then, lying back to back, they curled up on the hard ground, wrapping their coverings around them. They closed their eyes. It wasn't long before both had fallen into weary sleep.

A sweet, floral breeze brushed over them, coloring their dreams.

Chapter Seventeen

Liliya awoke the next morning stiff and tired. She felt as if she had just closed her eyes. But the sun was already up and climbing higher even as she lay there.

Groaning softly, she slipped out from beneath the coverings and sat up, automatically tucking Eli in behind her. Goosebumps began to form on her skin, and she shivered, wrapping her arms tightly around herself.

It's chilly this morning, she thought absently, rubbing heat into her arms. *Autumn must be just around the corner.*

She rose stiffly, shrugging off the heaviness of sleep. A thick, muddy feeling was in her head. It made it difficult to think. She reached for the water bag and, shaking it, frowned. *Empty.* With another groan, she made her way down to the stream.

Standing on the water's edge, she lifted her skirt and

waded in up to her ankles. It was cold. Small fish darted into the shadows, their sides flashing silver in the morning sun. Her teeth chattered.

Shivering harder, she bent over and splashed cold water on her face and neck until her skin tingled, and the last of the sleepiness had been driven far from her. Then, she filled the water bag and drank slowly. The cold water wet her dry throat and filled her empty stomach. When she had had enough, she rinsed the bag and filled it again. Then, she recapped it and climbed back up the bank. Shivering still, she stood in the sun, soaking in the warm rays. She glanced upwards. The sky was a hazy blue with not a cloud in sight. It would be warm again—no doubt too warm by the time the day was over.

With a lingering sigh, she turned and headed back to camp.

"Eli—"

She shook him awake.

He sat up sleepily and rubbed his eyes. He yawned loudly.

She began packing up their belongings, taking a mental stock of what they had left. It didn't take long. Eli handed her the cloak, and she placed it on top. She pulled the cinch tight.

He shivered. "It's cold."

"I know. Here."

Trying not to worry, Liliya handed Eli a few dried berries. She took a few more for herself.

"That's all there is, so eat it slowly," she said meaningfully.

He had already eaten half in one mouthful. He pouted slightly and cast her a dark look but chewed more slowly after that. When they had both finished, they rinsed the red stains from their fingers in the cold stream.

"Ready?" Liliya stood and stretched, leaning back until her muscles protested.

"Ready." Eli smiled.

Liliya smiled back. "Ok. Let's go."

They wove through the underbrush back to the road.

Ahead, as far as they could see, were unsettled and unpeopled areas, thin forests and stretches of flatlands, lands of fading greens and grays and browns. Not much. Certainly not enough.

The sack flopped against her shoulder as they walked. Liliya began to wonder where—in all that emptiness—she would be able to find more food. She knew there would be the occasional wild apple or plum tree and maybe a spreading tangle of berry bushes. She could definitely keep a lookout for those. But fruit would only get them so far, and it was late in the season. At some point, they would need more solid food— bread, potatoes, a bit of fish or meat. But how? They had no money, no possessions of worth that Liliya could barter even if she could find someone. She chewed her lip thoughtfully.

Her eyes fell upon her hands, and she flexed her fingers. A smile crossed her lips. She still had her hands and her strong young back and her willingness. Maybe there was some work she could do in exchange for food. That is, if they could find someone. She lifted her head once more, searching the road far ahead.

All they had to do was find someone.

They walked all day until night fell and then, disappointed, they made their sparse camp in the dirt among thin trees. Liliya opened the rucksack and pulled out the cloak, and they sat upon it. She took out the last of the figs she had carried so carefully. They were bruised and overripe. Choosing the smallest for herself, she handed the other two to Eli.

Eli's hungry eyes looked at them in disappointment.

"Sorry." She shrugged. "There's not much else left."

Eli nodded and accepted.

Liliya leaned back and ate hers slowly, letting it dissolve on her tongue before swallowing. It was sweet and fruity, and she felt a strengthening in her limbs even from the small amount. But she was still very hungry and knew the strength wouldn't last. She filled her stomach with water and tried not to think about it.

Eli licked the juice carefully from his fingers.

"I'm still hungry," he complained.

"I know, Eli. Drink some water. It'll help."

He took the water bag and drank. Wiping his mouth, he pouted. "I'm still hungry."

She pressed a hand against her empty stomach. "I know. Me too," she said wearily. "But it's all I can give you for now, Eli. We have to make what we have last."

"Oh. Ok."

"Let's try to sleep. At least in our dreams we won't have to think about being hungry."

Eli sighed unhappily. "If you say so, Liliya."

The next day they walked again. Night followed day and day followed night and still, they walked. Liliya parsed out the berries, nuts, and most of the apricots with extreme care. Despite their relentless searching, they had found only one thin apple tree. Five wrinkled fruits had clung to the branches. They had eaten them, too. Since then, there had been nothing more, and Liliya's worries continued to grow. She squinted into the distance, looking as far as she could. But it remained empty. Like her stomach. She hardened her will and then pressed a hand to her middle as it growled rebelliously.

"Liliya, can't we eat yet?" Eli begged. "I'm so hungry." His shoulders slumped.

"Don't you ever think about anything besides your stomach?" she snapped. Then, her face heated. "I'm sorry, Eli. It's just—we can't yet. We have to go a little farther first. Ok?"

"I wish I had some of Grandmother's brown bread," Eli muttered. "It was always good."

"I know. Me, too," she said softly. She was so hungry, even a dry crust sounded good.

The afternoon passed slowly and the sun blazed hot overhead. Wiping beads of perspiration from their foreheads, they continued. Liliya didn't speak. She had too little energy. Even Eli had fallen unusually quiet. For a long time, the soft, rhythmic sounds of their footsteps were the only noise they heard.

Liliya sighed. "Well, Eli. How about taking a short rest?"

He continued walking, automatically placing one foot in front of the other.

"Eli?" Her voice rose slightly.

He still didn't respond.

"Eli, stop!" Liliya cried. She grabbed his arm and turned him around. Blinking, he slowly met her gaze.

"Hi, Liliya," he mumbled.

She searched his face anxiously. His eyes were dull, his face colorless.

"Eli, sit down," she ordered him. She handed him the water bag. "Now, drink."

She pulled the sack from her shoulder and began rummaging through it. She quickly counted out three of the remaining dried apricots.

"Here." She handed them to him with a shaking hand. "Eat them, ok?"

To her relief, his eyes brightened slightly as he took the fruit. Nodding, he bit into one.

"That will put some color back in your cheeks," she sighed. She rose to her feet and then took a long swallow of the water. "You ready?" She squinted at him. Her eyes were blurry.

He nodded. "Uh-huh."

She tossed the sack back over her shoulder. Even though it was nearly empty, she stumbled a bit, unbalanced by the swinging weight.

"Come on," she said, pulling him to his feet. She turned and began following the road, leading the way.

Eli walked beside her contentedly, slowly nibbling his fruit. He cast sideways glances at Liliya every once in a while, the bright happiness in his face slowly fading. Finally, he tapped her on the arm.

"Liliya?"

"What?" she muttered irritably.

He frowned and pressed his lips together.

"Eli—" She let out a breath, making an effort at patience. "What is it? Just tell me, please."

"I just—I just wanted to share, Liliya," he whispered, taking one of his fruits and offering it to her.

"But Eli," she protested, "I gave them to you."

"Please take it," he insisted. "You're hungry, too," he said quietly. "I know. You've been eating less than me. I saw it."

Her face heated, and she lowered her head. She tried to hide her shaking hands behind her back. *I didn't think he had noticed.*

"Yes, Eli," she admitted softly. "I am hungry."

He pressed it into her hand and smiled brightly. "Then eat it, Liliya."

"All right. I will. Thank you, Eli."

They ate their fruits and walked until evening. Then, they squatted beside the road. They had no energy to find a better camp.

Liliya wrapped the shawl around her, but Eli just threw himself upon the cloak. It wasn't long before both had fallen asleep.

Chapter Eighteen

Eli and Liliya awoke late the next morning. Thick-headed and heavy-limbed, they rose and continued. There was nothing else they could do. Liliya's footsteps dragged. Eli's dragged even more slowly beside her. The stories inside spoke weakly, encouraging.

"Just a little further," they whispered, their voices soft and breathy. "Keep going. Don't give up."

Clenching her jaw, Liliya didn't. She didn't let Eli, either. They plodded along grimly, one step at a time.

The morning passed slowly, with little change. The landscape remained flat and bare and empty. Then at last, Liliya caught a glimpse of dark shapes lining the distance. She blinked and squinted, doubting her own eyes. Then, she grinned.

A village!

"Eli!" she cried happily. A flame of hope flickered to life. They had a chance now. She looked down at her hands and squeezed them tightly. She would willingly give whatever strength she had left. She laughed softly. "Come on, Eli." If she'd had the energy, she would have skipped.

It was late afternoon when they arrived. Liliya lost no time in leading Eli into the village. She scanned the road quickly, approaching the first person she saw.

"Please," she begged a woman purchasing a loaf of sourdough. "We need food. I don't have any money, but I can work for it. Give me a chance. Please. Just tell me what to do."

"Sorry, I don't have any work." The woman turned away.

Liliya approached another.

"Just a little food," she pleaded. "I'll clean, cook, do whatever you want."

That woman, too, dismissed her. "I don't hire people for help."

"I'll do anything, anything at all."

Liliya approached villager after villager, but not one accepted her offer. They all turned away.

"I'm strong. Much stronger than I look," she called after their retreating backs. "Please." Her voice began to fade. "Please."

Eli stared at her. His dark eyes appeared much too large in his thin, pale face.

"I'm sorry, Eli." Her shoulders slumped.

He nodded, looking like he was about to cry.

The villagers hurried along without giving them a second glance. Watching them, Liliya's heart fell, and her hope disappeared. The stories within fell silent, too. They had no more words left to give.

This will be it, then. The end.

Liliya stopped and looked around dully. *Now what?*

Dimly—through weariness, hunger, and despair—Liliya heard the shouts of children. She turned in their direction.

"Come on, Eli," she said quietly. It wasn't like they had anywhere else to go.

Following the sound, they soon arrived at an old cottage. Leaning slightly to one side, it looked as though one strong gust would be enough to send it toppling over.

A woman stood in the yard in front of it. Sweat streamed down her face. Her graying hair was pulled from her temples in a tight, knotted bun. She was washing clothes—or at least that's what it looked like to Liliya. One by one, the woman was dropping garments into an iron pot of boiling water and then stirring them in wide, slow circles. After a minute or two, she pulled them out again—dripping and steaming—and dropped them into a basket on the ground beside her. Then, she repeated the process.

Liliya let her gaze wander. The yard was filled with children of all sizes running around half-dressed in various states of ragged clothing. She wondered if they were the same family. Some were screaming at one another, some fighting, some crying, some laughing. All were dirty and unkempt, with thin little bodies.

She walked more slowly.

Suddenly, a shriek tore through the air, rising above the din. It was followed by an even louder burst of angry sobs.

Liliya turned quickly.

A little girl was wailing, beating her small fists against an unruly-haired boy much larger than herself. The boy held a ragged doll high above his head, out of her reach. He was laughing.

"Whatcha looking at?" a voice broke in.

Liliya gave a start and turned. It was the woman. She had her dark glare fixed on Liliya.

"Ain't none of yer business what goes on here!" the woman spat. "Git along with ya!"

The little girl shrieked again, and the woman snapped her head toward her, fuming.

"Simon! Give Sarah that doll back!"

"Sure, Ma. Whatever ya say," the boy sneered. He threw the doll into the mud and ran away, laughing.

"Liliya," Eli whimpered beside her.

Liliya clenched her fists. Her eyes tightened.

"Sarah, stop that blubbering!" the woman shouted. "Ya got yer ol' rag back. Now, go git it!"

The little girl's lips trembled, but she didn't move. She stared at the doll lying face down in the mud. Tears ran down her cheeks and her nose needed a handkerchief badly.

The woman's face purpled as she screamed, *"I said ta pick it up!"*

The child ground her fists into her eyes, choking back a fresh set of sobs. More streaks of dirt smeared across her cheeks.

Liliya stared aghast. She was quivering with anger. With a glare toward the woman, she strode over to the little girl and plucked the doll out of the mud.

The woman's eyes bulged from their sockets. "Just who do ya think ya are?" She straightened to her full height. Her face was livid.

Liliya gave no answer. She couldn't. For as she stood upright with the doll, stories began swirling around her, words, and colors. A wave of dizziness passed through her, and she shook her head to clear it. Half-dazed, she brushed off the doll the best she could and then wiped its muddy face with the edge of her own skirt.

"Here," she said kindly, offering it back to the small child. Her voice sounded hollow in her own ears.

The little girl stared at her and then the doll, her brown eyes dark with mistrust. Cautiously, she reached out and snatched the doll from Liliya's hands. As she hugged it to her chest, her tears stopped.

Liliya smiled.

The girl began to smile back and then froze, her eyes going wide. She buried her face in the doll and whimpered.

"Liliya, let's go now," Eli whispered.

She barely heard him. The stories were becoming more active, their voices growing louder. Trembling, Liliya took a deep breath and prepared herself.

"Liliya." Eli spoke louder, touching her arm. "Please."

She gave him a slight shake of her head.

"Can't, yet," she panted, closing her eyes briefly.

He glanced around nervously.

Almost immediately, she let out a soft gasp as everything swirled around her, becoming both brighter and less distinct. Thoughts filled her. New thoughts gathered and formed, becoming words. Then, opening her mouth, Liliya spoke, and the story came into being:

Long ago, when time was still young, a forest of tall trees nestled against a backdrop of mountains. The earth was fertile there and green things grew and budded, wild creatures roamed freely, and people built their lives on the ground among them, she began.

The story surrounded her, enveloped her, pulling her into it. Liliya felt a freshness in the air, a coolness on her cheeks. She breathed deeply.

"I thought I told ya to git!" The woman dropped her wet laundry with a thud.

Liliya heard her vaguely, seeing her as if through a haze from the corner of her mind where her own thoughts waited. The woman was moving toward her in slow motion, dreamlike. The story continued, and Liliya's thoughts were swept along with it. The woman faded from her mind.

At first, all was well, and the people lived their lives free from trouble, content and at ease. No one was touched by fear or sorrow. Then one bright fall morning, everything changed. The children went to play in the forest, just as they always had. But this time, they didn't return.

For days, the villagers combed through the trees, calling their names from sunup to sundown, but it was no use. The children had vanished. They continued their searches, but as more days passed, becoming weeks and then a month and more, the searches dwindled to a stop. The villagers had lost all hope.

Then, one cold night, as the trees were beginning to turn, an old couple was startled by the sound of a knock on their door. They opened it to find the lost children huddled together, hungry and cold, but alive.

"How did you find your way back?" the old couple asked in amazement.

"We saw the light from your window and followed it," the children said.

The woman broke into Liliya's story, screeching, "Doncha be speaking that nonsense to her! Sarah, git away from her!"

A sickly-sweet smell passed between them, and Liliya pressed a hand over her mouth. The story's words caught in her throat.

No. She swallowed hard, her eyes watering. The smell of rotting fruit and decay grew stronger.

More words formed, and Liliya tried to speak, but nothing came out. It was as if her throat had been closed. Fear rose. *This has never happened before.* She struggled, sweat beading her forehead. Then, the words began to re-gather and her tongue loosened. Liliya opened her mouth and continued, hurriedly:

And from that time, the villagers adopted a custom. They kept a light shining in the middle of their village, day and night, a light that never went out. It was called a "Hope Light," a light to help the lost find their way home.

Panting, Liliya rested her hands on her knees. *I did it.* The story unwound, releasing her.

The small girl was staring at her, a filthy finger in her mouth. A hint of something more shone in her eyes. Colors swirled faintly around their feet.

Liliya moved to lay a hand on the girl's shoulder, but the girl shrank from her touch. Sadness filled her heart as she stared at the child.

"Even a small light is enough to lead you out of the darkness," she said softly.

The girl gave a timid half-smile.

Suddenly, the woman took Liliya by the shoulder and began screaming into her face, *"That child don't need none of yer stories!* Git outa here. And I mean git!"

Liliya froze. Fear filled her. The woman had dug her fingers into her shoulder so hard it hurt. "But—" She winced as the woman squeezed tighter.

"*Git!* Or I'll make ya wish ya had." The woman let go as if she had been burned.

The last of the story's lingerings faded from Liliya's lips, forgotten, blown away by a gust of wind. With it, the smell of rotting fruit circled her one last time and then scattered. Gone.

The woman grabbed the small girl, yanking her roughly.

The girl cowered, whimpering.

"Git back in the house. Now!" she yelled, slapping her hard.

The girl, stumbling, gave a mouse-like squeak and then ran the rest of the way, sobbing. The woman turned in her fury, her eyes raking over the rest of the children staring in terrified silence.

"And that goes fer all of ya. *Now git!*" She wiped spittle from her chin.

Without a word, the children scurried toward the house.

"Liliya." Eli took her hand and tugged.

Chest heaving, the woman turned her face back toward Liliya.

Liliya trembled as she found herself staring into eyes that were dark and cold and filled with hatred, eyes that seemed to pull at her with their great emptiness—and their even greater need.

The wind blew again.

"Liliya, we need to go," Eli repeated, tugging on her with even greater urgency. "Now."

Numbly, Liliya rubbed her arms, smoothing the goosebumps that were trying to form. She couldn't pull herself away from the woman's eyes.

"Liliya!" Eli begged, his voice rising in pitch. Another gust of wind tugged and pulled at their clothing. Eli's eyes widened.

The woman took a step closer, a cruel smile forming on her lips.

"Come on. Let's go," Eli cried. Using all his strength, he pulled desperately. Liliya stumbled backward, tripped, and fell to the ground. The gaze was broken.

She looked up at Eli in confusion. "Eli—" she whispered, half-dazed.

"Take my hand. Hurry," he urged. "We have to go." His eyes darted fearfully all around them. "*Now!*"

Liliya stretched out a hand.

Chapter Nineteen

The stranger stepped out of the shadows. Looking around, he paused and stiffened. His eyes clouded as a soft voice reached his hearing, washing over him in waves. He turned his head, searching for the source. A sharp hiss passed between his lips as his gaze came to rest.

That one. That's the one.

His eyes narrowed to slits as he stared at the slight figure, half-hidden between the buildings and the trees. He took in the long, light-colored hair, the skirt swirling below her knees.

Female.

Young.

The voice continued, but he was too far away to make out the words. Even so, something within him was stirred, something deep. The familiar dull ache started and spread and he clutched at his stomach. He had no memories for the words to touch, no visages, only dark wraith-like shadows that teased the edges of his thoughts. It was all emptiness inside, but it was an emptiness that remembered what it was like to be full.

The wind turned, and suddenly he caught the edge of a scent—a sweet scent. The man raised his nose and sniffed. He recognized the smell immediately. Bile rose up in his throat and he swallowed it down with a grimace. He hated the smell almost as much as he desired it.

"Come swiftly." He lifted his head to the wind. A thin smile formed on his lips. "I've found it."

Instantly, the Wind began to rise and gather. Lightning flashed in the distance. Faint laughter reached his ears.

The man felt his skin tingling with the increasing charge in the atmosphere. He lifted his nose, breathing in the faint smells of rain and dust and the pungent, sweet-burn smell of dry lightning that precedes a storm.

Perhaps it will be tonight. His thoughts whirled about. *Perhaps tonight I will be filled.* He rubbed his palms together.

Wails and shrieks filled his ears, growing louder. An icy finger scraped across his cheek. The man's muscles jumped and twitched.

It's here.

The Wind curled around him like a great snake, its breath cold on his bare neck. "Where?" It quivered in eagerness.

"There," the man hissed just as eagerly. "Between those buildings and trees."

"At last." The Wind's shrill laughter sliced through the man's heart—laughter like the shattering of icicles. Then, it uncoiled and hurried on.

The man smiled coldly. *The Wind will do what it will do. Then at last, I will receive my reward.*

Wrapping his dark cloak around himself, he melted back into the shadows, just as silently as he had come. No one watched him go. No one remembered he had been there. It was as if he had never come.

Chapter Twenty

Liliya wrapped her fingers around Eli's outstretched hand and grasped tightly. He pulled her to her feet. Then, taking the lead, he hurried her along as fast as he could toward the outer border of the village. They passed houses, open spaces, and then more houses. Finally, they came to the last house—a split level house with peeling white paint. Empty road lay beyond.

Clutching their sides, they continued. A low stable had been built off to one side with a large fenced area stretching all the way up to the road. Liliya and Eli skirted alongside it as quickly as they could manage. Inside, nearly invisible in the shadows, was a black horse nibbling at the sparse dry grasses.

"Eli, look," Liliya pointed, breathing heavily. "A horse."

"A black horse." He frowned, glancing around. "Come on. Something's not right here."

She continued to stare, her steps slowing to almost a walk.

The horse had a powerfully-built chest and long slender legs. Even Liliya, who knew next to nothing about horses, could see that he was both strong and fast. The horse stopped eating and turned, arching his neck proudly. His black eyes locked on Liliya. Suddenly, he opened his lips and whinnied, tossing his head up and down.

Liliya stopped mid-stride.

"Liliya, what are you doing?" Eli said in alarm. "You can't stop now." His eyes darted around nervously.

"Wait, Eli." Liliya stared at the horse. For a moment, the colors around him had blurred and brightened as if a story were coming.

"Liliya?" Eli glanced behind them.

"Just give me a minute. Please."

Liliya remained where she was, staring at the black horse. He had gone back to nibbling the grasses. The colors faded. An icy coldness passed over her, and for a moment, she smelled the sickly-sweet smell of rotting fruit. She wrapped her arms around herself and shivered uncontrollably.

"Let's get out of here, Eli," she said quickly. Her voice was trembling.

"That's what I was trying to do," he grumbled.

They hurried along once more—out through the borders and onto the open road. They did not stop. A strange urgency had come over them. A fear. But as they went, Liliya began to slow, her steps growing heavier. She was struggling with the usual weariness of storytelling.

"Eli—" she panted.

"Keep going," he gritted through his teeth. "Can't slow down yet."

Her lips were pressed tightly together. She began to rub her arms. Suddenly, a lone gust circled them from behind and then hurried past. There were voices in it.

"Oh no," Liliya gasped. She looked around wildly. "It's coming." She glanced back the way they had come. "The

Wind."

"I know." Eli's face was hard. "I heard it, too. Just keep going. Whatever you do. And don't look back."

Story voices rose up in her, driving her forward. The Wind pursued from behind. Liliya found herself caught breathlessly in the middle—with Eli.

"I will. But you'll have to help me." Liliya struggled for words. "Getting tired—"

Eli nodded, understanding. Taking her arm, he pulled her beside him.

The wind grew stronger. Gust after gust began slamming into them from behind. Their footsteps staggered under the blows. Then, the leading edge of the storm arrived, swirling up around them. Cries and screeches tore through the air.

"It's here, Eli! Run!" Liliya wailed.

The screeches and wails became deafening. They both held their hands to their ears as they ran. The Wind curled around their ankles. Then, Liliya felt them—those terrible cold fingers—plunging into her mind and reaching deep into her thoughts. They seized eagerly upon a handful.

"No!" she heard herself screaming.

Pain and icy coldness came, followed by numbness and forgetfulness. She stopped running, her thoughts and will frozen.

"Liliya," Eli cried, staring at her in horror.

She couldn't talk, couldn't respond, couldn't move. She was still there, but it was as if she were hearing him through a layer of icy fog. Everything was muffled and confused.

"Liliya, what's wrong?" Eli grabbed her hand. When she didn't speak or look at him, he shook her. "Liliya, speak to me. Please," he begged. He began looking around desperately for help. But Liliya was no longer quite here or there, being lost somewhere in the middle. And he was all alone.

Time slowed, and the seconds ticked by. The Wind, for the moment, withdrew and waited, being content with smaller teasing gusts. It was like a cat toying with its prey. The brunt of the storm was rapidly gathering behind.

Eli stared at Liliya, his face flushed red. Slowly, he clenched his fists. "It won't have you!" His eyes filled with hot tears. "I won't let it!" he shouted angrily. He pulled her again, half-running, half-stumbling.

Liliya followed without conscious thought. But as they continued, her mind began to thaw, and her awareness returned. She glanced around in confusion.

"Eli—" she said faintly.

They kept running. He hadn't heard her.

"Eli?" she tried again.

Still, he had not heard her. He ran, dragging her along behind.

Finally, she dug in her heels. "Eli, stop for a minute, please!" she begged.

"Liliya—" he staggered to a sudden halt, staring at her. He broke into a relieved smile. "You're ok again."

"Eli." She spoke slowly, trying to catch her breath. "Why are we running?"

Eli's dark eyes fastened on her sharply.

"Where are we going?" she continued, shaking slightly. A hard knot was forming in her stomach. *Why can't I remember anything?*

He swallowed, his face blanching. "North, Liliya. We're going North." His voice shook.

"North." Her mouth formed the word awkwardly. She pressed a hand to her forehead in confusion. She knew there was something she had to do there, but she couldn't remember what or why.

Then, from behind, they both heard it and trembled. Laughter.

Eli paled even more.

"Wind," Liliya said softly, amazed that she had remembered something. More confusion came, and she looked to Eli for help.

"Yes. Wind," he said angrily. But his anger was not directed toward her. "We have to keep going, Liliya. The Wind is bad." He didn't try to explain more. "Come on, I'll help you," he said. He locked eyes with her. "Just whatever you do, don't stop."

"Right." Liliya nodded. She stared at this new Eli, wondering who he was. Fear began knotting her stomach again.

There was too much she didn't understand, too many disjointed fragments. She just wanted to gather up all the loose pieces, to figure out what was happening. But first, she had to trust Eli. First, she had to follow him.

"Wind. Bad," she echoed. She knew that much, at least.

Eli looked at her, his eyes tight with worry. Taking her hand, he held it firmly in his own. "Just stay beside me, ok?"

Nodding again, she tightened her own grip. She had to.

The laughter grew louder. Cries and screams of terror began rising up from the village behind them. The Wind had found a distraction.

"At least it will buy us a little time," Eli said heavily.

Liliya turned her head, grief-stricken.

"Come on," he said quietly.

Hunched over, they sped along once more, their bare feet pounding the hard, dry earth. It was a long time before the cries behind them fell silent, and even longer before Eli and Liliya stopped hearing them.

Chapter Twenty-One

Liliya's memories lay in tatters. She sifted through them as they went along, picking up and putting back together the broken fragments. One by one, pieces of her story re-formed.

She remembered the village by the sea and her stories and her grandmother. She remembered Eli and his father and much of her journey so far. She even remembered the old blind woman and her strange tale of the Mysteria. The memories gave her substance and grounded her—but she knew that pieces were missing, that her story was still incomplete. Too often, she glimpsed fragments of a memory or heard voices that seemed familiar but which she could not place.

She asked Eli about some of them, and he told her what he could. More bits and pieces were added to her recollections, small fragments of larger stories. It wasn't everything, but it was enough. Enough for her to know they'd better keep moving. Enough for her to be afraid. But still, she remained confused—and angry and hurt. It was disconcerting knowing that pieces of herself had been lost but not knowing what they were. For, try as she might, she could not remember why she was with Eli or why they were running. Nor could she remember why she had left the village and her grandmother in the first place. She had no memory of the Wind prior to this attack. In fact, if not for Eli's insistence, she would probably have turned around and gone back despite the warnings from her stories—and her own fears.

A cold drop stung Liliya's cheek, pulling her outside of her thoughts. She wiped it away, looking around in surprise. "Rain?" A few more drops fell scattered about her feet.

"Just starting," Eli said. A gust whipped past them, scattering more drops. The smell of rain thickened. "Do you think it's the Wind?" he asked quietly.

Liliya paused and rubbed her arms. "No. Probably not. It's been a while since we last heard it and… I don't feel anything."

"I'd bet it's from the Wind, though," Eli said, and his eyes darkened. He wrapped his arms around himself. The gusts blew colder and more scattered rain fell. "We should probably start moving again."

"I know," Liliya said with a sigh. "Maybe we can find some shelter somewhere."

He nodded. "Maybe." But his voice held little hope.

Hungry and exhausted, Liliya and Eli set out again, going until they could no longer keep their eyes open. Then, crawling under a bush, they snatched an hour of sleep—such as it was—and continued again. They didn't dare stop longer. There was no shelter from the rain, anyway.

The gusts blew colder and more rain came. The road beneath turned to mud. Liliya and Eli splashed along in their bare feet, growing colder and wetter and more miserable.

"Eli," Liliya said, and glanced at him, her teeth chattering. "Are you doing ok?"

"Yes," he answered bravely.

But he wasn't really, and she knew it, because neither was she. Both of them were hungry and cold and wet and scared. And all alone.

She fell silent, focusing her energy on staying upright on her feet.

They continued to search the area but found nothing among the flat, almost empty lands they passed, no refuge from the storm. Eli wrapped the cloak around himself and walked huddled within it. Liliya wore the shawl, clutching at it with cold and stiff fingers. Neither garment provided much protection or warmth.

"I wish I had a dry blanket." Liliya shivered.

"Or a loaf of bread." Eli gave her a faint smile.

"A warm bed." She smiled back.

It was an old game. A game they used to play at the end of the day when they were tired and hungry and ready to go home.

"A piece of baked fish."

"A fire."

Their voices grew stronger, more defiant. Stubborn.

"A barn."

"A cottage."

"Anything, as long as it got us out of this rain!" Eli shouted, splashing through a puddle.

"And mud." Liliya smiled.

Eli looked down at his feet and paused. "Especially the mud."

Night turned into day, and still the rain fell unabated. In the gray light, Liliya scanned the area in a renewed search for some kind of relief from the rain.

She was lightheaded and dizzy, and her eyes bleary with fatigue and hunger and the beginnings of fever. Her whole body ached. With every step, her muscles trembled. Eli walked beside her huddled in his wet clothes, staring at the ground.

"Eli?" she whispered.

He didn't answer. He was hovering on the edge, withdrawing into himself. Liliya sighed heavily. There was nothing she could do.

As she walked, she also became less aware of what was happening around her. Her thoughts began to slide and wander. Her feet plodded forward automatically, without thought or reason. She forgot their need for shelter and passed an old shack without seeing it.

Eli missed it, too.

Liliya's vision turned further inward, and she began to drift in and out of hazy dreams and memories. She blinked and saw her grandmother in their old cottage, rocking in her chair. The shawl, wrapped tightly around her shoulders, glimmered in the firelight.

This can't be, she thought thickly, looking around in confusion. *Wasn't I just somewhere else? With someone else?* She wrinkled her forehead but could no longer remember where or with whom.

"Liliya, come and rest by the fire," her grandmother said.

A great longing and deeper sadness rose up in Liliya, but she wasn't sure why.

"Yes, Grandmother," she heard herself respond numbly.

She was cold—shivering, really—and desperate for the warmth. She approached the flames eagerly. As she inhaled the familiar salty smell of driftwood and sweet, dry grasses, she smiled. Her face burned with the heat, and yet it couldn't seem to reach the deeper cold inside. She wiggled closer. Instead of growing warmer, though, she grew colder. She began shaking so hard her teeth chattered.

"Grandmother," she called weakly, glancing over her shoulder. "Something's wrong."

No voice answered back.

"Grandma?" she called again. But the woman looking at her was another old woman, a woman Liliya did not know. Liliya stared. There was something familiar about her face. Suddenly, she froze.

The woman has gray eyes.

Liliya blinked. The vision before her wavered, shrank—and then became familiar.

"Oh, it's just you, Eli," she said wearily, brushing a hand over her eyes.

The cottage had disappeared, and she was again following the road through cold, drizzling rain.

The next day the sun rose at last, friendly, warm, and bright. The storm had finally passed. Liliya, however, was too ill to notice, Eli too tired and hungry to care. Lost in her fevered memories, Liliya wandered in and out of visions, staggering forward, shivering and clutching at her damp cloak. Neither realized when their footsteps brought them to the border of another small village.

"Grandma, please help me," Liliya begged the visions wavering in front of her.

"Liliya, did you say something?" Eli mumbled, half-asleep.

"Sleep, Liliya," the old Healer's voice came to her softly. "Sleep, child."

"Sleep," she whispered faintly. Her eyes grew heavy. Liliya staggered a few more steps and then collapsed at the foot of a small tree on the side of the road, unconscious. Her body burned with fever. She knew no more.

"Liliya!" Eli was suddenly wide awake. He fell to his knees beside her. "Liliya?" he cried.

Liliya lay unmoving, her breath coming in quick, shallow pants.

"Liliya, wake up." He shook her. "Oh, what do I do?" he moaned. He took off the damp cloak and covered her with it. Then, too tired to think, too weak to do anything, he burst into tears.

A small three-legged dog found them there. Liliya was still lying in the same position into which she had fallen. Barking excitedly, the dog ran up to her and sniffed curiously. A boy in dusty clothes followed behind, whistling.

Eli looked up, his hollow face streaked with dried tears. "Please," he begged the boy. "Can you help us?"

The boy's whistling stopped. He looked slowly at Eli and then at Liliya. His eyes narrowed.

"Is it—is it dead?" he whispered. He grabbed a long stick and, standing back as far as he could, held it out in front of him.

"Stop!" Eli jumped to his feet, swiping at the stick angrily. *"She's not dead!"*

The dog barked and wagged his tail. He jumped and spun in a circle. Then, he bounced over to Liliya and licked her hot, dry face. She lifted a hand weakly and let out a soft moan.

"See?" Eli began crying again.

The stick dropped from the boy's hand with a clatter. He glanced at Eli and then squatted nervously. His eyes rested on Liliya's face, but her hair half-covered her, leaving only a part of a cheek visible. Leaning forward, he reached out and swept back a tangle of long, brown hair. Surprised at the face he had just uncovered, he fell back on his heels.

"She's just a girl," he gasped. "A kid."

Eli was crying harder. "See. What did I tell you? She's sick." He hiccupped. "Liliya?"

Another weak moan escaped her lips. Her eyes fluttered, but they did not open.

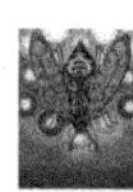

The boy's name was Ethan. As he stared at the girl, his heart began to beat wildly. He could see that she was very sick. He reached out and lightly touched her cheek. She was hot to the touch, but she was shivering. Whoever she was, she needed help right away. He stood up and looked around. "Wait here," he told the young boy. "I'll be right back. I'm just going to fetch my papa."

Then, without another word, he turned and ran away. Tanner, his little dog, followed at his heels. Ethan found his father on the north side of the field.

"Ethan. What is it, son?" His father dropped his hoe among the potatoes.

"Papa," Ethan gasped between pants. "A girl. Sick. Needs help."

His father grabbed him by the shoulder, his eyes darkening to almost black. "Where, boy? Where?" he demanded, looking over Ethan's head.

"Over there." Ethan swallowed and pointed in the direction of the road. "By that old plum tree."

Ethan's father ran from the field in his heavy boots. Ethan followed almost as fast. Arriving just ahead of his son, Ethan's father found a small boy on his knees beside another figure on the ground—both in little more than rags. He glanced first at his son and then fixed his gaze on the small boy beside the girl.

"Don't you worry none, boy," he said gently to Eli, giving his shoulder a light squeeze in passing.

He stared next at the girl's face, taking note of the flushed cheeks, the pale, almost translucent skin. Then, his gaze slid to the feather-light rise and fall of her chest. As he bent closer, his hand brushed over her hot cheek, and he froze.

A shadow fell over him. Suddenly, it wasn't this young girl's face he was seeing but another girl's face from another time, a memory buried deep in his own past. He wasted no more time. Bending down, he lifted the girl's limp frame in his arms. Then, straightening, he turned and began carrying her toward home.

"Come, boys," he called over his shoulder.

He took the shortcut, crossing the field. He didn't care if he was trampling potato plants.

"Martha!" he shouted. Using a hip, he pushed open the door to their cottage. "We've got a sick girl here."

He shifted the girl's weight in his arms to open the door wider. Then, he stepped into the small room. Ethan slipped in just after him, breathless and ruddy, the dog at his heels as usual. The young boy who'd been with the girl entered last, warily, not taking his eyes from her.

His wife turned. "Oh, the poor child!" She quickly began drying her hands on her apron. "Put her on Ethan's bed," she ordered, hurrying over.

She placed a cool hand to the girl's burning forehead, then gently touched a smooth cheek.

"Grandma," the girl moaned.

The woman clucked her tongue softly.

The young boy tiptoed over, watching her closely.

Her hand moved from the girl's cheek to circle her thin wrist, feeling for her pulse. It was slippery and faint beneath her fingers. The girl was very weak. Martha pursed her lips. The young girl's clothes were wet, too, she noticed. She would need to change her, get her cleaned and dried and warmed.

Then, her eyes fell upon the young boy, and she noticed he was in a similar state.

"Take the boy. Get him out of those wet clothes while I tend to the girl," she said sharply. "We don't want him to be getting sick too, now, do we?"

She quickly pulled several items from a drawer and pressed the small bundle into her husband's hands.

"Now, shoo." She hurried all three out the door.

Turning back to the girl, she shook her head. *The poor child.* She quickly stripped her of the filthy, wet clothing, dropping them in a heap on the floor. Then, after rubbing her clean with a towel, she dressed the girl in one of her own warm nightgowns. It was so large on the girl that she was nearly lost in it. The child had begun shivering again. Martha drew up the covers and tucked her in warmly.

"All clear, Martha?" Her husband poked his head in.

"Yes, dear, all clear." She smiled.

The young boy entered behind her husband, his eyes going instantly to the girl. "Is she ok?"

"Yes." The woman's smile warmed. The clothes the young boy was wearing were too big for him. They had been Ethan's just a few seasons before. She knelt down and began rolling up his sleeves and pant legs. "That is, she's going to be. What's your name?" She straightened.

"Eli."

"And the girl?" She nodded her head in the sick girl's direction.

"Liliya."

"Liliya." She felt the word in her mouth. "I don't think I've ever heard that name before."

Eli just shrugged.

"Come," she said kindly. "You must be hungry." She went to the table and removed a towel covering a loaf of bread. Quickly, she cut off a thick slice. "Here." She handed it to Eli along with a cup full of foaming milk. "Take this."

His eyes widened in surprise, and he grinned. "Thank you." He reached out with both hands.

"You're welcome. Now eat it all." Her eyes softened. "You must be hungry."

He nodded and then began eating with appetite.

The father turned toward his son. "Come, Ethan. I need your help to finish up in the fields."

"All right, Papa."

"We'll be back in time for supper," he told his wife. Then, his eyes flitted toward the girl, and he frowned.

"Don't worry." She smiled, laying a hand on Eli's shoulder. "We'll all be just fine."

In the far corner of the room, Liliya wandered alone, lost in her own dark dreams.

Chapter Twenty-Two

That night, Liliya tossed and turned, moaning in feverish half-visions. Martha bathed her hot forehead with cool cloths, speaking words gentle and full of encouragement. Whenever Liliya began to stir, soft hands reacted quickly to soothe and comfort her back to that place of restfulness. Sometimes a cup would be placed to her lips of which was she only vaguely aware but which she swallowed thirstily, anyway. All night long, she drifted through layers of sleep and wakefulness, nightmares, and visions.

Then, late in the night, the whole household was awakened by Liliya's screaming. *"No!"* She sat up in terror, sobbing.

Martha stumbled out of bed in her hurry to reach her.

"What's wrong?" Ethan mumbled, half asleep.

Eli lifted himself onto his elbows, his eyes wide as he

stared at Liliya's trembling shape.

"She's just sick," the father said quietly. "And had a bad dream. Go back to sleep now, boys." His eyes lingered on the girl as he watched his wife tending her—gently, patiently—coaxing her back under the covers.

"Easy now, child." He heard Martha's soft voice floating through the darkness. The girl's sobs quieted. "Drink this," she said. He saw Liliya's head lifted and watched as she noisily gulped something from the cup placed to her mouth.

Martha tucked her in. "Sleep now," she instructed.

Only after the girl's heavy eyelids had closed and she had fallen asleep again did he settle back into his own pillows and let sleep reclaim him. He was only vaguely aware when Martha slid in beside him.

Liliya slept and woke and then slept again for several days until the fever finally broke.

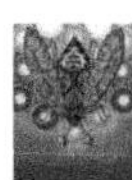

She opened her eyes.

The first thing Liliya noticed was the bright light streaming in through the windows. She squinted and blinked rapidly. Her eyes swept over the room. She didn't recognize anything. "Where—" Her voice cracked from disuse. She swallowed and raised a shaky hand to her throat. Her head felt thick and blurry.

"Don't try to talk, dear. You've been very sick." The stout figure of a woman moved into view.

Liliya lifted her head and then instantly regretted it as a wave of dizziness came over her. She sank back into her pillow, squeezing her eyes shut until it passed.

"You must be thirsty." A weight next to her caused the mattress to sag. "Drink this. It's some tea I made from the chamomile flower. From my own garden." Liliya could hear the woman smile. "It'll make you feel better."

A strong hand lifted Liliya's head, and a cup touched her lips. Liliya tried to raise her hands to help, but she had no strength.

"No, no, child. Not yet." The woman pushed her frail hands away. "Let me do it." She held the cup, and Liliya gulped the warm, fragrant liquid thirstily.

"Easy, easy. Slow down. You don't want ta be making yourself sicker." The woman chuckled.

"Who—" Liliya grimaced.

The woman smiled. "My name is Martha," she said. "My boy found you—you and the little boy—under a tree by the side of the road."

"Eli's here?" Liliya raised her head again and looked around eagerly. "Where?"

"Not *here*." The woman laughed. "He's out with the men-folk. In the fields."

"So, he's ok." She leaned back into her pillow, exhaling in relief. She closed her eyes to stop the spinning.

"As right as rain, dear. But you…." The woman's eyes lingered on her thoughtfully. "Don't know how you happened to be out there alone and so sick and all." She frowned. "But my man brought you here four days ago, and I've been tending you ever since."

Liliya gasped.

Four days. Her hands grew cold.

"I was that sick?" she said softly.

"You were," the woman said soothingly, patting her on the arm. "But it's all right now. You're gonna be just fine."

"Poor Eli," Liliya breathed. She turned her eyes back to the woman. "I—I don't know how I can ever thank you—" Liliya stammered. She felt her cheeks heating. "For me. And for Eli."

"Don'cha worry none about that. Never did turn away someone in need, and I'm not about to start now." The woman smiled warmly. "Now, child, here's a bit of bone broth. Drink up," she encouraged. "It'll help bring back your strength."

Liliya, once more, felt her head lifted and a dish placed to her lips. She took the rich, warm broth in small sips. Slowly, and with generous amounts of encouragement, she drank the entire bowl. With her stomach warm and full, waves of sleep began to wash over her. Her eyes grew heavy.

"That's just fine. Good girl." The woman took the bowl away and tucked Liliya in again. "Get some rest now," she said lightly. "That little boy of yours is gonna be mighty happy to see you've awakened."

"Eli," Liliya murmured drowsily, and smiled. Unable to stay awake longer, she closed her eyes and slid into quiet, peaceful dreams.

Chapter Twenty-Three

Over the next two days, Liliya slept, woke, and then slept again, her body doing what it needed to heal. Then, on the third day, she opened her eyes and sat up, looking around.

Martha was stacking and putting away the clean dishes. She hung her apron on its hook before turning toward Liliya. She smiled. "Yer looking better today. How about getting out of bed and stretching those legs a bit?" she suggested.

"Oh, yes. Please," Liliya responded eagerly.

"I thought as much," she said nodding. Walking over to her bedside, she wrapped a strong arm around Liliya and helped her to her feet. "That a girl," she murmured encouragingly. "Easy does it. Mind that long skirt, now. Don't get yourself tripped up in it."

Liliya carefully pulled the long nightgown up above her ankles before taking a wobbly step. She was surprised and a little frightened to find herself so weak. She leaned heavily on Martha for support.

"Don't you worry none," Martha assured her, tightening her arm around Liliya's waist. "You might be weak as a newborn kitten right now, but you'll be back to feeling like yourself in no time at all."

With Martha's help, Liliya tottered across the room to a chair set before what remained of the morning's fire. The short walk exhausted her, and she sank into the chair heavily, gasping for breath. Her legs trembled.

Martha, with a knowing smile, draped a blanket across her lap. "Absolutely no time at all." She clucked her tongue soothingly as she bent over and tucked her in.

Liliya frowned. She wasn't so easily convinced.

Chuckling, Martha put another piece of wood on the fire and then filled the kettle for tea. Liliya followed her every movement with her eyes. She had too little strength at the moment for anything else.

After a few minutes, Martha pulled up a chair near to hers and sat. "How're ya feeling now?"

"Better," Liliya said.

"Do ya need anything? Some tea or maybe a cup of water?"

Liliya shook her head. She stared at Martha shyly. "Could you—I mean, would you tell me a story?" she asked. Her voice was as fragile as dry leaves. "If you don't mind," she added quickly.

It was suddenly the one thing she really needed.

Martha paused. "A story?" She tilted her head and then spoke again. "Well, now, child. Of course, I can. Be right glad to."

Liliya leaned back in her chair.

"A story. Hmm. Let me think a minute." She tapped a finger to her lips. "Well, I guess I can recall a handful or two of stories," she said thoughtfully. She turned her gaze back to Liliya. "What kind of story do ya want, child?"

"Tell me about..." Liliya began slowly. Then, breaking

into a grin, she said, "Tell me about what you were like when you were a girl. Did you get into trouble, much?" she asked.

"Oh, ho! So you want a story about naughty me?" Martha laughed and swatted her knee. "You kids are all the same. I should have known."

Liliya giggled softly and nodded. She leaned back into the chair, resting her head.

"Well, then, a naughty little Martha it is." The corners of her eyes crinkled.

Liliya listened. The words washed over her, filling her—in their own way bringing more healing.

Martha told stories of her girlhood: her spirited adventures, her fun-loving ways, her mishaps. She told stories until both of them were holding their sides and laughing. She told stories until Liliya's eyes grew heavy, and her smile slipped. And then Martha, seeing that she had nodded off, let her voice drift, at last, into silence.

"I haven't thought of them stories in years. Years," she muttered to herself. She rose from her chair, feeling younger than she had in a long time. Lifting her arms high above her head, she stretched, letting out a groan. "Haven't done that in a long time, either." She laughed at herself softly. "Yer an old fool, Martha. Nothing but an old fool."

Asleep in the chair, Liliya mumbled something and stirred. Automatically, Martha leaned over and tucked her back in. Then, straightening, she gazed at the sleeping face. A small smile was flitting about Liliya's lips and dreams crisscrossing her brow. "I wonder what your dreams be, child?" she whispered, brushing a strand of loose hair from the girl's forehead. "Well, whatever they be, dream sweetly."

Still thinking of old memories, Martha slipped away to begin preparations for supper.

Martha had been right. With each passing day, Liliya felt more of her strength returning. She was soon able to move about the cottage on her own without losing breath. One morning after crossing the cottage back and forth several times, Liliya stopped by an open window. She looked out. Her gray eyes followed the greens and browns and blues as far as she could see. A gentle breeze outside stirred, blowing in through the window. It brushed past the curtains and tickled her cheeks. A second breeze soon followed, slightly stronger. It swirled around her, tugging on the long nightgown, sending it rippling in waves behind her.

Liliya trembled and crossed her arms over her chest. She stood there, unmoving, listening to the murmurs of voices awakening in her head. The breeze touched her cheek again, and her heart rose in her throat. Something else in her was awakening, too. Suddenly she had a desperate longing to be outside, beyond the four walls of the cottage—a real need to feel the warmth of the sun on her head and to fill her lungs over and over with fresh air.

"Here, child," a voice said softly from behind her. "From the look on your face just now, I thought you might be wanting these. I fixed them up a bit, added a stitch or two. Hope you don't mind."

Liliya stared at the clothes Martha held in her outstretched arms. She blinked and quickly swallowed the strange lump forming in her throat. "Thank you," she whispered. Her fingers trembled as she took the clean, sweet-smelling bundle and hugged it tightly to her chest. For just a moment, a sadness came over her—a premonition. Her eyes flickered back toward the open window before coming to rest on Martha. She sighed.

Martha looked at her thoughtfully. "Why don't ya get yourself dressed, now, before all them men-folk come back?" she suggested. "You might even have time to step outside before they return."

Liliya gave a quick nod and then glanced down at the bundle in her arms. She did long to be outside.

"Oh, yes, ma'am. Thank you, I will."

Wasting no time, she changed into her skirt and blouse and then slipped the shawl around her shoulders. The familiar golden threads caught the light streaming in through the windows and burned like liquid sunlight. She smiled.

"You know, ever since I first set eyes on it, I've been thinking there's something about that shawl of yours that's familiar," Martha said softly, studying the girl. "Reminds me of something. Something I saw a long time ago before I was married."

Liliya raised her eyes curiously. "Oh? Another story?" she asked.

"You could say that." Martha shrugged and returned the smile. "It's in here somewhere." She tapped the side of her head. "I just can't seem to draw it out. I'm sorry, child." She frowned.

"It's all right." Liliya hid her disappointment. She touched Martha's arm lightly. "It'll probably come some other time when you're least expecting it."

"I suppose so, child," Martha conceded with a sigh. She looked at Liliya again, her eyes running over her from head to toe, and her smile returned. "Just you wait 'til that boy of yers gets an eyeful of you."

"I know." Liliya laughed, running a hand down the front of her shawl. "I feel like I'm myself again."

Martha beamed. "Now, child, get yourself outside and get some of that fresh air in you. I can see you're nearly bursting out of your skin in eagerness. Just be sure not to wander too far."

Liliya turned toward the door. "I won't," she promised.

"And don't stay out too long."

"I won't," she called over her shoulder. Her hand reached for the doorknob.

"And don't be late for supper."

"I won't." She laughed, just before the door slid shut behind her.

Chapter Twenty-Four

The next morning, the day broke clear, promising to be warm.

"Probably one of the last warm days of the year," Ethan's father, Mr. Martin, predicted, "with autumn being just around the corner. Why don't ya come with me and the boys out to the fields?"

Eli had only been half-listening as he sat on the floor playing with the dog, Tanner. Suddenly he realized the invitation was for Liliya. He turned toward her, clasping his hands together in eagerness. "Oh yes, Liliya! Please come," he begged.

"The warm sun will probably do you better than anything else," Mr. Martin continued. He glanced at Martha for approval.

Martha nodded in agreement, then said to Liliya, "He's right, you know. Go with him. Just take care not to overtire yourself."

"I'll keep an eye on her," Mr. Martin promised solemnly, his dark eyes twinkling.

"Yay!" Eli shouted, then squealed as the little dog began barking in happy yips, running tight circles around him, jumping and licking his face.

Ethan grinned from the corner where he was stacking the last of the wood for his mother.

Mr. Martin laughed as he looked around. "Guess it's unanimous. Come along then, the whole wild lot of you, and let's be on our way."

Liliya followed them into the fields. She hardly knew where to look first. Her gaze swept rapidly from the blues above to the greens and browns spreading out from her feet below and then back again to the bright sun overhead. Her eyes never stayed on any one thing for long.

Once they reached the fields, Mr. Martin led her more slowly, placing his feet carefully between the straight rows. Already, he had dug down to the roots and overturned the green leafy potato tops. Bits of green poked, half-hidden, from beneath the dark, fertile brown of the field. The smell of the freshly turned soil was thick in the air about them, and the scent of the morning dew had mixed with it, creating a rich, heady aroma. Liliya paused a moment and breathed deeply, filling her lungs. Instantly, the field around her blazed into a swirling of color and light and scents. Her vision blurred. She knew then, the stories were beginning to awaken.

"This here looks pretty good." Mr. Martin squatted down. "Come." He patted the rich, dusty earth next to him.

Liliya shook her head, and her vision cleared. She took a step, and her bare toes sank deeply in the soft earth. Then, slipping and sliding, she imitated him, carefully picking her way between more rows. She continued until she had reached his side. Breathing heavily, she squatted beside him.

Mr. Martin waited patiently while her breath slowed, and her heated cheeks lost their bright color. Then, he began.

"We follow the roots with our fingers to find the

potatoes," he said simply. "Here." He took her smaller hand and pressed it into the soft, crumbling earth. "Feel that?" His eyes were bright.

The surface was already warm from the sun. Liliya wriggled her fingers deeper—into the coolness within—and felt her fingertips brush against something solid. Her hand froze.

"Yes," she said, her excitement rising.

"Now reach around it and pull it out," he encouraged her.

Biting her lip in concentration, she began wiggling and working her fingers deeper into the earth. Surrounding the hard, round object, she took a firm hold and pulled. The potato came loose in her hand. She held it up in surprise, examining it under the bright sun. It was brown and cool and dusty—and alive. It filled her hand completely. She gazed at it in wonder. Her heart swelled with the warmth of simple joy, growing until she could hold no more. Suddenly, she burst into laughter—her own sweet, girlish laughter—a laugh she had not laughed for a long time, not since she stood untroubled on the hill above her cottage overlooking the sea.

Mr. Martin rocked back on his heels.

"Good girl," he laughed with her. "That's all there is to it." He stood up and dusted his hands on his trousers, then cupped his hands around his mouth. "Ethan!" he shouted. "Take that row over yonder. Eli, you take the one next to him. I'll take the one here." He pointed to his left. "And our girl, here, can work this row." He turned to her, his eyes twinkling. "Slowly now," he cautioned. "Or Martha'll have me head."

Liliya grinned and nodded.

The four of them set to work. The sun was bright overhead, the earth below warm as they plunged their fingers into its depths searching for the hidden treasures.

Liliya worked slowly, pulling out potatoes, one after another. She followed her row all the way to the end and then turned back down to follow the next. As she moved along, the reawakened stories began to gather around her, very much like the potatoes she was unearthing. *They will be ready soon,* she realized. She kept her back bent to her work and continued, the joy in her work fading. Slowly, her fingers turned cold. It was because of the stories that the Wind was chasing her. It was because of the stories that the Wind had attacked—and would again. *And yet, I made a promise. I have to keep telling them.*

The stories formed slowly, speaking softly. Little by little, Liliya felt herself giving into the gentleness of their touch. Words came, brushing aside her own thoughts. The words connected—forming phrases and then complete sentences. She opened her mouth, and the words tumbled out. The first story had begun.

Liliya saw a series of pictures before her—pictures of wide fields with green leafy tops blowing in the breeze and orchards full of fruit-laden trees. Sunshine and rain and golden harvests followed. It was a land of plenty, a land that had never experienced hunger or want, a land that knew no words for them. More pictures came, and she saw families seated around tables sharing meals together, laughing and smiling and talking. The families were like the Martins and the McClellans, like Eli and his father and even like her grandmother and herself. They were just simple people sharing their lives together, sharing their stories. More pictures came. The seasons changed. Crops continued to be sown and harvested. There was no fear for tomorrow. Then, the words ended and the pictures faded. But the feeling of hope remained.

Liliya opened her eyes and let out a gasp.

There were changes in everything around her: the grasses, the sky, even the dust beneath her feet. The green and brown potato field, stretching out in all directions, blazed with color and vibrant life. She could almost see the potato plants growing—their roots and stems uncurling and lengthening as they stretched, the potatoes swelling beneath the surface.

And the air—she took another deep breath—*the air is so sweet. Almost like flowers.* She sniffed again, giving name to the scent: *the blossom of the wisteria.*

Then, her eyes fell upon Eli.

Eli—

She hadn't known until that moment how much she had missed him during her illness—his happy-go-lucky smile, his companionship, even his never-ending plea for more stories. She shook her head in fondness, noticing that his clothes were already half-covered in dirt. *Some things never change.* She watched him as he crouched over, digging deeper for more potatoes. His head was tilted in her direction, and what she could see of his face was relaxed and peaceful. *It's my stories,* she realized. Then she smiled. *He's always enjoyed listening to my stories.* She looked more carefully. He seemed different. Complete. He was like the Eli she glimpsed from time to time, the Eli she had known before his father—*Before I—*

Her eyes suddenly burned, and she blinked rapidly.

Oh, Eli.

And as if hearing her call, Eli lifted his head and turned. Their eyes met across the rows of green and brown tops. For a moment, they shared a smile—not the empty, dull smile he usually wore but a real smile, a smile that spoke more than words. It was a smile of knowing. A smile of belonging. A smile of trust. Then, looking away, he plunged his hands into the dirt once more.

Liliya continued to stare.

That is him, all of him. I'm sure of it. And maybe—she thought—*maybe he's still there. Maybe he won't go away this time. Maybe he is just waiting for another story. Waiting for me to tell it.*

More words were stirring. Liliya opened her mouth eagerly this time. *For Eli.*

In another part of the field, Ethan and his father were moving up and down their rows, pulling out their own brown potatoes. Behind them, the piles grew. Mr. Martin began muttering to himself as time went on, shaking his head in amazement. His eyes kept glancing back over the field, taking in the many potatoes already unearthed, knowing more were still hidden. He flexed his strong hands and smiled.

Liliya's words continued, surrounding and soaking into them. The words worked deep into their hearts and took root. A peacefulness spread through them. Worries fell away, burdens lightened. Seeds of hope started to grow.

Then, at last, her voice fell silent. Gazing upwards toward the bright sun, Liliya smiled and wiped away the sweat collecting on her forehead. Behind her, potatoes dotted the spaces between the rows. There was something satisfying about hard work—whether it was stories or potatoes. With a grin, she rose to her feet and stretched. Then, grabbing the water bag, she drank deeply.

"You needing a break, there, girl?" Mr. Martin asked. Liliya could hear the concern in his voice.

"No, thanks. I'm fine," she responded lightly.

Then, bending once more, she pushed her fingers deep into the earth. Feeling another potato, she wrapped her hand around it and pulled. It didn't budge. She tightened her grip and planting her feet, pulled harder. The potato broke free in a shower of dirt, and she fell backwards, landing hard. She sat up in surprise, blinking and spitting out dirt and grit.

"You sure ya don't be needing that break?" Mr. Martin began laughing.

"Yes." She straightened. She could feel her cheeks burning. Quickly, she rose to her feet and began shaking the dust from her clothes. "I'm sure," she said. Then, more carefully, she wiped the remaining dirt from her eyes and lips with the edge of her skirt.

"I suppose I probably should have warned ya beforehand," he said. "But sometimes them potatoes can be a mite stubborn."

"A *mite* stubborn?" Placing her hands on her hips, she turned toward him in mock disbelief.

Eli and Ethan began giggling.

"Yup." Mr. Martin winked at the boys and then his face turned sober. "So, you might want to be careful."

"Thanks," she quipped dryly, brushing more dirt from the front of her blouse. "I'll have to try to remember that. For next time."

"Just saying." He shrugged.

Liliya rolled her eyes and gave a long-suffering sigh.

The boys laughed harder.

When she finally bent her head to resume her work, she couldn't hide the smile forming on her face. There was no need to. A lightheartedness had settled over them all. Joy was springing out of the ground like new plants. Even the hurt and damage done to her by the Wind was becoming lighter and less painful. Her smiles came easier.

The change of season was upon them, and summer was quickly giving way to fall. Every day, Liliya worked in the field with Mr. Martin and the two boys. Every day, she told her stories with greater confidence and more joy. Every day, her body grew stronger and healthier as she dug for more potatoes.

Finally, the last potato was harvested and put into storage—and the work was finished. Liliya knew then, with heaviness of heart, that their time with the Martins had also come to an end. And as if by some special understanding, they knew it, too.

"Yer welcome to stay," Mr. Martin offered quietly. "The both of ya." He and Martha looked from Liliya to Eli in quiet hopefulness.

Liliya just shook her head. She had grown very fond of the Martins during her stay with them—and owed them her very life—but she knew she had to go. "I'm sorry." She lowered her eyes, blinking away her tears. "I'd like to. Really. But Eli and I can't. We have to go. I—"

But she didn't have to explain. Martha laid a hand on her shoulder. "It's ok, dear," she said gently. "We just wanted to let the both of ya know ya *were* welcome."

"Thank you," she whispered.

Slowly, Liliya drew her shawl over her shoulders and Martha, watching her, made a small sputtering cry.

"That shawl!" Her voice rose in excitement. "I remember." She gave an embarrassed laugh. "There was a young man used to come through our village when I was a girl. He wore a cloak with those same shiny threads. Strange, don't ya think? Haven't seen him for years now." She shook her head. "Mighty similar, though." Her forehead wrinkled, and then she shrugged. "Sorry. I guess that's all I can remember. Glad it finally came to me, though."

Liliya eyed her shawl thoughtfully and then turned her gaze back to Martha.

"Thank you. I'm glad, too," she said, and smiled.

Martha looked relieved.

"Oh, and this is for you," Liliya added quickly. She handed Martha the last of what she had brought from her home village, the small bag of barley. It was the one thing she had left, the one thing she and Eli had not been able to eat.

"Why, thank you, Liliya." Martha's eyes widened in surprise as she wrapped her hands around it. "It's a fine gift. Barley's a thing hard to come by. Our land's a bit more suited for potatoes, as you know." She smiled. Then, her face grew somber. "I have something for the two of ya, too."

She presented Liliya and Eli with several small bags of dried meat and fruit and something she called biscotti. She said it was a kind of dry, sweet bread that would keep for many days. She also gave Liliya a dozen boiled eggs—still in their shells—and a wedge of hard, dry cheese.

"I wish it were more," she said softly.

"Thank you." Liliya's heart was overwhelmed by their generosity. "It's more than enough." She carefully packed everything into her rucksack. Just as she was finishing, Mr. Martin came up behind her and spoke softly in her ear.

"It ain't much, but perhaps it'll remind ya of us." His face turned pink as he handed her a small bag of the potatoes they had dug together. "Take care, child," he whispered. He placed a calloused hand on the top of her head. "We're gonna miss ya. Both of ya."

"Thank you, sir." She wrapped her arms around his neck and kissed him lightly on the cheek. "For everything." She pulled away. "Goodbye."

"May the winds always blow soft, child."

Tears were blurring both their eyes.

"And may the waves bring you home," Liliya whispered.

Hefting her rucksack over her shoulder, she turned quickly and hugged Martha and then gave an awkward hug to Ethan who ducked out of it as quickly as he could. Eli, too, found himself enveloped in pairs of arms.

It was time to go.

"Stay safe now, children," Martha called out, her eyes bright with tears.

"We will. Thank you all again." Liliya choked back a sob as she and Eli waved goodbye. Eli sniffled loudly beside her.

They turned away. Liliya's heart burned in her chest and in her throat. Eli was crying openly beside her. She wrapped an arm around him.

"You could have stayed, you know," she said gently.

"No, Liliya." He quickly swallowed his tears. "I won't leave you. I'm coming, too."

She looked at him intently, her gray eyes meeting his brown. Eli was there, looking back. All of him. Her eyes held him.

"Nor I, you," she whispered. And she meant it.

They began the walk back toward the road. The land was far richer and more colorful than when they had first arrived. Liliya could feel the promises of good things to come. She breathed in deeply for the last time. There was a sweetness still lingering about, a trembling in the air. She managed a wobbly smile through her tears. She took comfort in knowing she had been able to leave so many stories behind, so many good stories.

They reached the road. As they turned their faces North, Eli slipped his hand into hers. Neither spoke. They didn't have to. They walked together, hand in hand, under a golden autumn sun.

Chapter Twenty-Five

Liliya and Eli followed the road all day until it became too dark to see. Then they made their camp on the ground beside it. The next day, they simply rose, dusted themselves off, and walked again. Falling back into the old pattern had been much easier than Liliya had imagined.

Night followed day and day followed night. They walked and slept and walked again. The landscape around them slowly changed. Flat tilled farmlands gave way to uninhabited lands of yellowing grasses, long low rows of blueberry bushes, spreading tangles of wild blackberries, and the occasional broad-limbed tree. Most of the fruit was gone by now or lay rotting on the ground. Fat yellow-and-black-striped bees buzzed and crawled over the last of them, eagerly lapping the sticky sweetness.

In the distance, Liliya saw what looked like a dark

smudge rising up against the horizon. Wiping away the dampness clinging to her forehead, she squinted. Hills or village or something else, she couldn't make it out. But she would soon. Straight as a ruler, the road was leading them to it. The land was changing again.

"Whatcha looking at, Liliya?" Eli asked, following her gaze. "The trees?"

"Yes, Eli." She pressed her lips together. She forgot, sometimes, how good his eyes were.

He shrugged. "It's just another forest."

She suppressed a groan. *Of course, Eli would know that.* They kept walking.

The smudge became a forest, and the forest became trees. The trees spread and grew taller, finally separating until even Liliya could distinguish the individual tree from among the whole. Then, the trees rose up on either side of the road and they were walking among them. Shadows lengthened. Evening was coming and dusk gathering behind. Liliya looked up. Already, the broad, leafy branches were darkening against a pink-purpling sky.

"I guess we might as well stop here," she said, at last.

Eli nodded happily. "Good. Because I'm hungry."

"You're always hungry, Eli."

He grinned.

They made their camp between two large trees. They ate and then fell asleep. Leaves rustled overhead.

In the middle of the night, Liliya awoke shivering. The cold surprised her. She glanced beside her and saw the dark shadow of Eli, curled cat-like into a tight ball. He was shivering, too. Frowning, she sat up. With chilled fingers, she quickly pulled out the cloak and shawl from where they had lain unneeded.

"Thank you, Liliya," Eli murmured as she spread the cloak over him.

"Go back to sleep, Eli," she said softly, tucking him in. Slipping the shawl around her shoulders, she lay down beside him. It wasn't long before she, too, had fallen back to sleep.

She didn't wake again until morning.

Sunlight worked through the cracks in the leaves, falling on their faces. Liliya opened her eyes and stared. A soft gasp escaped her throat.

"Eli! Eli, wake up!" She shook him.

"Liliya, what is it?" he mumbled.

"The trees, Eli," she said excitedly. "Look up at the trees!"

Eli rolled to his back and looked up groggily. Slowly, his eyes widened.

"Liliya!" His mouth hung open. He was suddenly wide awake.

"I know." She laughed.

Above them, the leaves blazed in criss-crossings of color: yellow, red, brown, pink, and purple. Autumn had come overnight.

They rose quickly and broke their fast. Both were eager to begin the day, eager to plunge into the forest, eager to see more. It wasn't long before they were packed and on their way. As they walked, Liliya's gaze slid easily from autumn color to autumn color, tracing the brilliant ceiling, the intricately woven tapestry of leaves. Her breath caught in her throat at its beauty. She sometimes had to remind herself to breathe.

"Eli," Liliya said slowly. "You know who else would have liked these trees?"

He glanced sideways at her, shaking his head. "No."

"Grandma," she answered quietly. She kept her gaze fixed ahead.

"Oh," he said simply, but there was an unusual warmth in his voice. His eyes saddened. "I'm sorry, Liliya. I know you must miss her."

"Eli—" She turned suddenly to search his face. "Eli?" For just a moment, she was sure he had been himself again. Complete. "Eli?" Then she frowned. "Oh, why do you always leave me?"

He looked at her dully, a blank smile on his face.

Liliya kicked at the leaves scattered along the ground. *I bet Grandma would have liked them.* She brushed away a bitter tear.

"Come on." She took his hand.

They plunged deeper into the forest. More leaves came drifting down. Liliya watched them as they fell, fluttering in ever-widening circles until they came to land softly about their feet. The sound as she waded through them reminded her of the gentle lapping of waves on the shore. She closed her eyes and tried to imagine the sea. It was easy. She could almost feel the sand turning beneath her feet, the cold sea spray on her cheeks. She smiled faintly, letting her thoughts drift and spin lazily around her like the falling leaves.

The forest around them deepened, becoming moist and dark. Older. Long beards of ivy and moss now hung from the branches. Little air moved. The dusty smells of the earth, the rich scent of woody trees, lay about thickly. Then, the treetops above rustled, and Liliya smelled another scent—sweeter, floral—almost like wine. It was the scent of time and age and many years. It was the scent of story.

Words were released with it. Liliya began listening in wonder. She learned that the trees in this part of the forest were old, far older than she had at first imagined. They spoke in a tongue heavily and deeply accented. And although it was a language she had never heard before, it was not unlike the language of the wind and the waves of the sea, both of which *were* familiar. The stories told of great hunts through the forest—men on horses with arrows notched. They told of caravans with travelers in bright-colored clothes, and songs and dances around the firelight. They told of winters with heavy snowfall and long seasons of drought and the joy of the first rain.

They told their own story.

The more Liliya listened, the more understanding and respect she gained for the old forest around her—and the long memories of the trees. She came to realize they, too, were Storytellers—whisperers of the stories of old. Like her, they had breathed the air of the distant past and now exhaled it into the present.

For the first time in her life, Liliya found her stories weren't needed. And it felt wonderful.

Chapter Twenty-Six

Liliya and Eli passed through the forest of fiery trees and out the other side. They entered another wide, empty land. Liliya immediately felt the difference as she swept her eyes over the pale flats. The stark emptiness was more than just emptiness she could see with her eyes. If the forest they had just left had been filled with story, this, then, was a place devoid. But it had not always been that way.

As they followed the road, their feet stirred the dust beneath them. Stories, Liliya realized, were also being stirred—stories from years long past, stories long forgotten. Their ghostly echoes rose up in dry whispers around her, disjointed fragments that flitted through her mind. They were memories of voices that once had spoken, voices that had now grown silent. The whispers faded, and the memories returned to the dust.

Liliya and Eli walked in silence. The land was, by far, the oldest that Liliya had ever seen—older than the bearded trees they had just left. It was an ancient place with an even more ancient history. But it was a history that no longer was. Stillness and emptiness pressed in around them. There were no voices.

But inside, her own stories, once again, began to stir. Liliya could feel them nudging at the edges of her consciousness, reaching outside of her into the silence. She was vaguely aware as they began collecting the fragile remains of the land's stories—like plucking withered fruit from a tree—giving them substance and texture and a form of new life.

Soft murmurs began to fill her ears. Liliya held her breath and waited.

The stories began re-forming, growing, swelling in her thoughts. Many stories. Then, without warning, heat rushed through her, and the ground beneath her shifted. Swaying on her feet, she staggered.

Eli grabbed her arm and steadied her just before she fell. He stared at her, not saying anything.

"Thanks," she gasped, squeezing her eyes shut. Her mouth filled, and words began pouring out. The long silence was broken. Stories that had been stilled suddenly found their voice in Liliya.

The land shuddered.

Liliya shouted out the words, one after another, as they formed. She was only half-aware of Eli trotting along beside her, trying to keep up. The words she spoke shifted rapidly— like the wind—changing with each turn in the land. Bold words came for the proud and old lands that had once hosted great battles and won, words of encouragement for the jagged ruins of a castle still remembering the days when it was strong and ruled over the land, gentle words for the wild grapes spreading over the hillsides, once a well-tended and praiseworthy vineyard. She spoke their own stories back to them, to a land that was once filled with stories. She told of a noble people who had lived there and died on the land, their proud accolades and achievements. She told how those same people had been forced into an exodus. She told how the land had been left behind, empty and grieving—story-less.

Days of silence followed, and the land waited. The silence stretched into months, months into years, years into decades and then centuries. The people never came back, the voices never returned. The once-great gardens that had dotted the land were lost and forgotten. Weeds grew, choking out the flowers. The once smooth and well-tended paths were no longer walked. Tangled briars hid them. Buildings crumbled into ruin. Trees wizened. Memories faded.

The land tired of waiting and grew hard. Everything passed into forgetfulness and silence. No more voices were spoken, no more stories told—until Liliya.

Words continued pouring through her. Never had she had so many stories. From sunup to sundown, Liliya spoke their stories back to them. Her voice grew hoarse, straining in effort. But she did not stop. She could not. The words scattered and fell wherever they walked, sinking deeply into the dry earth. Liliya spoke until she could speak no more. Then, at last, the stories and voices in her stilled and her own voice grew still with them.

Silence fell, again, over the land—but no longer was it voiceless and empty.

Slowly, tentatively, the bent and aged trees, the coarse breezes and yellowing grasses, all rose up into that silence and began to speak in Liliya's stead, growing stronger and more confident with each word. They had found their own voices at last, they had remembered their stories. Liliya had given them back.

Liliya spent the next days listening to them telling *their* stories, in voices that were brittle with disuse, in a language she could understand only little. As she learned more of their story, she was moved to compassion for the land, for the people who had once lived there, for the tragic ending of their story. A heavy sorrow came over her, and she began to weep.

Great round tears rolled down her cheeks.

Once more, the land paused and trembled. Once more, the voices fell silent and waited.

Liliya's tears pooled under her chin and then fell, landing on the hard, dry earth below. Colors burst open at her feet, swirling and blurring like a water-coloring. A new breath of life was released into the air, a sweetness, bringing with it the first gentle touches of softening to the hardened land. It had been remembered, had remembered. And once again, it had been loved.

Liliya dried her tears and smiled. She recognized the new grape-like scent drifting with the breeze. Then she realized her voice had returned. It seemed she had one more story to tell, after all—the last.

Lifting her voice, she began. The story she told was not a story of the past but of the future—a story full of new promises. A new people would come to the land and live in it—and tend it carefully and love it. Hope would return—and life—and a new story would begin. In time, the old sores left festering would turn to scars, and the bruises fade into memory.

Liliya closed her mouth. It was finished. Looking around, she smiled wearily.

Already, recognizable changes were taking place. The hardness and bitterness of the land was lifting, the trees and grasses playful in the breaking of their silence. They were full of voice, full of words, full of joy. They had come alive.

Eli slipped his hand in hers and she looked down in surprise. She been so full of words, so busy telling her stories, that she'd forgotten he was with her.

"Did you do all this, Liliya?" he whispered, looking around.

"No." She smiled. "It was the stories."

"The stories—" A look of longing came over Eli's face, but Liliya didn't see it. She was listening to the voices.

Liliya's and Eli's last days in the land were very different from their first. As they walked, the wind would often ruffle their hair in passing, tickle a cheek or break into sudden, exuberant laughter before racing on ahead of them. At night, when they lay upon the soft, pale grasses with the clear sky black overhead, winking with stars and silver moonlight, Liliya felt as if she were being rocked to sleep—by the wind, by the grasses, by the Earth. Those nights, Liliya's sleep was the deepest and most restful she had ever had. And there had been no need for dreams.

They came, at last, to the far edge of the land. Voices began dropping away behind them—one at a time—until only one voice remained. A last and final voice to wish them off. "Fare thee well. May the winds always blow soft."

"And may the waves bring you home," Liliya cried in return. "Goodbye."

"Goodbye…" The voice faded and was gone.

Liliya glanced over at Eli. "I guess it's back to just us again," she said softly.

"Just us, Liliya."

"Just like always." She ran a hand lightly across the tops of the dry grasses.

Healing continued in the old lands they left behind even after they were gone. Near the ruins of the great castle, the first tender leaves on a dead tree were unfurling. A wisteria tree had come to life.

Liliya had given the land the greatest gift: a future.

Chapter Twenty-Seven

The road cut straight and bare before them, and they followed it. Eli began casting furtive glances at Liliya as they walked. He cleared his throat several times. His brow wrinkled and then unwrinkled.

He was troubled and that troubled Liliya.

"Liliya," he began, then hesitated.

"What is it, Eli?" A knot formed in her stomach.

"I—" He puffed out his cheeks and frowned. His face reddened. "Can I ask you something?"

"Of course you can, Eli. You know that," she said warily. "Always."

"Liliya, how come you never tell *my* story?" he blurted.

Liliya opened her mouth in surprise before quickly shutting it again. "Why Eli, I've told you stories before," she spluttered.

"No, not *those* kinds of stories, Liliya." He shook his head. "I don't want to hear about how I learned to walk when

I was a baby or the first word I spoke. Liliya—" He began trembling almost to the point of tears. "I want to hear *my* story. I need to. I need to hear who my mama was. And my papa, too. I need to know what happened to them. I need to know what happened to me."

"Eli…" Liliya's voice trailed off.

"I've waited such a long time, Liliya, but you've never told my story. Ever."

"Eli, I—" She stopped. She wanted to protest, to disagree, but she was much too honest with herself to do so. Besides, she knew he was right.

"Why, Liliya?" He stared at her, his eyes filled hurt and confusion. "Why haven't you? You have all those stories for everyone else. Don't you have any stories for me?"

"Oh, Eli," she said softly. "Of course I do. I have many stories for you."

"Then why haven't you ever told them?"

"It's because…" She sighed. "Because I was afraid."

"Afraid? You? Of what?" He blinked away his tears.

"Of you," she admitted, lowering her eyes. "Of what you'd think when you found out. Afraid that you…" Her voice lowered to less than a whisper. "That you would hate me, Eli."

"What!" he exploded. "I could never do that!"

"I wouldn't blame you if you did," she continued hoarsely. "What I did was terrible, Eli. And I did it to you."

"Liliya, I don't understand—"

"Please let me finish, Eli." Now that she had started, she didn't want to stop. She took a deep breath. "Next to Grandmother, your papa was the kindest person I have ever known." Her voice softened. "He's the one who found me," she said quietly. "On the shore. Grandmother said I was more dead than alive when he brought me to her."

Eli nodded. "Go on." He already knew that part of the story.

"Grandmother took me in, but your papa took care of me, too. He made sure grandmother and I always had enough to eat." She smiled. "Later, he and your mama married. Then you came along. They were so happy, Eli. You made them happy."

He smiled wistfully, and then a shadow fell over his face. "Liliya, how did my mama die?"

"I—I don't know very much, Eli. Only that she became sick. Grandmother did everything she could—but she couldn't save her."

"What about my papa?"

"He was a broken man."

Eli sighed heavily. "I don't remember my mama, but I do remember him. At least a little. I know that after mama died, we'd sometimes visit you and your grandmother." He looked up at Liliya and smiled. "He always brought you sweets, Liliya."

"He did." She nodded. "And we'd eat them together, Eli—you and I—up on the hill, overlooking the sea."

"And you always gave me more." He laughed softly, but his heart wasn't in it.

Liliya half-laughed, half-cried with him. "You knew I could never resist those big brown eyes of yours." Then she lowered her head in shame. "Eli, I'm the reason you are alone. I'm the reason you have no family. It's all my fault."

Eli's face paled. "Liliya, what do you mean?" he said slowly.

"I told a story," she began hoarsely. "After your mother died. I didn't know any better. I was too young, I guess. Anyway, at that point, none of my stories had come true. I was just having fun and trying to tell the most frightening story I could—and it came out. I never thought it could happen for real."

"What happened, Liliya? What did you say?" he demanded.

Her voice became a whisper. "I told how a great Wind came from far over the sea, a Wind that set the waves tossing and rolling. I told how the fishing boats were caught in the storm and had no chance against it. Then, I told how the sea itself rose up like a great hungry mouth and swallowed all who were in it. I told how no one survived—"

"Liliya. No," Eli whimpered. "The storm?"

She nodded. "It was my storm." She covered her face with her hands and moaned. "Your papa should have just left me on that beach—"

Eli wrapped his arms around himself and turned away. He was shaking, staring down at his feet, but he made no sound.

"I'm sorry, Eli," she said softly to his back. "You have no idea how sorry." Self-loathing writhed in her stomach. "Eli?" Her voice trembled. "Eli?" The wait was terrible. She twisted her fingers together nervously. "Say something, Eli. Anything," she begged.

Eli remained silent. He didn't move. It was as if he had not heard her.

Suddenly, Liliya became angry. Her hands clenched into fists. "Eli, talk to me! Don't you dare run away again! Don't you dare go back into hiding." She began shouting. "I know I have no right to ask you. That I am next to nothing to you. But please—please don't go away. Stay here with me, Eli. Can't you understand how much I need you? Eli? Eli, please—" Her voice fell to a whisper. "I can't do this on my own."

The sun burst through the clouds above, setting everything ablaze in gold.

Eli turned around at last. Tracks of tears were visible on his cheeks, but he was no longer crying. He faced her calmly. "I don't blame you, Liliya. I could never blame you," he said softly.

"Eli, I—"

"It's not your fault," he continued.

"But I told that story. And your father—" she protested.

"It was the story, not you," he interrupted.

"But I *am* responsible, Eli," she said bitterly. "Don't you understand. I'm a—*Storyteller*." She spat the word with disgust.

"No, Liliya." He held her with his eyes. He was not hiding now.

Liliya waited, the pain in her heart growing, swelling, until it was almost unbearable.

"No," he repeated softly, slowly. "To me, you're Liliya. Just Liliya. Just as I am Eli." He looked at her, fully and completely. "Just Eli."

She stared at him, the pain in her heart now excruciating.

"No!" She took in a breath, her fierce passion surprising even her. "Not *just* Eli. Never *just* Eli. You are so much, much more. You are…*my* Eli." She paused. Tilting her head, she listened. The stories she had expected were already rising and filling her thoughts. "It's time, Eli. Time I told you your story." The ground shifted beneath her. She cried out loudly, "For you, Eli!"

She opened her mouth as her own thoughts were swept away.

Chapter Twenty-Eight

The black horse pawed at the hard ground and snorted.

"Easy, boy." The man stepped in front of him, raising his hands. "Easy." Reaching up under the mane, he gave a firm pat. The horse quivered and stilled though his ears continued to flicker uneasily. "We'll be leaving soon enough," the man continued.

Shivering slightly, he wrapped his dark cloak around himself and stifled a cough. His eyes stared far down the empty road. Anger and disappointment writhed and twisted within him. Despite his best effort, the Storyteller was still out there, free, and bloated with stories. Stories that should have been his.

"Blast the Wind's relentless demands. Blast its incompetence," he hissed.

For days, he had tracked the Storyteller like a faithful

bloodhound—through blistering heat and pouring rain, through wind and storm and illness. But the Wind had not accepted the limitations of the flesh as a reason for failure. *My failure!* He clutched the hollow of his stomach.

It was the Wind who lost her. The Wind who let her get away. Not me!

He gazed further, squinting against the sun. He would find her again—that Storyteller. He would hunt her until he did. He only needed the scent. *And then—*

He stiffened suddenly. Icy fingertips were trailing across his exposed face and neck. Then he felt the Wind curl around him.

"When—" the cold pressed against him.

"When *I* am ready," he growled, balling his hands into tight fists. "And not a moment before." As much as he wanted the Storyteller, he refused to be bullied. He raised his nose and sniffed at the breeze, feigning indifference. But he could not hide the tremble that passed through him, nor stop the cold fear that settled in his heart.

The Wind laughed softly in his ear, stroking a finger down his cheek. "You amuse me. A little."

"Bah!" The man turned away and sniffed again. There was still no trace of that elusive floral scent.

Where? Which way?

Undecided, he stood with one foot in the stirrup and one on the ground. He swept his gaze slowly from South to North. The last appearance of the scent had been in the Great Forest, many days past, just before he had taken ill. The last time he had glimpsed the Storyteller, she had been heading North through the village. His home, also, lay to the North.

So be it.

He made his choice and mounted.

"You *will* deliver her this time." The frigid breath stung his ears, his cheeks. There was no amusement in the voice now.

The man said nothing, only lifted his chin slightly. His eyes glittered.

"You will." The Wind tightened its grip on him. Shards of icy cold bit into the man's flesh. His jaws clenched until he thought his teeth would shatter.

"*Yes.*" He felt the word wrung from him.

"I don't accept failure." The Wind slowly uncoiled, releasing him.

"No," he whispered back, gasping and trembling. He swiped angrily at the frozen tears clinging to his cheeks. "No."

He gripped the reins tightly, and with a sharp cry spurred his horse into a run. Thick, gray clouds of dust rose up behind them as they fled. But they could not outrun the laughter of the Wind that followed.

The man and his horse traveled all day, passing through straw-colored flatlands. Against the hard-packed earth, the horse's hooves rang dully. They heard no other sound—no tree, no bird, no Wind. They saw no other living thing.

Then, at last, the shadows the man had been expecting appeared ahead of them—a forest he knew all too well. Dread gripped his stomach. They rode hard all the way to the edge and then slowed almost to a walk.

Tall, dark trees loomed up on either side of the road, their branches locked and twisted above him. Looking up, the man grimaced and pulled his cloak tightly around himself. Then, as he and his horse disappeared beneath the shadows, he drew his hood up over his head, as well.

The air was much cooler under the trees, and darker. He knew from his many journeys that not much sun ever made its way through the leafy tops. Hunched over and silent, he rode, staring straight ahead. The forest deepened and darkened as they went. Every so often, he would lift his nose and sniff. The air was dusty and smelled of trees and the passage of many years—the way it had always smelled. Voices, too, rose up—the same voices he always heard. And as untouchable as ever.

A deep growl, almost a moan, escaped his throat.

Over the years, he had grown to despise this forest. He hated the stories that were in it, the stories that it flaunted. Nowhere else did his own emptiness feel so empty. Nowhere else did he feel so incomplete.

Straightening in the saddle, he tightened his knees. *It is better not to linger too long, better not to think. Too many dark thoughts. Especially here.* Pressing a hand into the hollowness of his stomach, he spurred his horse faster.

They continued until dark fell, riding until the man could no longer sit upright. Then, exhausted, he cast himself upon the broken leaves that were scattered on the ground, and he slept. In the middle of the night, the Wind entered his dreams, and he awoke in a cold sweat. Nightmares hovered before him. Staring into the blackness, he clutched his stomach. The emptiness inside gnawed at him, and he pressed harder.

He lay awake the rest of the night, tossing and turning until twilight was just beginning to edge in around him. Then, he rose and packed quickly. He was cinching down the last of the saddlebags when suddenly, he froze. Looking up, he took a deep, lung-filling breath. Cold laughter bubbled up from his chest. He had found it, drifting along innocently with the morning breeze—the scent.

The Storyteller has not escaped me, after all.

Laughing again, he leapt into the saddle, his fist holding the reins tight. A new eagerness was upon him. *I'll find her. That Storyteller.* His stomach rumbled loudly. *Her stories will fill me, yet.*

With a sharp kick, they were off, leaving only a trampling of broken leaves behind, a dark stain of reds, golds, and browns.

Chapter Twenty-Nine

The sweetness of the wisteria lingered about them. And on Eli, a permanent smile seemed to hover about his lips, ready at any moment to burst like sun through clouds.

Ever since Liliya had told his stories, he had remained with her, not retreating into himself as he had always done before. Liliya looked at him often, now, smiling in wonder. This was the Eli she remembered, the Eli she had known. Reaching out, she took his hand in hers. This was the real Eli.

The old lands they walked gave way to pale green marshlands surrounding a narrow lake of silvery waters. It was an oasis in the middle of nowhere. Many birds lived there, as innumerable as they were various. Liliya and Eli saw them everywhere. Birds hid in the tall grasses, skimmed over the waters, and flew in great flocks overhead. Noise and movement came from every direction. Chirps and squawks and honks filled the air.

Suddenly, Eli pointed excitedly. "Liliya, look! Swans."

A flock of large, white birds were just landing, their great wings stretched out wide. They touched down, skimming across the surface and then gliding to a stop. Folding their wings to their sides, they began paddling, their long, thin necks curved elegantly.

"Oh," Liliya whispered. "They're so beautiful."

"I know." Eli grinned. "I've only ever heard about them. I never thought I'd actually see one."

"I didn't know you liked birds, Eli." She gave him an odd glance.

"Uh-huh." He nodded happily. "Always have. Papa used to tell me all about them when I was little. And sometimes"— he stretched out his arms and ran ahead laughing— "I even used to dream I could fly."

"Eli, wait!" Liliya called after him as she hurried to catch up. She found herself grinning. She was starting to like this new Eli very much.

"Come on, Liliya. Fly with me!" he called over his shoulder.

Stretching out her arms, she laughed as she, too, began to fly. She was definitely liking this new Eli.

All too soon, they passed beyond the lake with its birds and their noise. Then it was just the road again, and dry, empty lands. Eli plucked a dry stem of grass and chewed on the end of it as they walked. His eyes held a faraway gaze. Liliya was certain he was still seeing and hearing the birds in his private thoughts. When she tried, she could still hear them, too.

Before long, a small village appeared on the horizon. Dark and shapeless, it grew until individual buildings finally separated from the whole. Liliya was surprised to see that the buildings lining the two sides of a single road. Their own road soon merged with it.

"Well, here we go, again," Liliya said, frowning slightly.

Eli nodded and then glanced at her sideways. "We could always go back to the birds," he teased.

A smile pulled at the corners of her own mouth. "Right," she drawled.

"Don't worry, Liliya." He smiled confidently. "We'll be fine. I know."

Eli's chin was raised. His brown eyes shone clear. Watching him, Liliya, too, felt a boldness. She turned her eyes ahead.

There was little to see when they approached the village. Faded buildings lined the road just like they had seen from the distance. The dust below was gray, the sky above gray. Even the people appeared gray and fading. The silence hung heavily. Everything was dull and slow-moving and colorless. Liliya felt washed-out and faded as she walked the dusty road, like clothing left out in the sun too long. Even her stories felt thick and dull-witted. She heard their voices inside, stirring, but little life was in the stories that came—and even less fragrance. Liliya tried to speak the words anyway, but they felt like powder in her mouth and came out like dust. The words scattered, drifting before her, aimless—until they were swallowed up in the grayness. Liliya closed her mouth, bewildered. *That's never happened before.*

Then, a faint scent curled around them, clinging to their clothes. She breathed deeply, and choked. It was not the smell of the wisteria, as she had expected. Instead, it was the smell of death. Liliya realized, then, that her stories had come to this place too late.

She and Eli passed through the village as quickly as they could. They forgot it soon after.

Chapter Thirty

Each day, Liliya and Eli walked the road a little farther. They began to catch glimpses of sharp jagged peaks in the distance, the same mountains they had seen before descending into the valley. But now they appeared much closer.

The lands they traveled were mostly empty of people, houses, and villages. The few inhabited places they did pass through were small and widely spread out with the residents preferring privacy to the companionship of their neighbors. In those places, Liliya's stories remained silent, and the color around her dull.

But though she had no new stories to tell, she was not discouraged. Eli chatted beside her as they walked. He remained with her, complete. He was so like his old self—the self she remembered from when his father was still alive— that she sometimes stared at him in bewilderment or shook her head to remind herself of the years that had passed. There were times, though, when he fell into a brooding silence, and a shadow would come over him. It was in those moments that she told him more about his mama and papa, stories that came from her own memories.

Fall was now advancing into winter, and the weather growing colder. Liliya wore her shawl most of the time—and Eli the cloak—even while they walked during the day. At night, they slept huddled together for warmth. When morning came, they arose cold and stiff with teeth chattering and resumed their walking. It was often a long time before the chill of the night was driven from their limbs and their bodies warmed through enough so that their shivers subsided.

Day after day, it was the same. Day after day the mountains before them grew larger.

They ate their small meals and then slept on the hard, cold ground. In the morning, Liliya slung the old rucksack over her shoulder, and they walked again. Food, once again, became a constant worry. Besides the small bundles of herbs Liliya had been gathering along the way, all they had left were a few handfuls of nuts and the bag of potatoes that Mr. Martin had given them.

That evening for the first time, Liliya struck a match and made a small fire. She and Eli huddled near, grateful for the warmth. When it burned down, she roasted four small potatoes on the bed of coals. Eli ate his so quickly that he burnt his lips and tongue. Liliya ate hers more slowly, her thoughts drifting to the family who had given them. To her, the memories of their love and friendship strengthened her even more than the potato warming and filling her stomach. They each ate one that night for supper, hot. The other two, they saved for breakfast. They did the same each night.

The days passed and the bag dwindled. Finally, they came to the last two potatoes. Liliya stared at them as they warmed her cold hands.

"This is it, Eli."

She handed him the larger of the two. Then, slowly, she

put her hands together in the old prayer and breathed thanks.

Eli did the same.

They would eat half tonight, saving the other half for breakfast, they decided, making them last as long as possible. But, as they tore into the steaming white flesh, they both ate their first halves so quickly that Eli just stared at her, pleading. She, too, was hungry, and the potato was so warm in her hands and in her mouth and in her stomach that, ignoring a twinge of guilt, she nodded. Eli grinned happily and wolfed the rest of his down. Liliya, more sedately, broke hers into pieces. Then very slowly she finished the potato, blackened skin and all.

Morning came, cold and dreary, and they wrapped their outer garments around themselves tightly and plodded forward. They had no more warm meals to look forward to at the end of the day—only more coldness and hunger.

Eli soon lost the spring in his step. Liliya's steps wearied, too. Even the stories in her mind grew quiet. They walked. There was nothing else they could do.

Trees closed in on them and then the road took a small turn. They came to a river that divided it and then continued to run parallel on the other side. Liliya and Eli crossed over on the narrow bridge and then carefully made their way down the slippery bank to refill their water bag. They drank thirstily, feeling their empty stomachs swell.

"Liliya, I'm so hungry," Eli complained. He rose unsteadily to his feet. "I'm tired, too. And cold."

"I know, Eli. So am I. But we don't have anything else. We already ate it all. Even that bit of nuts. Water is all we have left—" A flash beside the bank caught her eye, and she tossed a stone angrily. "You'd think growing up in a fishing village, I'd know how to catch a fish." She sank down and hugged her knees.

"I know how," Eli said quietly.

"You do?" She looked up.

"Sure. All the kids did."

"Except me. Apparently," Liliya muttered. "Eli, why

didn't you ever tell me this before?" she asked in irritation.

"You never asked."

"Well, Eli, I'm asking you now. So, if you can catch anything, anything at all, do it. I'll go gather some wood. At least I do know how to make a fire," she grumbled.

Eli pulled a tangled string out of his pocket and began unraveling it. Then, he rewound it again carefully. Examining the hook tied to the end, he gave it a few tugs to make sure it was strong. He began wandering about. Lifting rocks and broken pieces of logs, he looked underneath them. Every now and then, he reached down and pulled out a fat grub or wriggling worm. After collecting a small handful, he baited his hook and dropped it into the deep, shadowed water. Sitting on the bank, he waited patiently.

Liliya watched him with amazement. It seemed that with each passing day, Eli managed to surprise her more. He was changing, she noticed. As a little boy, he'd always been clever, but the changes were more than that. Along with the reemergence of the old Eli, there was a stronger, more confident, and maturing Eli.

She smiled softly.

It's the Eli he was always meant to be.

"Hey, Liliya!" he called, holding up a silvery fish. "Looks like they're biting good. I already got one."

"Good work, Eli!" she cried. "Hand it here, and I'll clean it. Then keep trying. See if you can catch some more." She pulled out the silver paring knife.

"You bet." He nodded, his eyes bright.

Suddenly, Liliya's heart felt lighter than it had in a long time. They wouldn't go to bed hungry that night and perhaps—if Eli could catch more—not tomorrow night, either. Her eyes drifted toward the road and the North.

And who knows? We might just make it yet.

Eli had been right about the fish biting and managed to catch eight more before the sun set, and they stopped. That night, they feasted on freshly roasted fish. Then, finally, they let the fire burn low. Tired and full of warm food, they made their bed between the roots of the thin trees. Eli immediately threw himself down, dragging the cloak over him while Liliya banked the fire.

"Good night, Eli," she said softly, turning toward him. But he was already asleep. She tucked him in and then lay on the ground beside him. She pressed a hand to her stomach. For the first time in many days, she was not hungry.

"Thank you, Eli."

She glanced toward a faint red glow, all that remained visible from their fire. More fish lay in the coals, wrapped carefully in leaves. There would be enough to eat for several days.

The knot inside loosened just a bit.

Already, the night was growing colder, and Liliya wriggled closer to Eli. She checked again to make sure he was covered and then, leaning back, closed her eyes. She fell asleep almost at once.

Liliya awoke to the sun full in her face. She opened her eyes, stretched, and then sat up. Taking in a deep breath of crisp, cold air, she shivered. The sleep cleared. Suddenly, she became aware of her heart beating rapidly in her chest, her whole body tingling with excitement. She lifted her chin and filled her lungs again. A smile spread across her face.

"Eli, wake up. Hurry." She shook him.

"Liliya—" he groaned. "What do you want?"

"Eli." She smiled wider. "Can't you smell it? It's the sea, Eli. The sea!"

Chapter Thirty-One

All morning long, Liliya continued breathing deep lungfuls of sea air. It was different from the smell she had known—it was colder, wilder and less predictable—but it was still the salt-tainted smell of the sea that she loved. Eli, too, walked beside her in a happy daze, a smile fixed on his lips.

The road finally turned, taking them out of the trees and away from the river. The view ahead opened up. Mountains suddenly loomed before them. Liliya gasped.

The mountains! And the sea is just on the other side.

The road straightened again, hurrying onward. Liliya and Eli followed it at a quick pace. They traveled all day, straight as an arrow flies.

That night, they rested at the foot of the mountains.

Morning came, and they hurried through breakfast and packing. Both were eager to begin the climb. They stepped onto the road and followed it. Almost immediately, the road curved and began to incline. Liliya and Eli soon found themselves winding between rising hills. The hills hardened. The sun rose higher. A silence hung over the land, a stillness that increased the higher up they went. The silence deepened until they heard no other sound but their own flat footsteps, the occasional tumbling stone, and the ever-present wind racing down the path. The stories in Liliya, too, had become voiceless and silent.

Soon, the walking became more difficult. Hunched over and clutching their sides, they continued. Their breaths began to come in shallow pants.

"Keep going, Eli," Liliya gasped. "It's just a little farther."

"How much farther?"

"I'm not sure. Soon." She had said it so many times she was beginning to believe it herself.

Placing one foot in front of the other, she climbed higher. Her desire to see and hear the waves crashing upon the shore, to feel the sea spray on her face and taste the damp, salty air drove her to keep going. Not until the sun had dipped low in the west and the shadows stretched long before them did she let them stop again for the night.

When she did, Eli quickly threw himself on the ground, spent. "Finally," he groaned.

Glancing toward him, Liliya pressed her lips together.

They made their camp in barren foothills. It was a lonesome place and chilly, but with the wind blocked by the hills, it wasn't overly cold. They huddled together beneath the cloak and the shawl. Eli fell asleep almost at once. Tired as she was, though, Liliya could not. She lay awake in the darkness, her thoughts wandering up and over the mountain to the sea that lay beyond. What was to come after, she had no idea. The stories had not told her anything—if they even knew. She rolled to her side, pulling the edge of the coverings tightly around her, and sighed. Reaching underneath, she lightly fingered the shawl. The smooth fabric caught and snagged on her roughened fingertips, but touching it soothed her. Her thoughts drifted.

The smell of the sea was stronger. Closing her eyes, she imagined she was standing on her hill with wild grasses and flowers surrounding her. The gray sea was below, and the sun bright overhead. Then, she imagined her grandmother's voice, rising above the breeze, calling her home. With the smell of the sea lingering about her, she could almost believe she was there. Almost. Her efforts fell short as she heard rocks tumbling down the hard face of the mountain beyond, felt the sharp slap of cold air on her cheeks, heard the soft breathing of Eli beside her. Shivering, she slid closer to Eli and buried herself under the coverings. She closed her eyes and, at last, fell into a troubled sleep. All night, her dreams were plagued by shapeless shadows, fading memories of forgetfulness and the ever-present laughter of the Wind.

When she awoke the next morning, it was later than usual, and the sun already high overhead. Blinking in the brightness, she bit back a yawn and stretched. Her limbs felt sluggish and heavy. After shaking Eli, she rose stiffly to her feet. They each ate a mouthful of cold fish and then washed it down with a swallow of water. Then Liliya slung the rucksack over her shoulder and they set off, ready to continue the hard mountain climb. The morning air was still so cold that their breaths rose in white puffs before them. They wrapped their garments tightly around themselves and slapped their arms.

All day they climbed, straining their muscles until they ached. When evening came, they collapsed on the hard ground, choosing to shelter between two jutting stones. The next day they rose and continued again. It was their second day on the mountain.

The valley below grew smaller. The wind above increased. Every step of the path became rougher and more treacherous. They moved their bare feet carefully among the sharp, broken stones but kept a steady pace all morning and made good progress.

"Liliya, look." Eli, shielding his eyes, pointed. "The

peak."

The clouds had parted, revealing the top of the mountain above them. Liliya's heart began beating rapidly. She pressed her lips together. They were really almost there.

"Come on, Eli, let's hurry."

Their pace quickened. They climbed higher, following the rough, winding path up. They could still see the peak rising between pale and spindly pines. Wispy clouds passed beneath it. Then, the climb became more difficult, and their breath ragged and painful. Their steps slowed again.

"Liliya," Eli gasped. "Need...stop. Air...bad."

Liliya eyed the peak with longing. Black spots swam before her eyes. As much as she wanted to keep going, she, too, needed to catch her breath. She gave him a nod. Hands on her knees, she bent over, gasping for air. Eli sank all the way to the ground, to his hands and knees. Neither moved for several minutes. They just breathed.

A sharp cry came from high above. Another answered. Lifting her eyes, Liliya squinted. A pair of eagles were circling, growing larger with each turning. A chill worked its way down her spine. She was suddenly reminded of her nightmares from the night before. There had been eagles in them, too. Eagles with bright eyes and sharp claws.

Pressing a hand into her side, she straightened. "Ready to go, Eli?" She didn't want to stay there any longer than was necessary.

He nodded wearily.

"Come on, then." She glanced upward, but the eagles were already gone. Somehow, their disappearance didn't make her feel any better.

They began climbing again, carefully placing one foot in front of the other. The sounds of the wind grew louder.

Suddenly, Liliya stopped short. "Eli, did you hear that?" she asked.

"All I hear is the wind, Liliya."

"No. There was something else." She glanced around warily. "Sounded almost like..." She frowned.

"Like what?"

She didn't answer.

They continued again, Liliya's steps slower. She kept an ear tilted as she walked, listening. Then, once more, she stopped.

"Eli, you heard it that time, didn't you?" She stared at him.

"Yes," he said in confusion. "But dogs? Up here? How?"

"I don't know…" Her voice trailed off.

The sound of growls and snarls were becoming clearer, louder.

"We'd better keep going," Liliya said.

They set off, using their hands, now, as well as their feet, in their effort to climb. Suddenly, the clattering of sharp hooves against hard stone came from above them. They ducked. A mountain goat leapt over their heads, landing on a rock behind them. Liliya stifled a scream. Leaping from rock to rock, the goat hurried down the side of the mountain, the clattering of its hooves fading to an echo. Liliya pressed a hand to her racing heart. All of a sudden, she understood.

"Eli!" she said excitedly. "The dogs are chasing that goat."

Eli's eyes grew round. He nodded slowly.

Sure enough, rhythmic footfalls soon warned her of an approaching dog. Liliya quickly stepped off the path, pulling Eli beside her. They flattened themselves against the hard, rocky mountainside. The dog emerged at a full run, his feet barely touching the ground. They glimpsed a flash of red from his long tongue hanging out of his mouth as he passed.

Liliya turned to Eli and placed a hand on his shoulder. "Stay here. There may be more," she said quietly.

He nodded.

She stepped onto the road and peered ahead. Cautiously, she walked forward. Suddenly more sounds—barking and panting—came down the trail. Liliya hurried to scramble out of the way.

"Eli, stay where you are. Don't move," she hissed loudly.

They both froze as more dogs emerged from a wide cleft in the side of the mountain. The pack followed the same path as the first dog.

"Eli, I think they might be hunting dogs," Liliya whispered.

A few more dogs appeared, stragglers, panting even more heavily. They slowed in confusion when they saw Liliya and Eli and came to a stop.

They seemed to ask one another with their eyes, *Is this a new kind of prey?*

Liliya trembled slightly as a red tongue ran over sharp teeth. The rough surface of the rock behind her dug painfully into her back.

"Good dogs." She put up her hands. "Nice dogs. Your friends went that way." She tried to point them in the direction. "Why don't you follow?"

Several dogs growled deeply and bared their teeth. She shrank back. Their ears flattened against their heads.

"Liliya," Eli said worriedly, taking a step toward her.

The dogs lowered their bodies to the ground, muscles tightening like coiled springs.

"Don't move, Eli!" she cried. But it was too late. The dogs leapt toward Eli, barking, and snarling.

"No!" Liliya shouted. She yanked the rucksack off her shoulder as she ran. "Eli!" She began swinging wildly. Dogs yelped as she made contact, rolling off of him. They scrambled to their feet, turning their glazed eyes on her. Growls rumbled from their throats. Liliya locked gazes with each of the dogs in turn.

"Eli," she said calmly. "I want you to go. Slowly, now. Up the mountain." Inside she was quivering like jam.

Picking himself off the ground, Eli took two steps and then stopped. He turned back toward Liliya.

"Liliya, I—" he began.

"Just go, Eli." Cold sweat collected on her forehead.

The stories stood with her, roused from their sleepy silence. Liliya felt their strength flowing into her shaking limbs, giving her courage.

Eli took another step and then stopped. "But Liliya—"

"I'll catch up with you later." She reached down slowly and picked up three large stones and dropped them into the bag. Then, she wrapped the strap firmly around her hand.

"Liliya—" he whispered.

"I'll find you, Eli. I promise." She didn't dare take her eyes from the dogs.

Eli took a few steps. She watched him hesitate from the corner of her eye. "Don't stop," she said through gritted teeth. "Keep going. Good. Now run, Eli!"

Picking up his feet he ran—limping—up and over the top of the mountain. Watching him disappear from view, Liliya exhaled slowly. She turned her full attention back to the dogs.

"I'd rather not have to fight you, you know. But I will." Her throat tightened.

The dogs' crouch deepened. Liliya felt her own muscles tense. They leapt. Liliya swung her sack. Yelping, dogs rolled to the right and left of her in a blur of motion and howls and flying fur. Liliya swung until her arms burned, swung until she was trembling all over. Then, suddenly, everything stopped. She blinked. Dogs lay in tangled mounds around her, legs and bodies moving and wriggling as they scrambled to find their feet. Tossing the bag aside, Liliya turned and ran for the nearest rock face. Her hands gripped the uneven edge just as something hard slammed against her. She slipped and fell, hitting the ground hard. Pain shot through her arm.

The momentum of the dog had sent it tumbling to the side. Already, Liliya was back on her feet, grabbing hold of the crumbling ledge above her. This time, using her feet and toes, she managed to scale the side.

The dogs gathered below, snarling and snapping at one another. Liliya pressed herself against the cold face of the rock and gasped for breath. Terror filled her as she realized what she had just done.

"Eli," she choked. "Please be safe."

Stones crumbled and shifted beneath her feet. She didn't

dare move. She glanced around, looking for a safer perch, but there wasn't one. Below, the dogs were waiting. She was trapped.

Liliya had no idea how long she had been on the ledge when a man came jogging down the path. He held a bow ready in his hands, an arrow notched in place. He looked at the dogs and then at Liliya. Quickly, he lowered his bow. Raising two fingers to his mouth, he blew. An ear-piercing whistle sounded. The dogs immediately came to heel beside him, their tails wagging. The man signaled for them to stay back.

"You all right up there, girlie?" he called.

Liliya nodded shakily, tightening her grip on the rock face.

"You can come down now," he said.

Liliya looked at him askance and then frowned. There was no way she was going to come down while those dogs were still there.

When she didn't move, he added in a lighter tone, "They won't hurt you."

"If it's all the same to you, I'll just stay up here," Liliya grunted, shifting her weight for better balance.

He chuckled and walked over to where she was. When he was standing directly beneath her, he reached a hand up.

"Come," he coaxed.

She gave him a withering look.

"You can trust me."

Once again, the stories in her began to stir, colors swirling around them. With a heavy sigh, she lowered herself on the ledge and then swung her legs over. The man helped her find her footing on the way down.

"Thank—" she started to say, but took several steps backward instead. More dogs had just arrived.

"Easy there," the hunter said, raising a hand. "No need to be taking off in a fright again. They just came 'cause I called 'em."

At a single glance from their master, the new hounds backed up and waited patiently. Then, the hunter gave a different whistle and slapped his thigh.

"Bear, heel," he called.

A large brown dog moved up beside him.

"Sit," he commanded.

The dog sat, staring at Liliya with calm, liquid amber eyes.

"Bear's the leader. He'll keep the others from bothering you."

Liliya swallowed nervously and nodded, locking her eyes with the dog's.

The dog blinked.

The hunter was staring at her arm. "Them hounds do that?" he asked quietly.

Liliya looked down at her sleeve and then up again in surprise. "I—I'm not sure," she stammered. "Maybe." Her blouse sleeve was torn, bright lines just visible under the fabric, and a slow red stain was spreading.

"We'd best get you cleaned up. Come." He motioned. He reached down and picked up her discarded rucksack, slinging it over his shoulder. Then, he picked up the water bag and slung that over, too.

Liliya watched in silence. She didn't want to go anywhere with the man, and for just a moment, she hesitated. She was worried about Eli, wondering where he was. But already the stories were speaking again and she knew she had no choice.

"I'll come for you, Eli," she whispered softly. "Just as soon as I can."

The man was already walking away, and she hurried after him. The dogs followed. Liliya glanced over her shoulder, nervously. Bear seemed to be keeping the others at a distance like the man said, but she didn't feel any less unease. She glared at them, letting them know that she would be watching. All of them. Then, she turned and fell into step, once more, beside the stocky hunter. She had to walk quickly to keep up with his long strides.

As they hurried along, she studied him. He was, in a

word, hairy. His black, wavy hair fell nearly to his shoulders. A full beard covered most of his face. His two eyebrows stuck out from his forehead like wooly caterpillars. But when he glanced at her jogging along beside him, his eyes were kind.

"What's your name, sir? What do I call you? Mr.—?" she asked hesitantly.

"Patrick. It's just Patrick. I ain't got no other," he growled. "But since we're swapping names, who you be, girlie?"

"I'm Liliya," she replied curtly.

"Liliya?"

She nodded. "Just Liliya."

They wove through broken stones along an unseen path the hunter and his dogs seemed to know well. Patrick led her to a small, well-hidden gorge where trees were growing. She spied a narrow ribbon of stream winding between them with green-gray bushes growing thick along the edges. She would never have guessed such a place existed so high and secluded on the barren mountain.

"Well, Liliya," Patrick said, looking at her thoughtfully, "I suppose this will have to do. Now, let's take a look at that arm of yers."

Dogs began lapping water from the stream. Others waded into it, snapping at water bugs. Liliya's eyes darted nervously between the dogs and the man.

"Sit," he said as if giving a command to one of his dogs.

Liliya pressed her lips together. Stories or no, she still didn't like this man very much. Deliberately slow, she made her way toward the rock he had pointed to and sat down.

Patrick produced a piece of clean leather from one of the many pockets in his coat. He wet it in the stream. Coming back to Liliya, he pushed the torn sleeve up and began dabbing roughly at the long, angry scratches. Liliya winced and tried not to whimper. The cuts were not deep, but they stung and burned.

"Not too bad," Patrick murmured to himself. The tightness in his jaw loosened. He rinsed and washed the cuts several times until he was satisfied they were clean. "You want a dressing?" he offered.

Liliya pulled her arm back and cradled it to her. "No." She shook her head. "Like you said, it's not bad."

"Make sure you keep it clean."

She nodded. "I will."

He squatted down on the ground near her, studying her carefully. "So what brings you up to the top of this mountain—and all alone, by the looks of it?"

"Just traveling," she answered guardedly.

"Surely ya got some reason or another," he persisted.

"Maybe."

"Where ya be heading?"

She pressed her lips together.

"The village? Or…is it the sea?"

Crossing her arms over her chest, she lifted her eyes and met his. "I go wherever my feet take me, sir, and nowhere else."

He nodded. His moustache twitched. Leaning back on his heels, he shook his head slowly from side to side. "Fine," he grinned, "You can keep yer secrets. Yer a spirited one, though. I'll grant ya that much."

Liliya felt her cheeks heating, but she didn't uncross her arms.

The corners of his moustache twitched again.

Suddenly, Liliya made a small gasp. She grabbed hold of the rock beneath her. Colors brightened and blurred before her. She squeezed her eyes shut.

Patrick rose to his feet in alarm.

"What's the matter with you, girlie? You hurt after all?"

She heard him distantly and shook her head. Voices filled her thoughts, pushing them to the side. More came. Words wrapped around her tongue. She opened her mouth:

Many years ago, there was a young man who wandered his village. A dreamer by nature, he badgered his neighbors for stories. But it couldn't be just any story—it had to be a story he had never heard before, she began.

The villagers found themselves searching deeper and deeper in their memories to appease him. They began telling stories from long ago, stories all but forgotten. The stories told of a creature who gave birth to Storytellers and a Wind who devoured them. To the young man, they were strange and wonderful and filled his mind with even stranger thoughts. Yet, as soon as a story was finished, no one else seemed to remember.

As the words poured from Liliya, Patrick sat rigidly at her feet. His face could have been carved from stone but for the glitter in his dark eyes.

The more the young man heard these old tales and saw the forgetfulness in the others, the more he began to ask why. He wondered if the Mysterious creature and the Storytellers could be more than just old tales. He wondered if the Wind was actually real.

Then one day, a Wind came from across the sea, roaring like a dragon. It swept through the seaside village, devouring and destroying. A strange dullness spread over the villagers, a forgetfulness.

And when the Wind moved on, there were no more stories left in the village—except those the young man still carried.

Liliya's voice trailed into silence. Her eyes were fixed on Patrick. He met her gaze, warily. High above them, the cold sun dimmed. The clouds cast gray shadows across their faces. Swallowing nervously, Patrick blinked and looked away.

Liliya held her gaze steady. "This is you?" she asked quietly.

He shivered. "Maybe. Once upon a time." He stared at the ground.

"I'm sorry." She didn't know what else to say.

"So am I," he said.

"Why?" she asked curiously.

The silence between them stretched. Finally, Patrick spoke again. "I guess—I guess, I've always wondered if maybe it was my fault." His foot kicked at a stone.

"What? The Wind?" She looked at him in surprise.

"Yes. Maybe just by believing in the stories—in the Wind—it brought it to my village."

"Maybe," Liliya said thoughtfully. "But what if there was another reason? What if your belief actually saved the stories. For everyone else."

Patrick turned toward her. For just a moment, Liliya glimpsed a lifting of shadows from his face. Then, the mask slipped back into place, and he stood.

"You're a special girl, Liliya, and I've enjoyed yer companionship. But I guess it's time to be getting you back to the road. I've no doubt you have a work to do." He stared at her with a mixture of awe and respect.

This time it was Liliya who broke the gaze.

Patrick picked up Liliya's belongings from where he had lain them. Then, kneeling by the stream, he began carefully rinsing and refilling her water bag. Liliya watched in bewilderment. When he finished, he turned toward her, extending his hand. Liliya took the offered hand firmly, without hesitation, in trust, and in friendship.

He pulled her to her feet.

"Thank you," she said shyly.

"Yer welcome." He smiled.

Gently, he slipped the rucksack strap over her head and shoulder and followed it with the now full water bag. Then, without another word, he turned and began walking. Liliya fell into step beside him. Neither spoke until they had reached the road.

"Well, here we are. Back where we started," he said quietly.

Liliya nodded.

"Goodbye, Liliya," he said.

"Goodbye, Patrick."

Bringing his fingers up to his mouth, he blew. The dogs fell in behind. Without another word, he turned and left.

Liliya watched as they disappeared into the rocks and trees. Then, she turned her gaze back to the road. *Now, to find Eli.*

Carefully, cautiously, she picked her way up the side of the mountain. Voices began speaking in her head. *On. On,* they said. *To the sea.*

Liliya nearly stumbled. She had forgotten about the sea. In her heart, she repeated the words. *To the sea.*

She stared at the peak. She was nearly there. Her breath quickened.

But first, I need to find Eli.

Chapter Thirty-Two

Eli ran as fast as his legs could carry him. His heart pounded in his chest.

"Liliya," he sobbed.

He ran blindly up the mountain path and over to the other side. He ran on and on until he was clutching at the pain in his side, and his lungs were begging for breath. And still, he ran. It was a long time before he finally slowed and came to a stop. Only then did he become aware of the tears streaming freely down his face and the stinging pain in his leg.

He staggered and limped and then lowered himself to the ground. Pulling his knees to his chest, he wrapped his arms around them. He was shaking all over. Never had he been so frightened in his entire life.

"Liliya," he whimpered, looking back up the road. "Where are you?"

The winds rustled the few trees around him. Stones tumbled noisily down the side of the mountain. An eagle cried far above, its voice echoing off the rocks.

Never had he been so alone, either.

He turned his attention to his leg. Fingering the bloodied and torn skin, he winced. This was much worse than a skinned knee.

"Oh, what do I do?" he moaned, choking back another round of tears. He looked up toward the empty path once more. "Liliya, please come. I need you."

But she was nowhere to be seen.

He hoped she was ok, that she was even now on her way to him. *But what if she isn't? What if I never see her again? What if she just went away—like Papa? What if I'm left all alone? Forever.*

"Liliya—"

Suddenly, he could hold his tears back no longer. He buried his face in his knees and sobbed, releasing all the fear and hurt. He cried until no more tears could come, he cried until he was empty. Then, at last, his sobs quieted and stilled, and he raised his head.

A sea breeze was blowing. It cooled his hot, damp cheeks and ruffled his hair. He wiped away his tears.

"She's all right, she has to be." He lifted his chin higher. "She promised me."

He looked around for the first time, beyond the trees and rocks nearby. Slowly his eyes widened. He began to breathe deeply, eagerly. There below him, at the foot of the mountain, he saw a wide village hugging the shore. Beyond that, stretching out to the distant horizon, was the silvery spread of the sea.

The sea! It's right there. Just down the mountain.

His heart leapt into his throat as his eyes drank in the sight.

"Liliya!" he wanted to cry. But she wasn't there.

Chapter Thirty-Three

The man rode slowly, now that the road beneath them had become uneven and rough. At times he was forced to dismount and lead his horse. The going was tedious, but not unexpected. It was not their first time along this way.

Back and forth they wound, rising higher and higher. The familiar sharp smells of salty sea air grew stronger with each turn. They made another hard left turn, and suddenly the man caught a different scent—faint, sweet—but by this time, no less familiar.

Bile rose into his throat, and he grimaced, swallowing it down. Memories wavered on the edges of his thoughts, wraith-like and untouchable. The emptiness inside him groaned.

He quickly searched the path ahead, as far as his eyes could follow the road. But, he saw no living thing except for a few scraggly trees. The emptiness around him just echoed with the emptiness within.

But, still, he knew: *She's up there, somewhere. Just ahead.*

Returning his gaze to the road at his feet, he frowned and slid from the saddle. He took the reins and began leading his mount through another section of difficult ground. *We'll meet soon enough.* He pressed a hand into his stomach.

They walked, the roar of the wind blending with the dull thud of his boots and the sharp clatter of his horse's hooves on the broken stones. The peak rose above them. Suddenly, the wind gusted cold. Faint shrieks and wails were carried along with it. The man began trembling as a finger trailed across his neck.

"Now?" came the voice.

"Not yet," he hissed. "But not long."

Faint, cold laughter reached his ears. "I will wait."

His stomach growled, and he looked down. He smiled. "So will I."

It would not be long, now—he chuckled to himself—*not long at all. And this time*—his laughter deepened to match the roar of the Wind—*all would be done right.* He pulled on the lead, and his horse followed.

The hard-packed earth gave way to more broken stones, and their progress slowed. The incline grew steeper and they slowed even further. They had reached the last and most difficult stretch.

Wind came down from the tops of the mountains in angry, cold gusts. It whipped around them. The scent of the North Sea saturated the air with salt and sea and dead fish. All other scents faded. He took a breath and exhaled slowly. Then, shielding his eyes, he gazed upwards. The peak was hidden behind trees, but he knew it was there, just a few paces ahead. Rocks tumbled and rolled underfoot as they continued the final ascent. He caught nothing more of the floral scent nor the Storyteller. Not that it really mattered.

There is nowhere else for her to go.

Finally, they reached the top. Breathing hard, the man paused and gazed outward. The village, the place he considered home, lay sprawling at the foot of the mountain. Beyond it stretched the gray North Sea. Sunlight glittered off the choppy surface.

Glancing upward, the man frowned. The sun was still high up and bright, too bright for his liking. He wrapped his cloak around himself and pulled up the hood. Then, he returned his gaze to the village below. It had been many years since the Wind had come to his home. *It's too bad there are so few stories left among the villagers. Then again, the Wind isn't coming for them.* His hand went to his stomach, and he smiled.

He pulled on the reins and began to pick his way down. Once more, his horse followed obediently.

He would summon the Wind when he reached the bottom. *And then, well—* He chuckled into his hood.

Chapter Thirty-Four

Liliya hurried along, her eyes darting everywhere as she searched for Eli. She had stayed with Patrick much longer than she had intended. She could only hope that Eli was all right and that he wasn't too worried.

"Eli!" She put her hands to her mouth and called, "Eli, where are you?"

He can't be that far ahead.

"Eli!" she called again, louder.

She crested the mountain without even noticing and then began the descent on the other side. She was hurrying along so fast that her knees threatened to buckle underneath her. But she didn't slow.

"Eli! Eli!"

Where is he?

She called his name several more times before she finally

heard a faint answering response.

"Eli!" She let out a breath, breaking into a relieved smile. "Eli, where are you?" she called loudly.

"Liliya, here—" His voice carried through the trees.

She shouted, "Stay right where you are. I'm coming." She half-slid, half-ran down the path.

"Liliya! Liliya!" came his eager cries.

She found him further down the road. He was sitting on the ground, his knees pulled up to his chest.

"Eli," she cried breathlessly, rushing to his side. "Eli, I found you."

He wrapped his arms around her neck. "Liliya." He began to cry. "I thought you'd never come."

"Eli." She held onto him tightly, comforting him. "Eli, it's all right. Everything's fine, now," she said softly. "Shhh. I'm here."

He clung to her, and she let him, murmuring softly as she stroked his back. After a while, he quieted. She pulled away and searched his face. "Are you ok?"

His pained and frightened eyes locked onto hers as he shook his head. "Liliya." He swallowed. "I'm hurt."

"What? Where?" Her eyes immediately swept over him.

"My leg." He winced as he straightened it out.

"Oh, Eli." She stared at the injury. "Hang on. I have to think a minute." She chewed her lip. Then, opening the rucksack, she began pulling out bundles of herbs, selecting some and putting others to the side. "Don't worry. I know exactly what to do," she assured him.

Glancing again at his injury, she tore a wide strip of fabric from the bottom of her own long skirt. Then she began tearing it again, making several smaller strips. She worked methodically, calmly. She'd seen and helped her grandmother multiple times. Her calm presence helped calm Eli. His tears stopped. He watched her in silence.

"This is going to hurt, Eli. But I promise to be as gentle as I can," she said.

He nodded, his lips pressed tightly together.

She tucked her hair behind her ear in an impatient gesture. Then, she poured some water on a strip and began wiping away the dirt and dried blood clinging to his skin. New blood began to flow freely. She dabbed at it and then let it flow. She knew it would clean the wound.

"I'm going to wet the herbs now," she said.

Carefully selecting and then wrapping various plants in a small square of cloth, she wet the fat bundle and then began squeezing and massaging it gently between her fingers. A sweet aroma rose up from it, mixing with the salty smell of the sea already in the air. She could see Eli relaxing as he breathed it in, his fears lessening. After wringing out the excess water, Liliya applied the packet directly to the wound. The cold seeped in, soothing.

"Hold this," she said. "Tightly, now."

Eli held it against his leg.

Quickly she prepared more bandage strips. The largest she folded into a thick square.

"Ok, Eli."

He removed his hand. She placed the dry bandage over the damp herbs. Then, she began to wind other strips around his leg to hold them in place. She made them tight, but not too tight, just like her grandmother had taught her. When she had finished, she sat back and looked at him.

"That should help. A little," she said softly. She was concerned that his face was still so pale. She handed him the water bag.

"Here, drink," she ordered. Then she handed him the last bit of fish. "Now, eat this. All of it."

Obediently, he ate and drank all she gave him. A little color returned to his cheeks. Liliya rose stiffly and glanced upward. The sun was still high overhead, having just passed the noon hour position. Much of the day still remained.

"Do you think you could try to walk?" she asked. She had just seen one of the eagles circling high above. "I don't think we can stay here any longer."

Eli gave a brave nod.

Smiling encouragingly, Liliya reached down and helped him to his feet. "Just lean against me," she said.

"Wait, Liliya." He began tugging on her arm. His voice rose with excitement. "Did you see it yet?"

"See what?"

"Over there." His eyes brightened as he pointed. "The sea, Liliya. The sea." He broke into a wide grin.

"The sea?" She turned around slowly and looked. A painful knot formed in her throat, and her vision swam. No. In all her worry and fear and concern for Eli, she had not seen. "Eli," she whispered.

"I know." He laughed.

"The sea, Eli. It's the sea." She blinked away her tears. "At last."

Chapter Thirty-Five

Shadows marched up and over the mountains—large, fluffy clouds pushed along by ocean breezes. Every now and then, the sun would break through long enough to fall warm on Liliya's and Eli's heads. Then, more clouds would pass over, and the air would grow chill again.

With their arms wrapped around one another, Liliya helped Eli down the mountain path. The going was slow, but Liliya hardly noticed. Her eyes saw only the white-capped waves in the distance. As her excitement grew, so did voices of the stories inside her—so loud they spoke over one another in their eagerness. Her own thoughts joined them. All of them shared a common theme: they were going to the sea.

Eli began to lean more heavily against Liliya. His limp, too, became more pronounced.

"You all right?" she asked.

"Yes," he answered faintly.

"It's just a little farther. Can you make it?"

"Yes," he said again.

She nodded and then frowned. Something inside was telling her she had to reach the sea that day. The stories were echoing it. She knew she would. Wiping her sweaty palms, she shifted her grip to provide more support. "Lean on me," she said.

Liliya struggled with Eli all afternoon until her back and shoulders were aching and her legs wobbled. Finally, she lowered Eli to the ground.

"We can't stop long." Her voice was breathless, though steady. "I have to—" But she didn't finish what she started to say. She just shrugged and handed him the water bag.

"I know," he said quietly.

She gave him a tight, weary smile. Straightening, she stretched her arms high over her head and groaned. Then, more slowly, she lowered them. Eli handed her the water. She took a swallow and then slung it back over her shoulder.

"Time to go." She offered a hand.

"I'm ready." Eli grabbed hold, and she pulled him to his feet.

They could no longer see the village or the sea, only the path ahead of them. Stones rolled underfoot, and the way, at times, was slippery. But going down was much easier than going up and they moved along steadily. Gradually, the path began to widen and smooth. Then, just as the sky was beginning to turn pink with the coming of evening, the ground finally leveled beneath them.

"Eli, look." Liliya pointed toward the village and smiled. "We made it."

"We made it," he echoed.

She turned to look at him, and her smile faded. His face was eerily calm. "The sea is just ahead," she said.

"I know."

"Come on." Her voice was faint.

Eli walked more and more slowly, each step more

labored, more painful. It was as if he had used all his energy in getting down the mountain and had nothing left. As they came within sight of the village borders, color drained from his face, and he sank to the ground.

"Eli!" Liliya cried, crouching beside him.

"Sorry—Liliya." He grimaced, clutching his leg.

Liliya looked at Eli, looked in the direction of the sea, and then back at Eli. "I can still help you. We can still make it."

He shook his head. "No. You'll have to go on. Without me," he panted.

"Eli, what are you saying?"

"Liliya, it's ok. It was meant—to be this way."

Words froze in her mouth.

"I understand," he continued calmly. "I really do. It's the story—the story you told me before. You said we would be separated. That I would be left behind. I thought it might be the dogs—when you sent me over the mountain." He looked at her, his brown eyes somber. "But this is what it really meant."

She shook her head. "Eli—"

He smiled bravely. "I know you'll come back for me."

Liliya stiffened. "No, Eli! This can't be right. I—"

"I'll be right here," he said softly. "Waiting."

Her lips trembled. She felt like her heart was being torn in two.

"You have to go, Liliya," he said quietly. "The stories never lie."

"But—"

"You know I'm right."

Liliya wrapped her arms around herself. Her head lowered. *He is right. Just like he always is.*

"All right," she whispered. Then, her voice turned angry. "But not like this. Not out in the open. I'm going to get you off the road a bit, where you won't be seen."

Setting her jaw stubbornly, she half-carried, half-dragged him off the road and into some trees. It didn't provide much shelter, but it was more secluded—and invisible from the road. She eased him to the ground, making him as comfortable as possible.

"You should be safer here," she said. She placed the cloak over him and tucked him in warmly. Then, she handed him the water bag. A few swallows were all that remained.

"I wish it were more," she sighed.

"I'll be fine, Liliya."

She nodded. Then, she gave his shoulder a squeeze. "I'll be back as soon as I can. I promise."

"I know you will."

"Goodbye, Eli." She turned away.

"Goodbye, Liliya." His voice trailed after her. "May the winds blow soft."

Blinking rapidly, she walked faster. She didn't want him to see her crying.

The stories within grew louder. Her heart began hammering in her chest. Suddenly, she had a great, overwhelming need to cast her eyes upon the sea, to place her feet in the footprints of the waves. Brushing away her tears, she began jogging, running.

I'll be back, Eli—she promised fiercely—*just as soon as I can.*

Liliya passed though the borders and entered the village. From there, it was only a short walk to the sea. She could already hear it ahead of her.

The stories inside were shouting.

Her legs carried her straight through the village, past shops, through narrow alleys and through a little wooden gate. Then—joy of all joys—her bruised and aching feet sank into the soft, cool sand. A small sigh of delight escaped her lips but even then, she didn't linger, she didn't stop. She kept walking. The sounds of the waves and the wind roared in her ears, calling her. In the distance, white cresting waves shone silver in the moonlight. She licked her lips and, tasting the salt, nearly cried with joy. Her cheeks grew numb in the chill breeze but she didn't care. She listened eagerly to every last sound—each crashing wave, every whisper of the wind, every roll of sand underfoot. Her eyes darted everywhere, seeing everything. She walked until the sand became wet and her toes were covered in seafoam. She walked until she had reached the water's edge.

Then, her feet stopping at last, she burst into tears.

Chapter Thirty-Six

Darkness was gathering, and the long evening shadows just beginning to merge as the man and his horse galloped through his front gate. They had just outpaced the coming of night. Breathing heavily, the man swept his eyes over the familiar blackening shapes—the steep angular house, the stables, and the smaller servants' quarters. Beyond lay the tangle of unused fields, withered vineyards, and crumbling sand dunes. No matter how much time had passed, it was always the same when he returned—silent and still but for the restlessness of the shadows.

He slid from the saddle and stretched, taking in deep draughts of cold sea air mixed with the smells of the village and his own lifeless lands. He exhaled slowly. The weight of the miles dropped from his shoulders. Other smells reached him—dust and travel and the warm horse nearby. Then, faintly—almost as an afterthought—he caught a sweetness of flowers.

He smiled slowly. *At last.*

The horse stamped an impatient hoof, and the man turned. Black eyes glared at him.

"So, you smelled it, too," he said quietly. His smile twisted.

The horse snorted and shook his mane.

"Don't worry." He gave a mirthless laugh. "I'll tend to you first."

He led the horse to an enclosure and then began unbuckling the straps of the saddle. He worked quickly.

"There," he grunted, setting the heavy saddle to the side. "You're free."

He reached for a clean rag and began drying the horse's long, powerful legs. He did the same for his horse's back and chest, rubbing until the damp, black coat was dry. The horse stood patiently, only occasionally flicking his long tail.

As the man worked, the sweetness in the air grew stronger. He grimaced and swallowed. His stomach soured, and he swallowed again. Then came the familiar deep ache, rising out of his emptiness. Memories teased the edge of his thoughts—thin shadows that appeared and then faded like dreams upon awakening. The pain spread and grew. His stomach howled and he clutched at it.

"By the Wind, it shall be finished this very night," he gasped, nearly doubling over. Lifting his head, he spoke one word. "Come."

A flash of lightning lit the far horizon. He felt the surge of the Wind's response. An eager gust roared past, lifting the hair on his scalp. His emotions rolled and twisted as the Wind wrapped around him.

"You found it?" the voice hissed.

He quivered. "I will."

Cold laughter caused the hairs on his arm to rise, his throat to go dry. The Wind's sharp breath tickled his ear. "I am coming" —an icy breeze rushed past him, taking his breath— "tonight."

The man pressed a hand to his stomach and looked down. "Tonight," he echoed.

Stillness followed—the lull before the coming of the storm. The Wind was mustering and gathering all its strength. The same mistake would not be made twice.

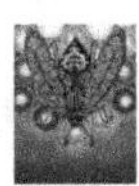

The man slowly pulled his cloak up around his shoulders. *It is done.* Releasing a breath, he tossed the last of the used rags to the side. *Now for my part.*

Leaving the horse in the enclosure, he slipped out through the gate and began to run—his boots thumping loudly against the cobblestone road. He followed the scent down a narrow alley, past a bakery, an inn, an alehouse, and then a long row of gray, weather-stained cottages. He came to the end of the road—and a little wooden gate. Sand and sea spread out wide before him. The scent of blossoms grew stronger.

He pushed open the gate and stopped. There at the place where the waves met the shore stood a girl, alone. He glanced right and left. There was no one else. His gaze came back to rest on the girl.

He quickly took in the whole of her. She was a slight girl of average height but dressed in little more than rags. A dark shawl was wrapped around her shoulders. *Just a simple girl. No more. Hardly worth a second thought.* But even as he stood there, the floral scent was growing stronger.

He stared harder.

"You there. Girl," he called out.

The girl turned, and they faced one another. As their eyes met, he felt a shudder run through him. Even in the dim light, he could see that her eyes were gray, the color of the sea.

He stared at the smooth young face, the strange, almost

silvery eyes filled with starlight. Somewhere, he had seen eyes like that before. Somewhere—he was certain—among the memories he had lost.

"Who are you?" he demanded.

"I'm Liliya."

The vacant spaces in him groaned and ached. He felt himself drawn to her, attracted, and repulsed at the same time. She was full—full in a way he had never been full. Her eyes were so filled with story that he could see his own reflection mirrored in them.

The girl pulled her gaze away, and he sensed, more than saw, the brief tremor that ran through her. She turned toward the sea, her hands clasped in front of her. She was speaking. Her voice was like the sea—or the wind—old and filled with a wisdom far beyond her obvious youth. Color bled into the gray shadowy darkness around her as she spoke. The man listened and watched. Words were flowing, one after another, from her lips:

Many years ago, a ship was heading to port when a storm rose up out of the sea, she said. *Dark clouds thickened overhead, blotting out the sun. Then, the winds came, and heavy rains fell.*

The man could feel the rocking of the vessel under his feet, the splash of waves on his face as they slapped against the hull. The winds tore at the sails above, and he drew his cloak tightly around himself. Cold, hard drops of rain pelted him and he looked around in fear and surprise. He was on the ship. He was in the girl's story.

All around him, dark-skinned sailors were shouting. Their chests were bare, their muscles tight with effort as they struggled against the wind and the waves. Water streamed from their dark hair.

The man opened his mouth to speak, but no sound came. The words continued:

A great wave rose above the others and stood over their ship, taunting. Clinging to the slippery deck, the sailors stared in horror. The wave bent and fell, crashing upon them. The small vessel splintered, and the men were tossed into the foamy sea.

The man began flailing and gasping, choking for air. Then, some other part of himself reminded him that the sand was still firm under his feet, his clothes still dry. He let out a sharp breath, willing himself to breathe normally. His vision cleared.

He saw the girl again, standing in the same place by the sea. Bold colors were trembling around her feet. She was still speaking, though her voice had now quieted to almost a whisper. Her words reached him, and he felt his thoughts slipping, growing distant. Then, the waves swallowed him once more.

Only one man from the entire crew survived. Clinging to a piece of the hull, he swam all night, fighting against the waves.

Villagers found him washed up on the beach the next morning. He was shivering and exhausted, coughing up seawater.

"A storm," he gasped. "From the North. A great wave. The ship—"

As Liliya was speaking, the man's own lips began to move, silently forming the same words.

"Everything lost. Destroyed. Gone."

The man froze, his throat tightening until he could hardly breathe.

Suddenly, an icy breath of Wind gusted onto the shore and blew past him. A warning. He blinked and shivered, pulling his cloak up around his shoulders. But he could not look away. Images and snippets of the story were replaying before him, locking into place within his own empty spaces. A tremor ran down his spine.

This slip of a girl has just given me a memory.

His anger surged. "You *are* a Storyteller!" he roared. His hands tightened until his knuckles turned white. "And you're the One I've been following."

The girl jumped and turned, making a half-strangled cry.

His voice came out now like ice, hard, and brittle. "You are, aren't you?"

She clutched the shawl, trying not to shiver.

"Yes," she stammered. "Yes. I am a Storyteller."

"Then I was right," he said, his voice grating. His fingers began to twitch. With effort, he resisted the urge to press his hand against his stomach. His hunger roared.

The air about them grew colder and windier. The girl's shivering increased. Sand and grit and salt scraped against their cheeks and foreheads. The girl pulled her shawl more tightly around her. Golden threads caught the fading moonlight and glimmered.

The man gave a start. "That shawl," he croaked. "I know it!"

He forgot about his hunger as memories began to appear before him, wraith-like. His heart leapt into his throat. He almost remembered—something. But when he grasped at the fleeting vision, it was already gone. He growled in frustration.

The girl looked at him and then down at her shawl, her eyes wide. She took a step backward. Waves splashed over her feet. Fear flashed in her eyes. Once more, the golden threads caught the faint light and shimmered.

More memories moved to surround him, tease him— colors and scents. A strangled cry worked from his throat. He had actually heard them whispering. The memories had never been so close. His eyes remained riveted on the shawl, on the faint gold shimmers.

"That shawl. You must tell me. Where did you get it?" he whispered hoarsely.

The girl stared at him as if not understanding.

"The shawl, girl. Speak up," he demanded.

She opened her mouth and then froze. He heard her gasp. Her eyes widened as she turned toward the sea behind them. She began trembling from head to toe.

"It's coming." She gave a cry of dismay. "It's coming for me." She began rubbing her arms.

He stared at her for a moment and then smiled slowly.

"Of course it is," he said without emotion. "I called it."

She turned back to him, her eyes large and round. "Why?" she whispered.

His smile was like ice.

The Wind blew again, and the girl's face blanched. Her eyes darted around fearfully, like she was an animal, trapped.

He took a step closer, feeling a different hunger.

"The shawl, girl. Where?" His voice was hard. "I must know."

She stared at him.

"Where?" he demanded.

She licked her dry, cracked lips. "Please—" she said. She clutched the shawl to her breast—protectively and possessively. "It's mine. I was found with it. On a beach." She searched his face anxiously.

His tone was, for the first time uncertain. "You were found with it?"

She gave a slow nod and swallowed. Her eyes skittered about them.

"But that shawl—" He made a low grumble in his throat. "I've seen it before. I know I have." He closed his eyes a moment, pressing his knuckles into his forehead. "It's in here." His voice strained. "There's something. Someone." His thoughts spun backward, searching for fragments of memory.

Screeches roared past his ears, echoing with his emptiness. A gust of wind came with it, and his thoughts were scattered.

The man howled. "Oh, blast the Wind and its interference!" He held his head in his hands. "Why can't I remember?"

Laughter faded into the distance.

Chapter Thirty-Seven

Liliya turned back toward the sea, searching the darkening sky. The hairs on her arms were rising again, and she rubbed them, absently.

"Eli," she whispered.

She was suddenly afraid for him, afraid for herself. She bit her lip, hard.

The sounds she had been longing for just a few hours earlier—the sounds of the wind and the waves and the sea— roared in her ears but offered little comfort now. The moon— though still shining above—appeared only bitter, cold, and lifeless. The voices too, had changed their excited clamoring to words of warning.

But Liliya didn't need them; she already knew. *The Wind is coming.*

And the man?

The knot of fear in her stomach tightened. She could still feel his eyes boring into the back of her head. She glanced over her shoulder, and her unease grew. She bit her lip harder.

Something inside began to stir—a voice—rising above the roar of the wind, the crashing of waves. Words filled her mouth. Images played out in her mind's eye. It was the story she had told earlier, but it was continuing, telling a part she hadn't heard before. It was a story meant only for her. She opened her mouth, and the words began:

When the villagers found the stranger, he stared at them, convulsing with shivers. He struggled to speak. "Wave. Ship. Storm. Wind." Her lips moved soundlessly.

"Easy. Easy, sir," they said soothingly. The villagers gave him food and warm drinks and wrapped heavy quilts around him. "You'll be just fine."

"My mates?" he croaked, looking anxiously from face to face. "Anyone?"

The villagers shook their heads sorrowfully.

The man lowered his eyes and turned away. He sat alone in silence, blinking away his grief. When he spoke again, his voice was hard, his face old. "What is this place?" he asked.

"Why, don't you know?" a heavy-set woman asked in surprise.

"You're in Little Haven," another said stoutly.

"Little Haven." He mouthed the words, slowly. Then, he looked at them again, his eyes growing murky. "Please. How did I come here?" he asked softly. He glanced at his clothes, and his frown deepened. "And why am I all wet?"

The villagers stared in bewilderment. A slow understanding came over them. And then fear.

"The Wind—"

Several gasped, clamping their hands over their mouths. Others shuddered.

Fear and confusion filled the man. He realized he didn't know who they were. Then, with even greater alarm, he realized he didn't know who he was. His thoughts were slipping away.

"What's happening to me?" he cried. It was fading. All of it. His head sank into his hands, and he moaned, "Who am I?"

Then, darkness came.

Liliya shuddered, rubbing her arms once more.

She repeated the words slowly. "Wind. Villagers. Beach—" Then, she paused. Her fingers tightened around her shawl. The name dropped from her lips like a heavy stone: "Little Haven."

It was her own home village.

"That shawl. I know it. I gave it to—"

She heard the man behind her. Suddenly, the meaning came crashing around her.

"I gave it to—" Sweat was dripping from his forehead. "To my mother!" he gasped. Color rushed into his cheeks. "I remember," he said in amazement, his eyes glowing. "I gave it to my mother. I remember her. I remember my mother." His voice trembled. He turned toward Liliya, and his smile faded. "But who are you?" His brow creased. "My mother. The shawl. But you—" He stiffened, his voice deepening. "Unless you were—"

Liliya lowered her eyes and began twisting her hands together. "Your daughter," she whispered.

"My daughter." His eyes slowly widened.

The stories inside Liliya exploded into deafening cheers, the voices beginning to shout in celebration.

Then, the Wind came.

Liliya felt her hair lifted from her neck, then the scraping of icy fingers across the newly bared skin there. Her heart turned cold.

"No! Wait!" the man shouted, sweeping his eyes across the sky. The Wind curled around him and tightened. "Not yet—" he begged. His knees gave way, and he fell. He clawed at the sand, moaning.

Liliya started toward him but was knocked breathless as the Wind slammed into her, pushing her back. Wailing and screeching filled the air.

"No!" she heard the man cry again. His voice seemed farther away, now, distant. She saw him as if through a thick fog.

Another gust slammed into her, and she staggered. Wave after wave of scents began to assault her—sickly-sweet rotting fruit, the vinegary smell of soured wine, decomposing flesh, death. Her eyes stung and watered. She gagged. More gusts pummeled her. She no longer saw the man. She no longer saw anything. She waved her arms to ward off the blows but it was useless. There was nothing to block. Suddenly, invisible fingers clamped down and she felt the sting of icy pain, following by a growing, spreading numbness. Her mouth opened in a silent scream. The Wind was reaching for the stories.

No. Anger overcame her fear. She gripped the stories tightly. *No!* She would not give in, she would not give up.

The Wind howled. The air became colder and sharper. Liliya could see each breath, quick and erratic in her fear. The Wind beat against her, relentless, isolating her further. Then, the icy fingers plunged deeper.

"No!"

This time, Liliya's throat opened to her scream. Her anguished cry rose above the screeches.

The Wind attacked again, more fiercely. Great, powerful gusts began pounding her from all sides. The Wind was trying to rip the stories from her, to tear them out of her hands. Liliya groaned and staggered under the blows. A faint fragrance began drifting in the air around her, and she winced. It was the scent of bruised blossoms. The Wind smelled it, too. Shrieking excitedly, it stretched its fingers further. Now, it was reaching for *her* memories, Liliya's memories, to take them, too.

Her thoughts grew numb, and her grip on the stories slipped. They clung to her, precariously, like the seeds on a dandelion puff. Fragile. Then, from a far corner in her mind, a memory came: this had happened once before. With Eli.

Eli—who's alone and waiting. Eli—who I promised I

would come back for. Eli—who I will not forget.

"Eli," she whispered, drawing strength from his memory. She held onto his name, and it gave a steadiness to her own. Her hands tightened around the stories. She was no longer fighting for herself, she was fighting for Eli.

"No!" she yelled. "I won't let you take him."

The Wind blew her words away before she even had a chance to hear them.

"No!" she shouted again.

Once more, her words were swept away.

But the stories inside had been listening. The stories inside had heard her cries. They had been scattered once before—left voiceless and drifting. They would not be lost again.

Suddenly, the ground beneath Liliya's feet shifted, and she staggered. Heat rushed through her. The stories rose up— voices gathered together in strength. Colors blurred and brightened in brilliant shades. Liliya planted her feet firmly beneath her.

In her mind's eye, she saw Alanna and her mother and the old blind woman. She saw Ethan and his father and his mother, the Great Trees, Patrick and the Old, Old Lands. And she saw Eli—always and forever, Eli.

Their stories swirled together, strengthening one another. Liliya drew from that strength. The life, hope, and love that were in them filled her. They were her stories, too.

"No!" she cried again. This time she had more force. This time her voice rose above the Wind. This time she *was* heard.

With the release of her voice, the air around them shimmered and brightened and became sweeter. For a moment, the Wind faltered. But only for a moment.

It quickly re-gathered and strengthened, tightening the swirl around her. Clouds thickened overhead, blocking out the moon and stars. The night deepened. Liliya stretched her hands before her, blindly.

The blows continued, relentless. The Wind pulled at her, tearing her from herself. Battered and beaten, she began to forget who she was, forget her own stories. The colors were blowing away. She was fading, losing substance, losing herself. She was becoming like the Wind.

But the stories were not finished. Linking together, they surged and fought back with all their combined strength. Loud and strong, they shouted *their* stories with voices, pictures, colors, and sounds. Liliya called the stories out—as fast as she could—desperately, breathlessly. She spoke them to the sky, the wind, the sea, and the waves. Her voice rose and fell. Once more, the colors around her brightened. Light from the moon and the stars burst through the clouds to mix with the colors of her stories, adding their strength.

The Wind shuddered and took a step backward.

The stories continued one after another, without ceasing. The Wind took another step backward. Step by step, they began pushing it back toward the sea.

But Liliya could not keep up. The stories pouring through her were already taking their toll, draining her of her last bit of strength. Her voice grew faint beneath the steady stream of words. Her limbs trembled with final effort. She had no stamina, no endurance. The long journey had left her wearied; her worries and cares had left her bruised. Despair and hopelessness seeped into her heart. Her voice faded. Her lips moved, but no more sound came.

Laughing triumphantly, the Wind turned and roared back toward the shore. Liliya felt it curl around her, tightening. Her breath was squeezed from her lungs. A cold finger stroked her cheek.

"I have you, at last," a voice hissed in her ear.

Her heart failed.

Chapter Thirty-Eight

The Wind roared in the man's ears as he knelt in the sand. The emptiness in him writhed and twisted—but it was his heart that pained him the most. A deep ache that he had never felt before, deeper than his hunger. Gradually, he became aware of a soft, clear voice outside the Wind.

The girl, Liliya, had begun speaking again.

He raised his head. The strength of story resonated in her words, and he listened eagerly. But already, the Wind was circling back. It rushed past him, screeching angrily. He felt its icy fingertips as they raked over him.

"Mine," the cold voice knifed through his thoughts. Laughter trailed behind.

The man gasped as he clawed at the cold sand. The pain was excruciating. Fear and hatred for the Wind filled him. But he did not stop listening to the words of the girl's story. He could not have stopped even if he tried.

With each successive word she spoke, his heart beat stronger, faster. The stories she was telling rushed upon him in a blur of pictures and emotions. He found himself caught up in the words. As his knees sank deeper into the wet sand, he began to realize that they weren't just any stories—they were his stories—his lost memories coming back to him, filling the empty spaces within. He was reliving his own life, rediscovering, story by story, who he had been. He was remembering who he was.

Then, beyond the layers of words and images flashing before him, he became aware of a shift in the storytelling. Something was changing. Colors in the stories began wavering, bleeding out, fading. He felt the girl's struggle beneath her words. It was like she was calling to him from some great distance. Thoughts and images continued to fill his mind, but his awareness of her was outside of them. Straining, he turned his head again and looked.

The girl was barely standing on her feet. In the dim moonlight, he could see that her face was pale and colorless. Beads dotted her forehead. Her eyes were squeezed tightly shut, her cheeks wet with tears.

And still, her lips continued to move.

"Liliya," he whispered, staring at her. His heart wrenched. The name had risen out of his own memory.

A sudden protective fear for her came over him, and he staggered to his feet. The influx of memories slowed and stopped. His mind cleared, leaving only one thought—bright, like a beacon in the night. *This is my daughter.*

"No!" he cried fiercely—to the Wind he could not see, to the Wind he could not touch, to the Wind he knew was there— "You cannot have her!"

Laughter swirled around him, and he shuddered. He remembered the Wind. He had met it before. Anger gave strength to his heart and his voice. Love gave him courage. "No!" he cried again, louder.

Hearing him, the stories in Liliya lifted their battered

voices. A renewed determination filled them. "No!" they echoed, their weak voices mixing and blending with his.

"She is mine," he continued. "My daughter. I remember the night she was born. I remember her mother. I know her story—because it is my story. I remember. I remember it all. I know who I am!"

The Wind flinched.

Into the darkness, the man began shouting the story of Liliya's birth—her mother's and his greatest joy, their love for their precious little daughter. He shouted stories of those happy few months they had shared together before the Wind had come and broken them apart. He shouted the stories angrily, passionately. He was just beginning to understand how much had been taken away from him—his wife, his mother, his daughter. How much he had lost.

Then, his voice deepened and strengthened, and he began shouting in hope—hope for what was yet to come. His powerful story—along with Liliya's own fading Storytelling—pushed the Wind backward. It lost its grip on Liliya and on her stories. Screaming in fury, it spiraled out of control, spinning wildly. The smaller winds that were gathered around the Wind began to loosen, unwind and break apart. For a moment, the eye at the center deteriorated. The Wind slowed and turned, peering through dimmed vision. Then, twisting in the opposite direction, it re-gathered itself, tightening the inner circle. In powerful, frenzied gusts, it roared back.

At the same moment, the stories rose up and joined their voices to the man's and to Liliya's. All together, they began shouting as loudly as they could. Strength was in their words. And assurance of who they were.

The words weakened the Wind, diminishing it further. But still, it would not give up. Not now. Not when it was so close. Protecting its vulnerable center, it surged once more. It beat against Liliya and her father violently, trying to grab hold, to separate them—to silence their stories.

But the voices continued. Straining for each breath,

Liliya and her father clutched their sides and shouted their words. The stories poured from their mouths in an endless stream.

Once more, the Wind stretched out, scraping its fingers along them—and found no hold. The electrical charge in the air throbbed. Lightning ripped through the sky. Thunder rumbled. The sea air smelled of burnt dust and ozone. With another roar, the Wind redoubled its attack, turning and sweeping over them again. But this time, it forgot caution. This time, it came too close.

That was its fatal mistake.

For a brief moment, the eye was vulnerable. The combined words of Liliya, her father, and the stories filled the empty space and pressed outward. They broke through the wall, and the great seeing-eye collapsed.

Screaming in agony, the Wind unraveled, rapidly losing size and strength. Winds broke off and scattered. Its rotation slowed to a half-crawl. It was powerless. Scavenging what it could, it wrapped the shreds around itself. Then, blind and broken—a shadow of its former self—it fled, leaving behind moonlight and starlight to shine bright and cold in the clear sky overhead.

Breathing hard, the man stared at the horizon where the Wind had disappeared. Slowly, he wrapped his cloak around himself. Then, hearing a soft moan behind him, he turned.

"Liliya?" he said anxiously. He took a step toward her.

She was swaying, pressing a hand to her forehead. Suddenly, her eyes rolled back, and she crumpled.

"Liliya!" He caught her in his arms and carefully lowered her to the sand. Crouching, he cradled her limp body. He could feel her heart fluttering against his arm, beating fragilely.

"It's all right, child." His hands shook as he brushed a long strand of hair from her pale face. Her skin was like ice. "You're going to be just fine." Tears stung his eyes. He pulled off his cloak and wrapped it around her. "I'm not going to lose you again."

Chapter Thirty-Nine

Liliya was so cold, so tired; she was trembling, shaking like a leaf. She couldn't think anymore. She felt her thoughts drifting—like the waves of the sea—and she couldn't hold onto them. She didn't try. She sank into the welcoming darkness. She never felt her father's hand circling her wrist to feel for a pulse. Never felt him wrap his own cloak around her or rubbing warmth into her hands. She never heard him as he called her name. The sea breeze lifted his words and carried them away—carried it all away.

Liliya floated peacefully in that place between waking and sleeping. It was so quiet she could almost hear the stars breathing overhead. Into that space came memories— stories—washing over her like fragments of dreams. She saw visions from her past—her grandmother, the cottage, and the sea. The older memories gave way to newer ones, and she saw the people she had met along her journey—Alanna, Ethan, Patrick. Those memories, too, faded and passed, and everything was left dark and silent but for the sound of her own labored breathing.

Then, from deeper within herself, one last memory emerged, a memory she had forgotten. It was her oldest memory, by far. Liliya felt her body rising into the air and then falling. Strong arms caught her. She felt herself rising and falling again. She heard the squeal of her own baby laughter, heard a deeper laugh answering.

My father.

Dimly, through time, memory, and darkness, she heard him again—that same father in the present moment—now weeping softly. She heard him whispering her name over and over. The baby in her reached out her arms, trustingly, longingly. Liliya found herself following his voice, rising through the layers of darkness to wakefulness, and into the present. Blinking, she opened her eyes and looked around.

She was in her father's arms. Anxiety and worry lined his face. As her eyes met his, relief smoothed his brow.

"Liliya." His voice sounded hoarse. "You're awake."

She gave a small nod.

"Are you all right, child?" His deep voice resonated concern.

She nodded again and then, struggling, raised herself into a sitting position. The colors swirled around her, dizzyingly. She waited while they stilled. Suddenly, she realized where she was. Flushing with embarrassment, she pulled from his arms and rose to her feet, leaving the cloak in his lap. She stood unsure, awkward, her heart thumping loudly in her chest. She fingered the soft threads of the shawl at her throat, drawing strength from their familiarity. Then tilting her chin, she turned and met his gaze steadily.

The man's expression softened as he watched. He brushed a hand over his eyes. "So like your mother," he murmured.

She stared at him, her emotions tangling.

"You sure you're all right?" he asked softly.

"Yes." She wrapped her arms around herself. She was shaking again. "Father?" Her voice was uncertain.

"Yes," he answered quietly. "I am." There was no doubt, no hesitation in his voice.

Her feet shifted uneasily. In her heart, she had known, but hearing him say it made it that much more real. Thoughts and emotions whirled within her. She swallowed the lump rising in her throat. "So, what happened to the Wind?" she whispered.

"Gone."

"I'm glad." She smiled nervously, adjusting the shawl over her shoulders.

"Me, too."

"How?"

"The stories." He smiled faintly. "Yours. Mine. The ones in you. They weakened it, drove it away. It won't be coming again for a long, long time," he added.

"Oh," she said again. She stood in silence, letting the meaning of his words sink in. The Wind was gone. The stories were safe. She was safe. *And now I have a father.* She closed her eyes. It was almost too much.

A breeze was blowing in from the sea—a gentle wind, a healing wind. It washed over her, touching the broken and damaged places in Liliya's heart, the places where she had been bruised by the Wind. It swirled the colors around her— remnants of the stories just told—blending and mixing them together. Then, the colors began to deepen, brighten. Suddenly, she felt the ground shift beneath her, and her eyes fluttered open in surprise.

What? A story? Now?

She felt the familiar pumping of her blood, warm in her chest, flowing into her limbs. She planted her feet and waited—but no words formed. The colors continued to swirl at her feet, ready—but no stories came.

Why?

She looked around. All the voices had grown still. It was

as if the whole world was holding its breath. Then, she began to understand. This time the stories were waiting for *her* to tell the story—with her own words.

Her father interrupted her thoughts. "Are you all right, child?"

She smiled suddenly. "Better than all right."

My own story. My own words. My own tomorrow.

This is what she had dreamed of for years. She opened her mouth, ready to speak, and then hesitated. *What if I make a mistake?* Suddenly, she was afraid. *What if I say the wrong words?* Instinctively, she reached out with a hand, seeking the familiar comfort of another, but found only emptiness. Then, she knew what she needed.

She turned toward her father, breathlessly.

"What is it, child?"

"Eli," she said.

"Eli?"

"A boy. My companion. My—" She searched frantically for the right words. "My best friend. He's like a brother. I promised I'd take care of him after—" She bit her lip and then plowed ahead. "We've been through everything together."

"Where is the boy now?" her father asked.

"I had to leave him. Just outside the borders of the village. He was injured—his leg. He couldn't go on."

"Shall we go get him?" He offered his hand.

Liliya broke into a relieved grin. "Oh, yes, please. I mean—that's what I was trying to say all along." She laughed. "Hurry."

They raced across the sand, Liliya pulling him along. They passed through the town to the outer borders and then out to the road beyond. Eli was still where she had left him, huddled under the cloak, asleep.

"Eli." Liliya touched his shoulder.

He murmured in his sleep.

"It's me, Eli. Wake up."

"Come on, boy. Open your eyes. You're among friends," the man coaxed.

Eli blinked open his eyes. He smiled sleepily. "Liliya," he mumbled. "You've come back."

She nodded and grinned. "Just like I promised."

"I knew you would." He smiled again.

"Of course." She laughed lightly. "And Eli, you know what else?" Her words tumbled out in her excitement. "I have something for you."

"You do? What?" He struggled to sit up, wincing as he moved his leg.

"It's our story, Eli!" She spoke eagerly. "Yours and mine. And I'm going to tell it. Right now!"

"Our story?" he said slowly. "Together?"

"Together." She smiled. "The way it was meant to be."

His face brightened. "Like always, Liliya."

She nodded. "Like always."

"Come on, boy." Liliya's father picked him up. "I have a feeling this should be done by the sea."

Liliya found herself staring at the two of them. Seeing Eli in her father's arms, she realized something. She was wrong. *Her* story wasn't just her story or Eli's story. It was her father's story, too. It was also Alanna's story, the Martins' story, and Patrick's story. She glanced down at her shawl and smiled…*a golden thread in a tapestry of stories.*

"Come on," she begged. "Let's go."

They retraced their steps back through the town, across the sand, and all the way to the edge of the sea.

"Liliya." Eli's eyes went wide and round. "The sea."

She hugged herself and laughed. "I know."

All around her, the colors quivered in anticipation. *It's time.* She looked at her father and gave him a smile. Then, giving another to Eli, she took his hand and clasped it firmly in her own. His smaller hand fit perfectly, just as she knew it would. She was now ready; she was complete. Her fears melted.

"Go on," Eli whispered eagerly. His eyes were bright, his face shining. "Tell it."

Her father nodded.

Liliya squared her shoulders. The words had come, at last. She knew exactly what to say. Taking a breath, she turned her face toward the sea and opened her mouth:

Once upon a time, there was a girl who lived in a cottage by the sea. One day, she was visited by a Mysterious creature who gave her a precious gift—stories.

The words began to pour out of her, one after another. Words of hope, life, and beauty. Words of love and family. Words that surrounded them and bound them together—and words that brought them home. They were everyone's story. And they were her own. She spoke her story from beginning to end. Then, wiping tears from her eyes, Liliya shouted her final words, the secret words closest to her heart, her own greatest desire.

—And they lived happily ever after.

Then, at last, her voice fell silent. It was finished.

She looked out at the horizon and smiled. Colors had formed there as she talked—shades of silver, purple and blue—the brightening that comes before dawn. As she watched, the colors began to spread outward, filling the night sky. The colors deepened as they went, painting the surface of the sea below. Then, riding the tops of the waves, they tumbled at last onto the sand, where they came to rest, trembling, at Liliya's feet.

"Indeed, they did." Her father turned to her in amazement. "But how?"

"Like this." Liliya smiled mysteriously.

With the colors had come a delicate, sweet scent: the fragrance of the Mysteria. Voices were again awakening all around them—the stars, the wind, and the sea. Voices that had been silent. The voices added to those already present. Then words came, filling the spaces around them, saturating them all with story.

Her father's eyes widened.

Liliya took her father's hand firmly in her free one. "Forever and ever," she whispered, smiling.

"Forever and always." He chuckled, pulling her to him

and wrapping an arm around her. He held her close—close to his heart—where she had always been.

As she stood there, she pressed her forehead against his broad chest, smelling the sea, horse, and miles of travel that were on him. They were strangely familiar, strangely comforting. Her heart warmed. She wrapped an arm around Eli, and her father brought him into the embrace, tightening the circle.

Suddenly, shades of fiery pink, orange, and gold burst through the colored darkness above. Dawn had broken.

Epilogue

I tell my granddaughter's story because it was the story given to me. I tell it because I am the only one who can. I have no doubt, wherever she is, that she might even tell it differently. But she's not here, and that makes it mine. Mine to tell to the best of my ability.

But there's another reason I tell it, a more personal reason. I tell her story because—like all the others—I need her story, need the fragrance it releases—to remind me of who I am.

You may call this weakness or even selfishness on my part, and perhaps it is. But I think she would understand. And forgive. For even as my story is interwoven in hers, so is hers interwoven in mine.

I think she would also tell me that a story—especially a story shared together—is the greatest gift that we can give one another. That it is the ultimate act of love.